Series: Meant to Be
Title: *Worth Fighting For*
Author: Jesse Q. Sutanto
Imprint: Hyperion Avenue
In-store date: 06/03/2025
Hardcover ISBN: 978-1-368-11280-2
Paperback ISBN: 978-1-368-11281-9
Hardcover price: US $26.99 / CAN $35.99
Paperback price: US $15.99 / CAN $21.99
E-book ISBN: 978-1-368-11481-3
Trim size: 6 x 9
Page count: 288

We are pleased to send this book for review.
Please send two copies of any review or mention to:

Disney Publishing Group
Attn: Hyperion Avenue
7 Hudson Square,
New York, NY 10013
DCP.Disney.Publishing.PR@disney.com

WORTH FIGHTING FOR

A **MEANT TO BE** NOVEL

JESSE Q. SUTANTO

HYPERION AVENUE

Los Angeles   New York

First Edition, June 2025
10 9 8 7 6 5 4 3 2 1
FAC-004510-25079
Printed in the United States of America

This book is set in Adobe Caslon/Monotype
Designed by Marci Senders

Library of Congress Cataloging-in-Publication Data [[TK]]
ISBN 978-1-368-11280-2

Reinforced binding for hardcover edition

www.HyperionAvenueBooks.com

This book is dedicated to my grandparents, all four of whom weathered a tough journey from China to find a better life. My paternal grandparents, Chen Be Lin, Ho Ji Nio, and my maternal grandparents, Ho Ching Yen, Ung Xien Ze, are the ones who have made this book possible.

CHAPTER ONE

It is a truth universally acknowledged, that a woman working in finance must work twice as hard, worry twice as much, and get approximately 50% less sleep than her male coworkers. But if you met me, you'd never know it. I doubt even my male coworkers do.

I look at Josh, who's been talking without catching a single breath for the last five minutes, oblivious to the fact that I might want to respond. As one of the latest hires, Josh is the firm's most junior of analysts, and yet the way he talks to me is so patronizing that if anyone glanced at us, they'd assume he's my boss. Josh is the epitome of the finance bro. He's just so . . . there are no other words for it—*finance bro-y*.

I place my cup carefully on the table and take a deep breath, making sure my voice comes out evenly when I finally speak. When I first started working here five years ago, I made the mistake of raising my voice at one of the analysts, and it took me years to shed the reputation of being "hysterical." Never mind the fact that every male employee here has, at one point or another, straight-out yelled at people without any repercussions. I clear my throat, hoping it will be enough of a signal to Josh to stop talking. It isn't.

"Very good," I say, finally. It isn't good, actually. It's the most opposite of good that ever opposed. But that's the thing about this job, isn't it? It requires me to wear so many masks, layer upon layer of them: Fun finance bro who can let loose. Supportive supervisor who challenges the newer recruits to do better. Diligent, brilliant analyst who doesn't make a single mistake.

Josh leans back, a smug smile spreading across his face, and places his right ankle over his left knee. He looks ready to receive a lot of praise.

Over the years, the firm has only managed to hire two female analysts, and Lisa moved to the East Coast last year, leaving us with Hayley, who has just gone on maternity leave. I try not to dwell on the stress of losing both our female analysts in such a short period of time, but it's so hard not to. With Lisa and Hayley, I could just shoot straight to the point. But with the likes of Josh, I have to appeal to his male ego and give my critique with the same amount of gentleness that a mother would reserve for her newborn baby.

"Great analysis, Josh," I say.

Josh's smile brightens, and I wonder for the hundredth time how it is possible that he has a degree in finance from UCLA. The cash-free debt-free leveraged buyout model that he has created is technically sound, but also wildly optimistic. If it had been Hayley or Lisa present-ing these projections, the other analysts would have laughed them out of the office. Eyes would roll and comments would be made about how women live in fantasy worlds where dreams come true and numbers magically add up.

"I do wonder," I continue in what I hope is a neutral tone, "if the management team's projections are perhaps a tad optimistic." Sometimes, my nightmares are narrated by this neutral voice of mine. I hate the voice, hate that I have to use it so often around here.

The corners of Josh's mouth pull down and he straightens up. "Oh, not at all. Maybe you didn't understand the financial forecast—hang on, let me pull up slide seven—here we are. This is what we call multi-ple linear regression."

I grit my teeth and try my best to ignore the condescension in Josh's voice. "Oh, I understood it perfectly. Except you seem to have missed out the steep increase in production costs that would cut into the company's profit margin."

"Ah," Josh says in what he probably thinks is a cunning voice, "I did catch that. I had a talk with the management team and they said they're already in talks about opening up a factory somewhere in Southeast Asia to cut down on production costs, maybe in Indonesia."

I sigh. "That just opens up a whole host of other issues, like making sure that their factory is run ethically, not to mention that every country has different efficacy. Have you looked into how efficient factories in Indonesia are compared to factories run here? They might be cheaper to run, but if they're going to be sixty percent less efficient, then that also needs to be taken into account."

Josh opens his mouth, looking like he's about to keep arguing, but I hold up a hand. "Look, Josh, I'm not saying that your quantitative analysis isn't good—in fact, it is very good—" *God, how many times do I need to reassure him?* "But it must always be guided by a sound understanding of the underlying business. I think you could make it even better by coming up with more scenarios. Ones that are less optimistic. Just to make your analysis more complete."

"With all due respect—"

I bite back an inward sigh. Whenever a finance bro says "With all due respect," I know that what they really mean is: *You stupid little girl, let me tell you every way in which you are wrong.* Time for an intervention. I glance over Josh's shoulder. My office has glass walls, which means I can look out, straight into Mushu's wide eyes. Good old Mushu. I can always count on her to help end otherwise endless meetings with finance analysts who think it's their god-given duty to explain all the basics of finance to me, as if I hadn't graduated summa cum laude from

Princeton with a degree in finance. Now I scratch the tip of my eyebrow; a signal for Mushu to come in with some made-up reason.

It's a challenge not to grin when Mushu leaps out of her seat with her usual exaggerated movement and bursts into my office, out of breath. "Mulan!" she cries. "You have to come quick. There's an emergency."

Josh whirls around, his mouth falling open. "Excuse me, but we're in an important meeting?"

"Yeah, okay, calm down, you're presenting a small LBO model for review. I'd hardly call that important," Mushu snaps.

I choke on my latte. Coughing, I say, "Sorr—" I manage to stop myself from completing the apology, and switch instead to "Josh, thank you for your understanding. Please come up with more scenarios like we agreed on and I'll review it at my earliest convenience." I stand before Josh has time to formulate a response.

Visibly confused and annoyed, Josh picks up his laptop and strides out of the office, giving Mushu a dirty look as he brushes past. As soon as the door swings shut behind him, Mushu walks to me, holding out her fist. "Good job, cuz, you managed to not apologize to that jackass."

"Mushu, for the last time, we are a professional private equity firm, we do not bump fists in the office."

Mushu holds her arms up. "My bad. Butt bump?" She sticks her butt out.

I can't help laughing. "Stop that, everyone can see you."

"Uh, yeah, they'd better! You know how hard I've been working on these glutes? Plus, what's the point of working for my uncle's company if I can't behave badly?"

I sigh. "Easy for you to say," I mutter. If anything, I've found that working for my father's company has thrown even more roadblocks my way. For the first two years I was here, no one took me seriously, not even Hayley or Lisa. They all just assumed I was hired out of pure

4

nepotism, and even I started to doubt myself. It had taken years of me dedicating everything I have to the business to prove myself to my colleagues, years of seventy-hour workweeks, of making sure I'm always the first one in and last one out. Years of self-sacrifice, of making sure I'm prepped for every possibility, of pounding the pavement to look for potential investments. There is a reason I haven't been in a serious relationship since—well, since Princeton, actually.

Mushu, on the other hand, would be the first to tell everyone that she is, in fact, a nepotism hire. She doesn't ever try to hide it; in fact she owns the label completely and unapologetically, and somehow, it works for her. Everybody has accepted her presence and she gets away with—not quite breaking the rules, but doing things her way. Like barging into meetings with made-up emergencies and dressing like she works in the fashion industry instead of the finance industry. While my wardrobe is made up of pantsuits in various shades of navy and gray, there is truly no telling what Mushu is going to show up at the office wearing. One time, she wore an honest-to-god feather boa, and no one batted an eyelid, not until she accidentally flicked the feather boa into Kenny the analyst's eye.

But the key difference is, Mushu is here as the office assistant, whereas I'm here on a partnership track. Mushu has nothing to prove, whereas I have everything to prove—and to lose.

"For the millionth time," Mushu says, "I would like to point out that Work Mulan is no fun at all."

"Pretty sure that's true for most people," I mutter.

"Not true! I am as fun at work as I am outside it."

I smile and shake my head. I'm loath to admit that a part of me is maybe just a little bit jealous of Mushu. For as long as I can remember, Mushu has always been herself. I can't even begin to imagine what that's like, to be true to yourself and not put on different masks depending on the environment.

"Okay, I'm bored," Mushu says now. "Let's go grab lunch. There's a new place two blocks down—"

"Mushu, it's ten in the morning."

"And how long have you been in the office?"

"Since six o'clock."

"So you've been here four hours. Our hours are supposed to be from nine to six, so technically, you're due your lunch hour."

I narrow my eyes. "Didn't I see you sauntering in here twenty minutes ago?"

"I was doing the morning coffee run for the office. That counts as work," Mushu says with a wink. "Come on, I can totally tell you're hangry."

"What? How?"

"You've been twirling that pen incessantly and you're tapping your foot so much you might as well join my tap-dancing class."

I put down the pen that I have, indeed, been twirling furiously. "You got me. I'm not hungry at all, though. It's this Wutai Gold acquisition. It's stressing the hell out of me."

The expression on Mushu's face softens. "Oof, yeah, that's a toughie."

Wutai Gold is a family-run whiskey company that my father, Zhou, is keen on buying out. The thing is, I've studied the numbers and I'm not convinced that this would be a good investment.

"Have you seen their latest ad?" Mushu says, already taking out her phone.

"Do I want to see it, is the question," I grumble. With a sigh of resignation, I look at Mushu's phone.

The ad shows a freeway jammed with bumper-to-bumper traffic. As all the drivers curse impotently inside their cars, a grimed-up, ridiculously muscled Caucasian man riding a horse slips easily between the cars. A gravelly male voice intones: "Wutai Gold. The drink for real men."

"Oh god," I groan.

"It's not that bad," Mushu says. "The guy's really hot."

I give her a look. "It's just so . . . ugh. And why is there even a horse on the freeway? This ad makes no sense and just goes to prove how out of touch they are."

"Yeah, I lied. It's really bad. Do you know why he's so eager to buy them out?" Mushu says.

"As far as I know, he got along really well with the owners. But it's really not like him to get swayed by things like that. I have a meeting with him in an hour to discuss it, and I need to prep. Could you order me lunch?" I give her an apologetic smile.

"Consider it done. What would you do without me?"

"Probably get stuck in a never-ending meeting with Josh."

"True," Mushu laughs as she walks out of the office.

I spend the next hour brushing up on all of my preliminary research on Wutai Gold, at the end of which I'm even more convinced that this acquisition is the worst idea that my father has come up with in years. Not only has the company been overvalued at seventy million dollars, but there are other factors working against it as well, like its lack of a social media presence and thus lack of a customer base with younger generations. I can't believe Ba still wants to go ahead with buying them out.

"You've got this, Mulan," I whisper to myself as I walk down the hallway to Baba's office. But I know that I'm far from having got anything. Before going in, I take a moment to adjust my mindset. I can't just talk to Baba as Work Mulan, though that is of course one of the personas I have to put on. But no, with Baba, it's even more complicated than just being a finance bro.

At sixty years of age, my father is the picture of health. His posture is straight and confident and he carries himself with the vitality of a much younger man. The only signs he displays of his age are his salt-and-pepper hair and the deep laugh lines creasing the corners of his eyes. Eyes that crinkle up in the exact same way as mine when he smiles, which he does now.

"Ah, Nu er." Nu er is *daughter* in Mandarin, and Ba always says it with so much love that my heart squeezes every time he says it, though part of me can't help wondering if he often calls me that as a reminder that I'm not a son. God, I hate these intrusive thoughts that I get sometimes. Maybe more than sometimes.

"Hi, Baba." I settle on the sofa in his expansive office.

Baba walks over to a drinks tray next to the window and pours us each a drink.

"Bit early to start on the drinks, isn't it?" I say.

"Ah, but we have so many good reasons to imbibe." He brings over the two glasses of amber liquid and sets one in front of me. "Number one, this is the best whiskey I've ever had, and I know you're a whiskey fan as well."

I'm about to protest when Baba holds up two fingers. "Number two," he continues, "I can see from your face that you've come in here ready for a battle, and I like to soften my opponents up."

I laugh. "Baba, I'm not your opponent."

"Ah, you are correct. You're an even more formidable figure than an opponent. You are my daughter."

I roll my eyes, but pick up my glass anyway and clink it with my dad's. "Okay, Baba, you win."

He grins. "Don't tell your mother about the morning whiskey."

"Sorry, but you know I am firmly on Team Mom."

Baba gives a dramatic sigh. "Ah, the bane of a father with no sons to rely on." There it is again, that small jab to the heart. Does he mean it when he says things like these?

"Poor you," I say dryly. I take a small sip of my drink, and I have to admit that Baba was right; it really is the best whiskey I've ever had, and I've had plenty of whiskeys in years past. "Wow. What is this?"

Baba gives me a sly smile. "Wutai Gold Reserve."

I groan. "Ba, you're not going to sway me with how it tastes. Their numbers are a mess."

He merely takes another sip. "Drink up, then we will talk."

CHAPTER TWO

Ever since I can remember, Baba and I have always had a special bond. When I was upset or scared or sick as a child, I would ask for Mama, wanting nothing more than to lie in her embrace and feel her soft hands stroking my hot forehead. And even now, I'm still very close to Ma, still see her as the source of comfort and love.

My connection with Baba, on the other hand, is something different. We are, at our core, the same person—our sense of humor, the way we see the world and digest information, and the way we interact with other people are so similar that my mother often describes us as two parts of the same soul. She often says this with an exasperated smile when Baba and I are caught in cahoots yet again, like the time we both separately kept sneaking into the kitchen to steal slices of the crispy roast pork belly she was letting rest, until there were only two little pieces left before dinner.

Even with our special bond, however, it does not mean that Baba and I see eye to eye on everything. Unfortunately, Wutai Gold is one of the few things we do not see eye to eye on.

"What about the fact that their customer base is rapidly aging?" I say now. I realize dimly that I'm more than halfway through my first glass of whiskey and can feel the amber liquid burning a hole in my empty stomach. Breakfast was a bottle of green juice I'd grabbed out of the fridge before rushing out of the house, and that was over four hours ago. I need to stop sipping the whiskey; otherwise I'm going to be too tipsy for this conversation. With some effort, I place my glass down and will myself to focus on the tablet screen, on which I've pulled up a list of reasons not to buy out Wutai Gold.

"The product is of such high quality," Baba replies, taking a deep inhale of his whiskey. A slow smile spreads across his face and he shakes his head. "Ah, what a scent."

"Ba, focus," I scold, but I can't help meeting his smile. Baba has the best smile in the whole of the Bay Area. Once, when I was back visiting from college, he got a speeding ticket. After a friendly chat, the officer let him off with a warning and said, "That smile will get you out of trouble every time, sir!" People have told me that I have a similar smile, but mine is nowhere near as irresistible as his. He's basically Asian Santa.

"Mulan, it's like I always told you, quality will always shine through. This is true whiskey, lovingly crafted. It's only a matter of getting the product out there. Once people find out about it, it'll fly off the shelves."

"Actually, it's no longer about the product anymore. It's about its presence on the market. It's why junk food sells. The product isn't good, everyone knows it isn't good—heck, it's even called junk, for goodness' sake. The most important thing is market presence. And Wutai Gold doesn't have it, Ba."

He looks at me, and I could swear he's trying not to smile. His eyes are twinkling with obvious affection. "You're right that marketing is very important, and so far, Wutai Gold hasn't spent much on it at all. It's part of my strategy to increase its worth. We're going to do some restructuring. We also have special expertise when it comes to publicity and marketing, something Wutai Gold doesn't have, so we'll be adding definite value there."

"Speaking of value, their company is way overvalued."

"I thought you might have something to say about that."

"Their numbers are stupidly optimistic and I have no idea what they're basing them on, because their sales numbers have been falling steadily."

"Yes," he agrees, "they are on the more optimistic side. I believe they are basing the numbers off the company's potential."

I release a long, frustrated sigh. "Yes, the whiskey is delicious, I'll give you that. But aside from that, I don't see any potential here." *Am I being too harsh?* I check myself, going over every word I said. It's a habit of mine, watching myself, monitoring, making sure I don't put a foot wrong and disappoint my parents.

"Ah, that's why I asked to have this conversation with you. You're right. The quality of the whiskey alone isn't enough to sell me on the company as a whole. The real reason why I believe so much in Wutai Gold is because of the people running it."

I roll my eyes. It's a childish move, I know, but *argh*, seriously! "Ba, the fact that it's a family-run company is a con, not a pro."

Baba merely raises an eyebrow and gives me a long, meaning-ful look.

I throw my hands up. "Yes, I know you hired me because I'm your daughter and—"

"Whoa," Baba says, and for the first time, a flash of anger ignites in his eyes. "No, Mulan. Do you really think I hired you because you are my daughter?"

For a moment, neither of us speaks. I lick my lips. They feel dry all of a sudden. "Well, I mean . . ."

"Mulan, the fact that you are my daughter worked against you. I didn't want people to think you got hired here because of that. And I knew you'd get better offers elsewhere."

I open my mouth, but no words come out.

"I hired you despite the fact that you're my daughter, not because of it. I hired you because you graduated top ten in your class. From

Princeton, let's not forget! I hired you because you are the brightest mind I've come across in the last few decades. I hired you because you work hard." His expression softens, almost turning sad. "I know you are the first one in the office every morning and the last one out every night. When was the last time you went on a date?"

"Hey! I go on dates."

He gives me a look. "When was the last time they actually turned into a relationship?"

"Is it my fault that men in finance have such fragile egos?" I shoot back.

He laughs. "We do, don't we? I don't like men in finance. I see the way your hard work and success make them feel threatened."

I have no idea what to say. Baba sees all that?

"I see how much you give to this company, Mulan. I don't want you to ever think that you were hired because you are family."

There's a massive lump in my throat that keeps me from speaking, so in the end, all I do is nod.

"Now, Mushu, on the other hand . . ." he says dryly.

I laugh through unshed tears. I take a deep breath and give myself a mental shake. I need to focus on the matter at hand. "Thanks, Ba. I know, the only family you've hired are Mushu and me. Everyone else we employ is unrelated to us. But Wutai Gold is a true family company. I mean, everyone from the board of directors to the sales associates are all family. It's a mess."

"So we'll have to let some of them go, this is true. But I've been exchanging emails with the person running it and I believe in him. His vision, his passion . . ."

"Why emails?"

"There is beauty in writing long-form messages," Baba says. "It's an art that text messaging is slowly killing."

"Okay, Ba. God, you are such a nerd."

He brightens up, as though something has just hit him. "He reminds me of you, actually."

"And that's a good thing?" I tease.

"The best thing."

"Oh, Ba." I reach out and give his hand a squeeze. Then I frown. "Your hand's really cold."

"Don't try to change the subject. I have set up a meeting with the Wutai Gold directors tomorrow and I'd like you to attend. Now, from what Shang has told me about his family, they don't like dealing with women, but I'm hoping that once they meet with you, they'll realize how silly they've been."

"Of course."

He holds up a finger. "There is a problem I haven't mentioned."

"Uh-oh. What is it?"

"Foreman and Byrde are also looking to acquire them."

"Ba," I groan. "Are you serious? Is this going to turn into an auction? You know we never go into auctions. We're not big enough to compete with firms like Foreman and Byrde."

"Don't you think I know exactly our limitations?" he grumbles. "I'm hoping we can avoid an auction situation by getting ahead of the competition. We meet with them, we show them the value we bring to the table, we get along well with them on a personal level. . . . Surely they'll see that we have much more to offer than Foreman and Byrde."

"They'll only outbid us, and that will be that. Waste of our time and energy. You always told me that time equals money. And why is Foreman and Byrde even trying to buy them out? Surely Wutai Gold is too small for them." Even as I say this out loud, I know why. Richard Foreman's college sweetheart, who happens to be my mom, dumped him for Baba. Mama and Baba ended up getting married right after college, something that Richard has never quite been able to forgive. Over the past decade or so, I've watched helplessly as Richard went out of his way to cut in on our buyouts, and now beating them has become not just a point of pride for Baba but a financial necessity as well.

"You know why," Baba says with a shrug.

"I can't believe your feud is all because he can't get over Mom."

"It's romantic, isn't it?" he says. "And your mom's special. A once-in-a-lifetime kind of woman."

"Oh, ew. Change of subject, please and thank you."

"Well, something tells me that the people behind Wutai Gold aren't just in it for the money," Baba says.

I give him a flat look. "Ba, we're literally in finance. Everything we do is for money. In fact, don't let anyone hear you say it's not just about the money; they'll think you're aging fast, old man."

"Old man?" he laughs. "I'll have you know I'm a young sprite. I can still touch my toes. Can you? When was the last time you exercised?"

"Like you said, I'm first in and last one out. When do you think I have time to exercise?"

"You need to have a better work-life balance. Look at me, look how limber I am."

To my horror, my gray-haired father is climbing out of his seat and bending over to touch his toes. "Ba, people are looking."

"Let them look! They'll be inspired to do more stretches."

"Okay, you've proven your point. You are basically a human rubber band, now will you please cut that out before you hurt yourself?"

"Hah, silly daughter, I— *Oof!*" Whatever else he was about to say ends in a pained grunt. He tries to straighten up, but totters forward a couple of steps instead, still bent over. Before my brain can register what's happening, Baba has collapsed onto the lush carpet.

It feels as though time has stopped moving. For a split second, I sit there, frozen, not quite understanding what's just happened. My mind gibbers: *Why is Baba lying on the floor?* Then reality rushes back in, strong and fast as a roaring waterfall, and I leap up, my veins on fire.

I practically pounce on him, turning him over so he's on his back. He's so pale, so incredibly, deathly pale. Shaking, I press a finger to the side of his neck. There's still a pulse, although it feels so weak.

"Help," I say. The word comes out weak at first, wobbly and unreal. I take a deep breath, then scream it out loud. "Help!"

Vaguely, I'm aware of people rushing into Baba's office. Someone calls 911, and I register the caller's voice loudly telling the phone operator our office address. Mushu is suddenly in front of me, crouched on the other side of Baba's supine body. She rolls up her sleeves and begins administering CPR, and I think dazedly: *Wow, Mushu knows CPR?* Meanwhile, I'm useless, frozen at Baba's side, clutching his hand. His cold, cold hand. I should've known something was wrong when I'd touched his hand earlier and found it cold. *Isn't it a sign that his heart isn't functioning well enough to pump blood into his hands? Is it? Why am I thinking such stupid thoughts?*

Then paramedics flood the office space. We are told to clear a space. I don't react fast enough. Mushu has to pull me away, and when I feel Baba's hand slipping out of mine, I cry out, "No, wait—" But my view is blocked by a paramedic, and I know there's nothing I can do to help Baba but get out of the way of the professionals. I watch, leaning against Mushu for support, as the paramedics hook an oxygen mask onto Baba and cart him out of the office, and when they tell me I can join them in the ambulance, I almost weep with gratitude He looks so small and helpless on the stretcher next to me. "Ba, it's okay. It'll be okay, I'll close Wutai Gold for you, you can count on me, I promise." *Can he?* The last thing I call out to Mushu before the doors close is "Call my mom!"

CHAPTER THREE

My mother is a petite woman who does things like wear a dainty dragonfly pin on her sweater and cook at least three different dishes to accompany the rice every dinner. In other words, on the surface, Ma seems to be the type of person who'd crumble at the news that her husband of thirty years has had a heart attack. But when Ma arrives at the hospital, she strides in with a puffed chest and a determined glare on her face, like she's ready to take on the laws of the universe, and win.

I jump to my feet when I spot her. "Ma!" Tears rush into my eyes at the sight.

"Be strong for her," Mushu mutters under her breath.

Right. Mushu's right. I need to step up and be strong for my mother. My poor, old mo—

"What is the diagnosis?" Ma says briskly. Her words come out clear, with only the slightest hint of a tremor.

"All they told me was that it was a heart attack," I say. "They're still working on him."

Ma closes her eyes and seems to deflate slightly. Then she takes a deep breath and looks at me. "Are you okay?"

"I—" To my horror, huge, body-racking sobs rip out of me. So much for staying strong for Mama. I hide my face under my hands and feel Ma's arms enveloping me.

"There, there," Ma says.

"I'm so scared of losing him," I weep into her shoulder.

"We won't," Ma says, and the way she says it is with such certainty that one might believe that she has the ability to manipulate fate and destiny.

"Fate and destiny?" Ma says with a small laugh, and I realize I've said it out loud. "Fate and destiny are my bitches, didn't you know?"

"Ma!" I laugh in between sobs.

Ma cups my face with both hands, wiping away my tears with her thumbs. "Ah, sweetheart. Don't you worry, everything will be all right."

As much as I would love to believe Ma, I'm no longer a little kid, and this isn't just some nightmare Mama can brush off with hugs and tender words. "You don't know that, Ma."

"Oh, but I do. I haven't had a chance to speak to him, you see. He won't leave until I do. We have unfinished business."

"Unfinished business?" I sniffle.

"He didn't unload the dishwasher last night," she says simply.

Again, I laugh, then more tears come and I hug Mama tightly. She feels so tiny in my arms. When did my parents turn old? When did I outgrow them? I can sense a slight tremor when Mama takes in a breath, and I know that she's fighting like hell to keep herself together. She's being strong so that I have the luxury of falling apart, and I wish I could've done this for her. But no, I reverted into a little kid as soon as I spotted my mom. Guilt washes over me. A very familiar feeling.

Up until I was eight years of age, I used to beg my parents for a younger sister. They'd smile sadly and tell me that they didn't want more children, that I was such a perfect child that they couldn't ask for more. I used to believe them, until Auntie Dongmei and Uncle Bao came to stay with us while visiting from China. One night, I was on my way to the bathroom when I overheard Auntie Dongmei say to Mama, *What a shame because of Mulan you had to have that awful operation. And she isn't even a boy!* Later, I found out that after giving birth to me,

Ma had contracted an infection in her uterus, and so had to have it removed. But at the age of eight, all I cared about were the words: *And she isn't even a boy!*

Guilt and shame became my most familiar friends then. Not only had I taken away Ma's chances of having another child, but I'm not even a boy. And so I resolved to do the next best thing: Be the son that my parents deserve.

When we release each other, Mushu comes toward us. "Hi, Auntie." She envelops Ma in a tight hug before handing her a steaming cup of tea. "The tea is nothing like that tea you usually get from your friend Vera, but it's hot, at least."

"Thank you, Mushu," Ma says, patting Mushu on the cheek before settling into a chair. She gestures for Mushu and me to join her. "Tell me everything that happened."

I try my best to recount how Baba had been trying to touch his toes, and Ma makes a sound that's somewhere in between a laugh and a groan.

"And before he decided to show off how flexible he still is, what were you two discussing?" she says.

I sigh. "Wutai Gold, you know that whiskey company he's been after for a while?"

"Ah, yes. He's told me quite a bit about them." Although Ma has never worked a day in the finance sector—she is a software engineer—Ba has always maintained that she has some of the best instincts he's ever come across, and he often discusses matters of the firm with her.

"Yeah, well, I was telling Ba that the numbers aren't great, and he was telling me that he sees potential in them." I pause. "What do you think of them?" Just like Baba would've been if he were in my shoes, I'm desperate to know what Ma thinks.

Ma purses her lips as she ponders my question. "Well, I can see why your father likes them."

19

"Really? Why? They're a huge mess. He did tell you that it's completely family run, right?"

"Well, yes, that part isn't ideal, but he really hit it off with some of the family members. Said they reminded him of himself when he was younger."

I know it's stupid, but I can't help feeling a stab of jealousy at that. Reminded Ba of himself when he was younger? Excuse me, that should be me.

Ma takes my hand and squeezes gently. "Mulan, I know you don't think much of Wutai Gold, but your father . . . I haven't seen him this happy about a potential buyout in a long time. Maybe when the doctors are done with him, you could tell him that you'll see the deal through."

"Or maybe he should be taking it easy and not be obsessing over buyouts," I grumble.

"I agree. It's time for him to take a step back and let you take the helm."

"Oh." I hadn't been expecting that. Anxiety stabs through my chest at the thought of "taking the helm." Of course, that's always been my ambition, but I've only ever thought of it in a very vague, blobby way.

"And I think that seeing this buyout through on your own will give him the reassurance that he needs to do just that," Ma continues.

I grit my teeth. "Or I could just, you know, show him that it's a terrible idea."

Ma levels her gaze at me. "There is a reason that your father has managed to build a successful firm from the ground up, despite people like Richard Foreman trying their best to take him down at every turn, and you'd do well to remember that, Mulan. You don't know everything. Do your due diligence, and do it with an open mind. Do not let Baba down."

I lower my head, feeling chastened.

"I'm sorry," Ma says, tucking a finger under my chin. "I didn't mean to be so harsh on you. The thought of something happening to your father . . ."

Just then, the doors to the operating theater swing open and the surgeon walks out. We stand, clinging to each other.

"Mrs. Hua?" she says, slipping her mask down.

Ma nods. "How is he?"

"Stabilized," the surgeon says.

It feels as though my limbs have turned to water. "Thank god."

"But he did have a heart attack and we did have to perform an emergency angioplasty, so his recovery will take a while. And he really needs to take things easy from now on. No stress, seriously." Though the surgeon can't be older than forty, she looks so stern that we all nod like children being told off. "He'll be taken to the ward in a bit. You'll be able to see him then, but only for a short while, then he'll need to rest."

"Thank you, Doctor," I say, and turn to give Ma and Mushu a big hug.

Baba looks so painfully small and pale that I have to pinch the back of my thigh to keep from sobbing when I finally get to talk to him. "Ba."

He looks up from Ma and though his smile is tired, his eyes are as bright and twinkly as ever as he takes me in. "Hi, Baby Cheeks." Baby Cheeks is a nickname he had given me when I was a toddler, and had stuck the moment I'd screamed, *I'm not a baby and that's a stupid name!*

"Hi, old man." I stand next to him and stroke his arm. "How're you doing?"

"Oh, you know, pretty uneventful day. Had a bagel, followed by a heart attack, but I understand I'm about to be given some Jell-O, so all in all I'd say the day's looking up."

"Ba," I groan.

"I have to say, Uncle," Mushu pipes up, "for someone who's just had heart surgery, you're looking very perky."

"And handsome, I hope?"

"Oh yeah, totally banging."

I spot the look that Ma is giving me, and clear my throat. I need to reassure him quick, before the nurse throws us out of the room. "Hey, so, Ba, we need you to take things easy while you recover. So please don't worry about work."

He grimaces. "The meeting with Wutai Gold tomorrow—"

"I'll handle it," I say quickly. "Don't worry about it."

Ma gives me a small nod and raises her eyebrows, a clear indication for me to keep going.

"I'll do the due diligence with them, and don't worry, Ba, I will do it with an open mind. I know how much this buyout means to you. I promise you I won't let my own bias get in the way."

"No, don't—"

Whatever Ba is about to say is interrupted by the arrival of the nurse, who says, "Hellooo! Time for you to rest, Mr. Hua. We're under very strict doctor's orders to minimize stress, so everyone out, please, thank you." Though her tone is friendly, it's also clear that there will be no discussion about staying another few minutes.

In the rush, it's all I can do to plant a quick kiss on Ba's forehead before I am ushered out of the room. We all stand in the hallway for a second, slightly stunned at how fast we'd been thrown out.

"I was really hoping I'd be able to get a bit more info about Wutai Gold out of him before we were asked to leave," I moan. At the expression on Ma's face, I add, "I know, I know, no shoptalk."

"Just go through his emails or something," Mushu says.

Ma shrugs. "Not a bad idea. I don't think your father would mind, especially since the meeting is tomorrow. The password is our wedding anniversary plus my birth date."

"Aww, Auntie Li, that is the most romantic thing I've ever heard," Mushu says. "But also the least secure email password. Anniversary and birth dates are the first things a hacker would try to break into your account. You guys really need a lesson on cybersecurity."

Mama smirks. "Ah, but it's not the actual date, it's the date plus the other date."

Mushu stares at her in confusion, until I say, "You literally have to add the two dates together, so it ends up looking like a random string of numbers."

"Damn, Auntie Li, that is some next-level nerd shit. I love it," Mushu says.

"The family that does mathematics together stays together," Ma says.

"No, Ma, still doesn't work. Stop trying to make that saying work."

"Never say never." Ma pauses, then adds, "If a saying as silly as 'never say never' can work, mine definitely can work, too. Anyway, I best go home and pack some things for the hospital."

"Are you staying overnight, Ma?"

"Your father and I have not had a single night away from each other since we got married thirty years ago, and I'm not about to start now." With that, she gives me a kiss and hugs Mushu before walking away.

"Aww," Mushu says. "Your parents are so cute. Have they really never spent one single night away from each other since they got married? What about, like, business trips and such?"

"When either one has to go on a business trip, they call each other before bed so they can fall asleep to the sound of each other's breath. Used to rack up some serious phone bills before WhatsApp and FaceTime and all that came about. So technically they have spent some nights physically apart, but they've always fallen asleep with each other."

"Oh my god," Mushu says, clasping her hands to her chest. "That is

23

the most romantic thing I have ever heard of. Well, romantic and also weirdly codependent, but codependent in a cute way."

I smile wistfully. My parents are probably two of the most in love people I've ever known. I love it for them, but it's also kind of set an impossible bar for my romantic interests. Even back in college, whenever I went out on a date, I couldn't help but compare our interactions with my parents'. *Is our banter as witty as Ma and Ba's? Is the way he looks at me as soulful as the way my ba looks at my ma?* A million and one little tests that I don't even realize I'm giving the poor guy up until the moment my subconscious says: *Nope, he fails.* It's probably one of the many reasons why I haven't been in a serious relationship for ages. That, and the fact that one of my exes once told me, *You're so strong and independent, there's no space for me in your life.* Which isn't completely untrue.

"All right," I say, taking a deep inhale to try and bring myself back to the present. "We have to focus. Tomorrow's the big meeting with Wutai Gold, and I promised my dad that I'm going to see this buyout through."

"What about all that stuff you said about the . . ." Mushu waves her hands in a vague gesture. "You know, the finance-y stuff?"

" 'Finance-y stuff?' " I cock an eyebrow at her. "Mushu, how long have you been working at the firm?"

"Long enough to know that most finance terms are fancy-sounding crap you guys made up to sound like you know what you're talking about."

"Okay, you have a point."

"It's funny, I started at the company right out of college because I simply had no other offers or prospects and I didn't know what the hell I was doing—"

"Did you say all that during the interview?"

"I did, yes," Mushu says without hesitation. "And your dad said,

'Well, you are my favorite niece, so there's always a place for you here.' "

"Did he really say that?"

"Okay, it was more like . . ." Mushu assumes a stern expression and pinches the bridge of her nose. " 'Mushu, don't ever say that at a real interview. And you know you can always work here if you need a job, but promise me you'll use this time to figure out what you really want to do with your life.' Your dad is a sweetheart."

I try to ignore the painful way my heart squeezed at that. "He is. Okay, back to Wutai Gold. Yes, I still think the projections are on the optimistic side—"

"Because you're a raging pessimist?" Mushu says helpfully.

I narrow my eyes at her. "Because I go by the numbers. But I owe it to Ba to—"

"Not be so pessimistic?"

"To give it a fair shot," I snap. "So I'm going to that meeting tomorrow, and you're going to help me prep for it."

"Only one problem," Mushu says.

"I don't care what hoops I need to jump through to get this done, Mushu, I'm doing it."

"Fine by me, it's just that, well, I've been helping your dad out with the correspondence and stuff, and . . ."

"What?"

Mushu shrugs. "I don't think these people are going to want to do the deal with you."

It takes a moment for Mushu's words to sink in. "I don't understand. Why not?"

"Um, they sound kind of, sort of, really—hmm, what's the word I'm looking for?—*traditional.*"

" 'Traditional,' " I echo.

"You know, sort of more on the conservative side . . ."

"So you're saying they won't want to deal with me because I'm a woman?"

"Well, not quite, but—well, yes."

I grin. "Oh, Mushu. Mushu, Mushu."

Mushu looks at me like I've finally lost it.

"Mushu, I am a VP at a private equity firm."

"I am aware of that," Mushu says warily.

"Every day for the past five years, I have had to deal with finance bros in all their human, and barely human, form. Analysts who think they are certified geniuses—and some of them are genuine geniuses, mind you. Partners who think they are destined to become billionaires, if they're only given the right opportunity. Manspreaders who are used to bullying and not taking no for an answer to get to where they want to be in life. And every single one of these men thinks they are god's gift to women."

"Yep, sounds about right," Mushu mutters.

"And yet not only have I remained in this male-dominated industry, I have excelled." I say this with a little bow.

"Yeah you have, sis!" Mushu cheers.

"So the fact that the Wutai Gold family is sexist? Doesn't faze me. In fact, I would've been surprised if you'd told me they weren't sexist."

"Right. Except they also said they can't possibly trust anyone aside from uh—your dad."

Anxiety claws up my chest, threatening to wrap its hands around my throat and squeeze, but I fight it back. No, I can't afford to fall apart right now. Not when I've just promised my father to bring this one home. The memory of my mother's sad, lined face floats to the surface, and I ball my hands into fists in determination. "I'm not going to back down. I can't afford to cancel tomorrow's meeting. Foreman and Byrde will cut in and sweep them away if we don't go fast. They're already competing for this deal. The stress of that would destroy Ba."

"Ugh, those creeps," Mushu mutters.

"Come on, we're going back to the office."

"To hack into your dad's email?"

"Does it even count as hacking if I know his password?"

Hours later, the sun has dipped well below the San Francisco hills, and I'm wondering if this is where I give up after all. Alone in my dad's office, I rub my tired eyes and scroll back through his emails with Wutai Gold. Most of his correspondence has been with Shang, who is the acting CEO of the company, and the messages are very . . . I struggle to describe them without being rude to Baba. No other word for it, the messages are so bro-y. Take this one, for example.

> From: Hua Zhou
> To: Li Shang
> Subject: Re: Wutai Gold & Jin Shan Capital
> Dear Shang,
> I think it's wonderful that your whiskey distillery is located at your family's ranch. Back home in Yunnan, my family has a large farm that sounds very much like your family's ranch here. We owned all sorts of animals and grew most of our crops. My fondest memories are of chopping wood and herding cattle. I could ride a horse before I learned how to walk, and the pigs and goats were my friends growing up. One day soon, I hope to visit your family ranch. Perhaps we could even have a bit of a race

on horseback?
Best,
Zhou

From: Li Shang
To: Hua Zhou
Subject: Re: Wutai Gold & Eighty-Eight Capital
Dear Zhou,
Hey I never back down from a challenge. Horseback
race it is.
My family is very much looking forward to meeting
you on Wednesday. Between you and me, they're
very traditional, as you can probably guess. They
feel strongly that whomever we end up selling the
company to needs to understand what our brand
stands for—strength, courage, and perseverance.
I've really enjoyed our correspondence and hope
that our meeting will go well.
I'll see you then,
Shang

"Strength, courage, and perseverance," I mutter. My forehead thunks onto the table and I lie there quietly for a while, savoring the silence in the office.

The sound of footsteps entering the room. "Uh-oh. Are we done for the night?" Mushu says, setting bags of takeout down on the table.

I peer up at her without lifting my head. "The patriarchy is so tiresome."

"That's one word for it." Mushu starts unpacking the bags, filling the room with the delicious, greasy smells of black pepper beef and Yangchow fried rice. She pushes the containers to me. "Eat. Your brain needs food."

"I've lost my appetite." On top of Baba being in the hospital right now, the images of him being raised on a farm hurt for some strange reason. For the life of me, I can't imagine Baba herding cattle or milking cows or whatever else they do on farms. And here he is, telling a complete stranger that he learned to ride horses before he could walk? What? Who is this man and what happened to him? The Baba I grew up with carries a microfiber cloth to clean his glasses every thirty minutes and takes two different antihistamines for his pollen allergy. He watches *Love Is Blind* and says, "Oh my" when the contestants inevitably get hurt on camera. He is a math nerd who plays the Xbox and cries at games like *The Last of Us*. I feel betrayed somehow, finding out that there's a whole side to him I didn't know about.

And not to mention the fact that this Shang has basically spelled out that his family will only deal with a man. What I said to Mushu earlier in the day about being experienced when it comes to dealing with finance bros is true. It's just that I never expected that my father would connect to a finance bro on such a personal level. *Maybe Baba lied to me all these years when he told me that he was glad to have a daughter instead of a son?* The thought stabs straight into the roots of my heart, making my eyes water. Historically, Chinese families have been known to favor boys over girls. Hadn't my own aunt said as much to my mother? I've always considered myself lucky that my parents are so untraditional, but maybe that was all a lie. *Could Baba have secretly wished for a son all along?*

The thought of this makes something click. Haven't I been playing different roles my entire life? This whole time, I've tried to fulfill the role of a son *and* daughter for my parents to make up for me being a girl. At the office, I've played yet another role. My life is nothing more than a series of roles. What's one more?

"I take it you've read all their emails?" Mushu says. Her mouth is full of fried rice, so it takes me a second to figure out what she just said.

"Yep."

"You read the emails that basically say they don't want to deal with anyone but your father?"

"I read the emails that say they don't want to deal with anyone but Hua Zhou," I say.

Mushu frowns, chewing slowly before swallowing. In the thick silence of the room, her swallowing is painfully audible. "I'm not sure what you're getting at."

"My dad never referred to himself as a 'he.'"

"Um . . ."

"He never mentioned his age, never mentioned his daughter or his wife or any other identifying details aside from his name. Zhou could be a girl's name."

"Mulan . . ." Mushu says with a warning tone.

"Mushu," I reply with a sweet smile.

"No," Mushu says.

"Yes."

"No."

"And you're going to help me."

"No!" Mushu groans.

I pick up my chopsticks, and grin. "You love the idea and you know it. We're going to save this deal, you and I." And, though I don't say it out loud to Mushu, I know that deep down inside me, there's a tiny kernel that burns with anger and frustration and a fierce longing to prove for once and for all that I, Hua Mulan, am a better, more filial offspring than any son could be.

CHAPTER FOUR

As a private equity VP, I have attended more introductory calls and meetings than I can remember. Most of these meetings take place at our office and are attended by an analyst, a principal if it's a highly desirable company, and me—as well as, in the case of a company that is being hotly pursued by other firms, Baba himself.

The meeting with Wutai Gold clearly falls into the latter category, and it would be the first time that I am conducting such an important meeting without Baba present. Not only that, but I've had to tell Brian, the analyst who prepped the Wutai Gold file, not to attend, because I have no idea how Brian would react to me telling him to call me Zhou. If I had to guess, Brian would not take it well. Brian is the kind of guy who thinks that taking more than one sugar packet from Starbucks is stealing, so it's probably best to leave him out of this chaos. The only person I'll have in the meeting room on my end will have to be Mushu. . . .

A decision I am second- and third-guessing as the hour draws near and Mushu fusses about me, dabbing more and more makeup onto my face. I flinch as Mushu prowls toward me, carrying what looks like an industrial-grade torture device.

"Stop moving, you're going to end up with second-degree burns," Mushu snaps.

I flail at her, batting her away. "Or maybe a device that can cause second-degree burns should not be used on my face?"

"This is the latest thing," Mushu says. "It's a heated eyelash curler that'll curl your eyelashes for twenty-four hours." She glances down at the curler, which has started smoking. "Or burn them off."

"Along with my corneas," I say. "You are not getting anywhere near me with that. Unplug it and step away from the weapon before you burn down the entire building."

"I saw it on TikTok," Mushu grumbles, but she listens, and puts the machine away. "All right, ready to see the new, fabulous boss lady version of yourself?"

With no small amount of trepidation, I nod. Mushu grabs me by the shoulders and turns me around to face the bathroom mirror. My mouth falls open. Dimly, I hear Mushu going *Ta-da!*

It isn't that the makeover is bad, exactly. But it's just so . . .

"What do you think?"

I search with increasing desperation for the right words. "It's very . . . The makeup is very Cruella de Vil," I say finally, staring with despair at my hyper-arched, hyper-darkened eyebrows and bloodred lips.

"Yes, but the Emma Stone version of Cruella, not the misunderstood version," Mushu says happily.

"*Okaaay.* And these shoulder pads are very . . . uh, padded." I poke at my left shoulder pad, which is so high it practically grazes my earlobe.

"Exactly. I was going for a Margaret Thatcher look."

"Is that who you were channeling with the hairstyle as well?" I say, my voice coming out weak.

"No, the hairstyle was inspired by Adele, but you do exude a matronly vibe, which I guess is why it ended up more Margaret Thatcher. Goes with the suit, though, right?"

I stare in horror at my cousin. Why in the world did I trust Mushu when she said she knew just the right look for me to pass as a managing partner? The urge to wail *Why, universe, why?* is almost overwhelming.

"I can't go in there looking like this."

"Why not? You look like someone people should fear."

"Exactly," I say with feeling, blinking at my shocking reflection.

The expression on Mushu's face softens. "I get it, it's very different from your boring day-to-day look, but trust me, this is what a badass boss bitch looks like."

For the millionth time, I thank my lucky stars that my father has decided against putting up any of our pictures on our website. There was a nasty incident a couple of years ago involving a jealous ex who tracked down one of the associates at the firm, and after that, Baba took down all our photos on the company website and instead only listed our names and work emails on the ABOUT US page. Proper bios are only given out to trusted individuals who have shown serious interest in becoming a client. As such, the people at Wutai Gold wouldn't know to expect a middle-aged man, or a young woman. They would see me and assume that this is how "Hua Zhou" looks all the time.

I poke my hair gingerly. After all the hairspray that Mushu has unloaded into it, it's more titanium helmet than hair. When I turn my head, the hair follows a split second later like a wad of cotton candy resting on my head. A wad of metallic cotton candy.

Stay calm, I think. *Take a long, deep breath in. Hold it for two seconds. Now scream—nope. Now exhale. Yes. Good. Unrelated, but this is what snipers do right before pulling the trigger on their targets.*

Great, now I'm thinking about snipers and death, which is not at all a bad omen. I check my watch. Only fifteen minutes before the Wutai Gold people are due to arrive. I force myself to take another breath. I can do this. And Mushu is probably right; this is probably what badass boss bitches look like. I wouldn't know it, because I've never dealt with a badass boss bitch, only spoiled, whiny finance bros. I lift my chin and assume what I hope is a strong stance.

"There you go," Mushu cheers. "Embrace your inner finance bro.

Rule number one, your one true love is your muscle tone. When in doubt, flex your biceps. Rule number two, never say sorry, even when you're wildly wrong about something. Number three—"

I laugh. "All right, I get it! God, it's scary how good you are at this. Okay, remember, you are not an office assistant, you are—"

"An associate, got it."

As I nod again, Mushu adds, "What is it that an associate does, again?"

I won't scream, I won't scream, I won't—

Somehow, through gritted teeth, I manage to bite out, "Just look business-y."

"Got it, Boss." Mushu gives a smart salute and marches to the door. She opens it with flourish. "After you, ma'am."

"Don't overdo it," I hiss under my breath. Keeping my gaze firmly on the floor, I brisk-walk to the conference room. The conference room isn't at all far away from the bathroom, but the walk there feels eternal. I can practically feel the stares from my colleagues, eyes growing saucerlike and mouths scraping the floor. Nope, I'm not going to be able to live this one down. Thankfully, no one dares say anything to me, though I do catch the sounds of Josh choking back a laugh. I should get him demoted from analyst to . . . uh, to something else even less cool than analyst.

As soon as I get inside the conference room, the first thing I do is lower the shades to give us some semblance of privacy.

"Let me do that," Mushu says. "That's not the job of a managing partner."

Heat flushes across my face. Mushu is right. No managing partner would stoop to lowering the shades themselves. God, I'm so bad at this. How am I ever going to fool anyone into thinking I'm Baba?

Mushu pulls out the biggest chair, at the head of the table, and gestures at it. "Have a seat, Boss. I'll take care of everything. In fact,

I'm going to run out for a second and tell one of the interns to make us some lattes."

I do so, lowering myself gingerly into Baba's chair. It feels way too big for me somehow, and I imagine myself as a little kid clambering up my dad's seat, feet dangling in midair. *Stop that*, I scold myself. I am not Mulan. I am Zhou. I am the founder and managing partner of Eighty-Eight Capital, a midsize private equity firm. As the managing partner, I am very comfortable, uh . . . doing management stuff, like managing people and five-hundred-million-dollar deals. I close my eyes and take a deep inhale, imagining my chest filling with oxygen as I do so and puffing up to fill up the space. Despite myself, the method is working. I envision myself filling Baba's shoes, running the company with natural aplomb, telling Josh where to shove it.

The door swings open, and without moving, still envisioning myself as Baba, I say in my most I-am-the-boss-around-here voice, "You have my coffee?"

Without missing a beat, a rich, velvety voice replies, "How do you take it?"

My eyes fly open. Everything stops. My heart stops, my breath stops, and I'm pretty sure that deep in my veins, my blood platelets have crashed to a standstill. Because the man standing in the doorway is the most beautiful creature I have ever seen. His figure is tall and imposing, and his face is surely chiseled out of pure marble. His jet-black hair is pulled up into a bun, drawing attention to his incredibly defined cheekbones and jawline. Thick dark brows draw attention to his eyes, which are the darkest shade of chocolate. Eyes I can really lose myself in. Something I belatedly realize I'm doing.

The man clears his throat, and I snap back to reality with burning shame. Damn it, just two seconds in my new role as the boss and already I'm flubbing it. Get a freaking grip! And, though I know I'm being unreasonable, I'm annoyed at this man for catching me out. How dare he be so gorgeous? He must be the new intern Mushu was just talking about. God, I should've put Mushu in charge of hiring new interns a lot sooner.

Lifting my chin imperiously, I say, "I'd like a latte, no sugar. And make some for the others as well."

His mouth quirks a little, then he says, "How many would you like, ma'am?"

Did he really just call me ma'am? Wow, I guess Mushu was right about the outfit and makeup, after all.

"Let's have eight lattes—you know how to work the espresso machine, yes?" I catch myself. Baba has always told me that micromanaging is the sign of an incompetent leader. "You know what? Figure it out. I believe in you." There. That's something Baba always says to his employees. *I believe in you.*

"I'm glad you believe in me. I'll see to those lattes." As the door swings shut behind him, I lean back in my chair, satisfied. There. That wasn't so bad. I've barely caught my breath when the door opens once more and Mushu walks in, accompanied by a bespectacled kid who looks like he's barely out of high school. They're both carrying trays full of steaming lattes and plates of pastries.

"Here we are," Mushu trills. As she sets the trays down, she catches sight of my expression. "What?"

"Uh. Is this the new intern?"

"Yep. Introduce yourself to the boss, Gerald."

"Hi, I'm Gerald."

My gaze ping-pongs back and forth between Mushu and Gerald. Then I leap out of my chair and grab Mushu's arm, pulling her aside. Ignoring Mushu's protests, I hiss urgently, "Mushu, is Gerald the only new intern here?"

"No, we hired three of them. Do you not like Gerald? We can get rid of him."

Gerald's face falls.

"No," I say hurriedly. "You're doing a great job, Gerald. Carry on."

He smiles and resumes distributing the lattes.

I turn back to Mushu. "The other two interns—is one of them really tall and, uh, sort of . . . devastatingly handsome?"

Mushu's eyebrows scrunch together. "Um. Well, the other two interns are women because of, you know, how we're trying to hire more women and all that? But I guess you could describe Wanda as 'devastatingly handsome.' She does Pilates."

"Oh no," I say. Just then, the door opens again.

"Oh yes," Mushu says.

There, standing in the doorway looking as dangerously gorgeous as before, is the stranger. And, to my horror, he's carrying a tray of foamy lattes. Beneath his sharply cut suit, the muscles on his biceps ripple as he lowers the tray onto the table. "Freshly made, as you asked for," he says. He gives a grim smile that doesn't quite reach his eyes, and deep-set dimples appear on his cheeks.

How dare you have dimples on top of everything?! I want to scream at him.

"But I already got lattes," Gerald says in a small voice.

Mushu, her gaze still glued to the newcomer and her mouth half open, raises her hand and places it on Gerald's face and pushes him to the side gently while saying, "Shh, Gerald." Then she swallows and strides toward the man with her arms wide open. "Hello, you must be Shang, I've stalked your IG. So nice to finally meet you in person!" She envelops the man in a tight hug.

Oh god, this can't really be happening.

"Um," he says, patting Mushu's back gingerly. "Thanks?"

With obvious reluctance, Mushu lets go of him and steps aside, still openly admiring him. Turning to me, she says, "Mu— I mean, Zhou, this is Shang."

Oh god, of course he is. Of course this distractingly good-looking man that I've mistaken for the intern is Shang. I fight back the urge to bury my face in my hands and wail. But on the other hand, Shang looks as taken aback as I feel.

"I'm sorry," he says, "you're Zhou? Hua Zhou?"

I nod, mustering up a winning smile that feels more like a grimace as it sits, wobbling, on my face. "Yep, that's me. Hua Zhou in the flesh."

Shang does a double take, but before he can say another word, there is a knock on the door, and the receptionist pops his head in and says, "The rest of the Wutai Gold shareholders and their spouses are here."

CHAPTER FIVE

I brush down my ridiculous suit, pretending not to feel Shang's curious gaze boring a hole into my forehead. Within moments, Shang's family spills into the conference room. I stand at the doorway, my mouth pressed into a thin smile, and remind myself to give them a firm handshake as they stream inside.

"Welcome," I say, and I notice how Shang's uncles and aunts and cousins barely spare me a glance. Even as they shake my hand, their eyes roam over my shoulder, probably searching the room for Zhou. I tell myself to stand taller.

Shang's family is an intimidating bunch. There are three uncles, four aunties, and—apart from Shang—four cousins present, and most of them are dressed in a style I can only describe as "old money." There is nothing overly ostentatious, and yet there is very clear luxury in their outfits, their hairstyles, and even the women's makeup.

One of the uncles says, "And where is Mr. Hua?"

Here goes nothing. Praying that my voice comes out even, I say, "It's Ms. Hua, actually."

Conversations pause. Eyes turn to lock on me. I can practically hear breaths stopping mid-inhale. I wrestle my mouth into a smile. "Hello, welcome to Eighty-Eight Capital. I'm so glad to finally meet you after all the correspondence that Shang and I have exchanged over email. I'm Hua Zhou, one of the partners of this firm."

The silence stretches on for a painful few seconds before someone says, "We're happy to be here."

The one who spoke is a middle-aged woman with a kind smile. I find myself returning the smile before realizing it. "Thank you, Ms. . . . ?"

"Ah, you can call me Auntie Jiayi. I am Shang's mother, also a shareholder in the firm."

"Auntie Jiayi," I say obediently. "Very nice to meet you. Please, take a seat," I add to everyone.

"Have a latte," Shang says to his family. "I made them."

He makes a point of not looking in my direction. It takes all my willpower not to dig a hole right then and there and disappear into it. How could I possibly have mistaken him for an intern? He couldn't possibly be less intern-y. *Focus. Let all that stuff about Shang go. You can't afford to lose sight of the real purpose of this meeting.*

Right.

I must remember that I'm in control here. These people are here because they're hoping to sell their company to me.

Somehow, though my legs feel like jelly, I manage to walk back to the head of the table without tripping. I lower myself into the seat. I fold my hands and place them on the desk. Is that something a managing partner would do? I consider unfolding them, but choose to leave them as they are. I open my mouth, ready to launch into my greetings, but someone says, "There must've been a mistake. Can we possibly speak to the man in charge of this firm?"

The speaker is a man who looks like he's in his late twenties. He wears a navy blue suit, with his hair slicked back and a huge gold Rolex gleaming on his left wrist. The older man sitting to his left, presumably his father based on the similarities in their faces, boasts an even larger Rolex on his wrist.

I smile inwardly. I've been feeling uncertain of how to behave the way Baba would at an acquisitions meeting, but casual workplace sexism? Ah, this I know how to handle. I've been facing it as far back as high school, where my fellow female friends and I often found ourselves vastly outnumbered by boys in our STEM classes. And there is nothing as hateful as nerd boys who find themselves being bested in calculus by their female counterparts. I can almost hear the click as the mask falls into place. I am not Mulan right now. *I am Zhou, managing partner of this company. Old-school finance bro.*

When I speak, my voice comes out loud, clear, and calm. "And you are?"

"James Li," the man says. He gestures to the older man who wears a similar Rolex. "And this is my dad, Hong."

"James, Mr. Hong, nice to meet you," I say in the same tone of voice, which is calm and yet firm. "The person in charge of this place is me, and I look forward to us working together very closely." Without giving them a chance to protest, I continue, "And now shall we commence?" Baba has countless tactics to steer business conversations in the direction he wants, and he does it so seamlessly that most people don't realize that they are being steered.

Mushu snaps her fingers at Gerald, and he rushes about, handing everyone a booklet we've prepared for this very meeting. Meanwhile, Mushu herself turns on the large TV behind my seat and it switches onto our presentation.

I know that the presentation is flawless: When I was working up the corporate ladder as an associate, one of the many tasks I was in charge of was creating sophisticated presentations for shareholders, complete with financial models and analyses of the ventures we were looking at acquiring. I've assisted Baba in numerous meetings to raise funds for new acquisitions and I know exactly what people want to hear, and can anticipate the questions they might have.

But what I haven't experienced in a long time is the hostility I am now sensing from the majority of the Li family. As I take them through my analysis and forecast, the waves of hostility coming from these people are so palpable that I can almost smell them, like a heavy stench that everyone is pretending not to notice.

What the hell is their problem? Sure, they may be taken aback by the fact that "Zhou" has turned out to be a young woman, but at the end of the day, business is business. Could these people be so sexist that they can't see what's right in front of them: that by offering to buy them out, I am, in fact, saving their failing company?

Still, I soldier on, presenting slide after slide to show them why Eighty-Eight Capital is the right home for Wutai Gold. I look each of them in the eye as I talk, and I am surprised to find that the only people who aren't openly glaring at me are Shang and Auntie Jiayi, so I end up directing most of the presentation at them. Well, I wouldn't describe the way Shang is looking at me as "friendly," exactly, but at least he looks like he's paying genuine attention to the presentation. When I finish, Mushu claps enthusiastically. Gerald follows suit.

"Woo-hoo, awesome job, Boss!" Mushu says. Then, sensing the frigid atmosphere in the room, she quickly stops clapping and nudges Gerald, who stuffs his hands in his pockets like he just got caught doing something bad.

"Thank you," Shang says. His voice is clipped, neutral.

I drag my gaze from his handsome granite face.

"That was the best presentation I have ever seen," Auntie Jiayi says warmly.

Hong snorts. "Oh? And how many presentations of financial analysis and projections have you sat through, Jiayi?"

Pink blooms on Jiayi's cheeks and she lowers her head, her lips pursed.

"My mother's read more on the theory of finance than you could ever know, Uncle Hong," Shang says.

"Reading *Rich Dad Poor Dad* hardly counts as learning the theory of finance. No offense, Auntie Jiayi," James says. *What a prick.*

A muscle pulses visibly on the side of Shang's jaw as he leans forward, about to say something, but his mother places a hand on his arm, and I catch sight of the invisible connection between mother and son. Shang sits back in his seat, taking a breath before transferring his attention to me.

"My mom's right, that was an impressive presentation, thank you," he says, and though he said it a bit stiffly, there's also grudging admiration on his face.

A warm glow spreads across my body, relaxing my muscles. I've done it. I managed to carry the presentation through.

"But we can't possibly sell the company to you," James says.

"Why not?" I say, my face remaining impassive. It's the only way I've learned to deal with misogyny in the finance industry. Keep calm and come across as innocuous, and ask them to explain themselves until they inevitably out themselves.

James laughs, and it's not a nice laugh, more of a snigger. "Well, obviously you don't know what our brand stands for."

"Well, I did do a lot of research into the history of Wutai Gold before approaching Shang for a potential investment opportunity, but perhaps you can tell me what the brand stands for."

James looks at me with an incredulous expression, as though he can't believe how slow I'm being. "It's a whiskey company."

I nod, giving him an expectant smile. "Yes, I am aware of that."

"And we've been known as the drink of choice of the man's man."

"Ah, yes, of course."

"And when our consumers find out that we've sold the company to a woman . . ." James shrugs and raises his hands. "I'm sure you can see why that would be a problem."

There it is. Sooner or later, they'll always out themselves. I reach deep down inside me, locate another mask, and give James the sweetest expression I can. "Hmm, no, I'm still not seeing the problem. But what I do see is the value our company can add to yours, a company that I'm sorry to point out has a shrinking profit margin every quarter. By my projections, you will be in the red by quarter three of next year."

James's expression goes from smug to angry. "What? You can't say that."

God, if only I could tell him, *You need to attend more of these meetings, because people have said much worse than that.* Instead, I turn to Shang and say, "Do you disagree with my projections?"

"I don't disagree, no," Shang says. "It's a fair assessment."

"This is preposterous," his uncle Hong says. "We came here expecting to meet with a man who was interested in buying our company because he saw value in it, not someone who comes in here telling us that our company isn't doing well!"

"I apolo—" I say, stopping myself in time as I recall Mushu's rules to being a finance bro. With some effort, I swallow the apology. "I did not mean to offend. But I'm hoping that the numbers make it clear what we bring to the—"

Another uncle talks over me: "You are much too young to be Zhou, my dear girl."

"Uncle Jing—" Shang says, but Uncle Jing ignores him and continues speaking. "Shang says you grew up on a farm in China!"

Uh-oh. Here we go. As long as we're discussing numbers, I'm in my territory, but now I'm about to venture into a subject I know next to nothing about. I channel my inner Baba once more. "Yes, I did. I moved here when I was a teenager."

They all look at me dubiously. Uncle Hong brandishes his phone and says, "Aha, over here, you say: 'Back home in Yunnan, my family has a large farm that sounds very much like your family's ranch here. We owned all sorts of animals and grew most of our crops. My fondest memories are of chopping wood and herding cattle. I could ride a horse before I learned how to walk, and the pigs and goats were my friends growing up. One day soon, I hope to visit your family ranch. Perhaps we could even have a bit of a race on horseback?"

It's a struggle to keep my expression even. "Yes," I say finally, "I do often miss the simple life." This makes me want to laugh. Baba does, in fact, often say that he misses "the simple life," though I've never thought to ask him exactly what kind of life he's referring to.

"You say you herd cattle back in China," Uncle Hong says.

"Um, yes, indeed that is one of the many things I had to do back home in China."

"You talk quite a bit about butchering the new year pig with the other villagers," Uncle Jing says.

Ew. What? The thought of my gentle, bespectacled father butchering a whole pig is a disturbing one. "Y-yes, that is something we do every year, yup."

"Butchering the new year pig is always done by men of the village," Uncle Hong says, "while women are busy cleaning and preparing the meats."

Silence clings to the air for barely a second before my instincts kick in. I raise my chin and smile. "You're right, of course. But my family has always raised me to defy traditional gender roles and expectations, which is why I'm sitting here before you, as one of the youngest, most accomplished managing partners of this firm." The uncertainty and wobbliness leave me and I charge forward. "I had to work twice as hard to prove myself back home in my village and I've had to do the same here in the finance industry, and I can prove to you that once we acquire your company, we will be working night and day to make sure it turns into the massive success story it deserves to be."

"It's already a massive success story," James says.

I level a calculated, polite smile at him. "Well, I would love to go

45

over the numbers with you to show just how much you are missing out on and what we can achieve together."

"Ah!" one of the aunties exclaims. "I sense romance! I don't see a wedding ring. . . ."

The blood drains from my face. No way I heard the auntie correctly. Surely this cannot be happening at a business meeting, for god's sake? "Uh—"

"How old are you, Zhou?" the auntie says.

"Um, twenty-eight?" Belatedly, I wonder why my answer came out as a question.

"Wah, good age gap. James here is thirty years old. He is a rooster, which means you are dragon, very good pairing."

"Oh, uh . . ." What the hell am I supposed to say to that? I don't even dare look at James. Never mind my cheeks, my entire face feels singed with embarrassment.

"Tsk," one of the other aunties says, "what rubbish. She will make better match with Ryan, he is a rat, they complement each other perfectly."

A young man, probably the Ryan in question, tilts his head back and groans, "Not again, Ma."

"Ryan did not even go to Ivy League," James's mother says. "I think Zhou can do better than that, can't you, Zhou? My James here went to Brown."

Ryan's mother's chest swells to about twice its original size, but before I can make what would no doubt be a caustic retort, Uncle Jing says, "Jamie, don't interrupt meeting with your womanly gossip."

I'm burning with even more embarrassment at having witnessed Uncle Jing publicly chastise his wife in such a horrible, sexist way. But the auntie, probably used to him being brusque toward her, doesn't seem to mind. With a shrug, she says, "We will talk more later about making a good match for you."

"She does have impressive credentials," one of the cousins says, and they all follow his gaze to the TV screen, which is now showing a large photo of me.

Next to the photo is my bio, detailing my graduating with honors from Princeton, and highlighting the biggest acquisitions I've spearheaded since joining Eighty-Eight Capital, each one over a hundred million dollars' worth of investments. I steal a glance at Mushu, who winks in return. Good old Mushu. I can always count on her to come through for me, no matter how ridiculous the situation. Growing up, the two of us were always as thick as thieves. Neither of us has any siblings, so we became sisters to each other in a way, and when I went to Princeton, Mushu chose to go to Rutgers, which meant we spent many a weekend in New York City painting the town red. I focus now on the strength that being near Mushu lends me. I can do this, I can carry this meeting through.

"Very impressive résumé," Auntie Jiayi says.

"Yes, you make very good daughter-in-law," Auntie Jamie says.

"Um, thanks," I say, "but let's circle back to the numbers. Ah, yes, here we are. This is your company's financials sheet, which includes your historical and capital structure. As you can see, there are things we can do to cut down costs—"

"No cost cutting," Uncle Hong says immediately.

Shang clears his throat. "Ah, what my uncle meant is we are hesitant to take cost-cutting measures because we don't want the quality of our product to suffer. Wutai Gold is a smaller whiskey company compared to what's out there, and what we have over our competitors is a reputation for quality."

"I completely agree," I say. "What I was about to say is that there are things we can do to cut down costs, but my proposed strategy is to focus on expanding the market."

"That's ridiculous," James says. "How do you expand a market?

This isn't some fairy tale where you can just magically conjure up more customers."

"How about you let her finish talking?" Shang says.

"I'm glad you asked," I say to James the Asshat. "There are a few ways of expanding the market. One way is expanding the distribution, looking at foreign markets . . . China, for example, has an ever-increasing whiskey fanbase, and the market is nowhere near as saturated as the US or UK. Another potential market is Southeast Asia, especially Indonesia. It's the—"

"Soon-to-be fourth-largest market in the world," Shang says at the same time as I say the same exact words.

There is a pause as we both stare at each other. Ugh, why does he have to be so gorgeous? Those dark brown eyes of his look as deep and rich as chocolate, and when he speaks once more, I'm momentarily distracted by the shape of his lips and how utterly kissable they look. Shang says, with grudging admiration, "Good to know you keep up with the global market."

Is that a compliment or is that condescension? I can't quite tell.

"Going worldwide?" James says, his eyes so wide they look like they're about to pop right out. "That's—"

"That's what we've always talked about doing, but never ventured into," Shang says.

"Because we're already bleeding money!" James snaps.

"Well, Eighty-Eight Capital is well connected in the import/export sector. Many of our partners are exporters of fine goods, so we would of course be cutting the most favorable export deals for the companies we invest in." *God, I hope that sounded as reassuring as it did in my head.*

The Li family turn to one another and burst into an animated argument about the pros and cons of going global. I study them as they debate. This is, so far, one of the most perplexing meetings I've ever attended. Usually, by the time a company gets to the stage where they're meeting face-to-face with me and Baba, it's because they've come to an agreement that selling would be the best decision for them. But now, the only thing that's clear is that the stakeholders of Wutai Gold are massively divided on their stance. James obviously is very much against selling, though I have a feeling James doesn't quite understand the business as much as he'd like us to think. Uncle Hong, James's father, and a few of the other uncles and aunts seem to be on James's side. The other three cousins, Ryan, Thomas, and Christopher, seem undecided, and the only one who seems to actually be open to the idea of selling is Shang.

Furthermore, in every board of directors, there has to be a clear leader. From Baba's emails, I would've guessed that the leader here would be Shang, but now that I'm meeting everyone in person, it becomes a lot less obvious who's in charge. I instinctively sense that Shang is perhaps the one who has been the most hands-on with the business, the person who knows the actual ins and outs of it. But the others, like James and Uncle Hong, seem to have a lot to say about the company, which makes it nearly impossible for me to deduce who I should be directing my questions or suggestions to.

This is why I hate family-run businesses. And it also begs the question: If Baba had been able to attend this meeting himself, would he end it still as keen on going forward as he had been before the meeting?

After a few minutes, sensing that the argument is now going around in circles, I call out, "Exporting the goods is just one of many ways of increasing the market. It's an option we can explore down the road. But there are also things we can do within the domestic market." Shang meets my eye, his expression unreadable, and I try to ignore the way my insides twist at his look. "I have noticed that currently, your market is very, very limited. It's niche, so to speak. Your audience comprises solely older men in the fifty-five to seventy-five age bracket."

"The real men," Uncle Hong grunts.

"Sure," I say, "but this market is, unfortunately, rapidly shrinking."

"They're dying," Mushu says dryly. Heads swivel to stare at her, and she shrugs and says, "What? I'm just saying. They old."

"Um, Mushu is right," I say. "Not that they're all dying, of course, but ah, they are aging, and as people age, they don't drink as robustly as they used to, so. This is the main reason why your sales numbers are falling."

"And how are you going to solve that?" James says.

"Well, here at Eighty-Eight Capital, we have a wide range of companies that we're invested in. Many of them are marketing and publicity specialists, they have an extensive social media outreach—"

"Social media!" huffs Uncle Hong.

I falter. "Ah, yes . . . Facebook, YouTube . . ."

"Hah!" Uncle Jing snorts.

"What am I missing?" I say.

Shang clears his throat. "Our family is very traditional. G-one— that's my uncles' generation—thinks we should only stick to conventional advertising. Magazines, billboards, and so on."

For a second, all I can do is stare blankly at him. "May I ask why?"

"Our brand is high-end, limited-edition whiskey," Uncle Hong says with obvious pride. "We don't pander to masses by flogging our product on social media." The words *social media* are said with as much venom as I've ever heard anyone say them. The other uncles and aunts nod in agreement.

I'm starting to understand why their sales numbers, so full of potential in the early years of the company, have started to fall. I understand now why everything else in their company has stagnated. I also know exactly what this company needs to revitalize it. But what I can't see, frustratingly, is a way of getting my ideas across without causing them offense. Because it feels right now like I've found myself in a minefield, and I'm completely unprepared for it because, again, all the companies

50

I've had these sorts of meetings with before have been eager to sell, whereas for some strange reason I need to woo these people.

Then, as I try to decipher what my next step should be, James says, "I don't think selling to you is the right move for us."

My chest constricts. A tide of pure shock washes over me. Not since my well-meaning parents had enrolled me in soccer have I felt this outmatched. No. I can't lose this now, not when my father is lying in the hospital, clinging to the hope that I will carry this through for us, for our company, for our legacy. I watch with increasing despair as Uncle Hong nods and straightens, ready to leave the room, and the words rush out of my mouth without consulting my brain.

"I understand completely what your company stands for. Wutai Gold is the gentleman's whiskey, and there is no other like it in the market," I hear myself saying. "We don't want to dilute the brand. We'll prove to the audience that Wutai Gold is just as masculine as ever. That what is stands for is strength and . . ." My mind scrambles for the right word. What would Baba do? You are not Mulan right now, you are Zhou. Think like Zhou! *"Audacity."*

Everyone stares at me, unblinking.

"Audacity?" James says, one eyebrow cocked like he's about to say something disparaging.

"It means boldness," I say, at the same time as Shang. Once again, there is a momentary pause as we lock eyes. Is it me or is there a hint of color in his cheeks? *Stop reading my mind*, I want to snap at him.

"I know what it means," James grumbles.

"I like it," Shang says, breaking eye contact with me. "It's catchy."

"Yes, but no offense," James says in a tone that is clearly meant to offend, "you're just not the kind of person we had in mind to run our family company."

Shang leans forward, opening his mouth, but his mother places a hand on his arm.

"You mean a woman?" I say, making sure I seem completely unfazed by this. Despite myself, despite knowing that I am above this, that I've spent years dealing with chauvinists exactly like James, a sourness churns in my gut. Baba has spent decades of his life toiling away, building this company from the ground up, and it had been painfully clear that he'd been passionate about acquiring Wutai Gold. And though his reasons might be a mystery to me, I'll be damned before I let him down. "Don't worry, I will prove to you that I can be just as manly as you are."

James scoffs, and then his smirk disappears when he sees the seriousness of my expression. "And how exactly will you prove that?"

"My résumé should be en—" But even as I say this, I can see the smug look of victory spreading across James's face.

Then Shang says, smoothly, without looking up, "How about we invite her to the ranch? We shouldn't make any decisions before Zhou can actually come to the distillery and assess it for herself."

Everyone stares at him, and he finally lifts his gaze to meet mine. He raises an eyebrow. "You did tell me you're a better rancher than I."

I did? I want to squeak. *Baba, what have you done?*

"That's a great idea. A ranch isn't a place for everyone," Mushu says. "Especially not weak-willed, city-bred women."

Welp. I'm not weak-willed—anyone who knows me well knows that—but I am very definitely city-bred. "Mushu," I try to whisper without attracting anyone else's attention, but it's no use. Mushu has found her stride, and when that happens, there's no stopping her.

"All right, it's settled! We will come with you to your ranch, where Zhou will show that she is no sniveling, high-maintenance city girl, but a man's man who is ready to grab the world in a chokehold and make it give your company the success it deserves," Mushu crows.

Oh god. What Mushu just said is so sexist I don't even know where to begin. But somehow, it's working. The Li family looks astounded at first, but now over half of them are nodding along. What is happening?

James snorts again, but before he can say a word, Uncle Hong says, "Fine. We are supposed to go in a day's time for our annual family trip anyway, so you can come with us then."

I gape at him until my senses slam back into place and I snap my mouth shut. I did not really just get the green light for a visit to the Li family ranch and distillery, did I? Somehow, I manage to eke out a "Great, thank you for the opportunity, I'm very much looking forward to it."

Am I really looking forward to it? Heck no. Still, it feels like the sort of thing one might say at times like these. As everyone shakes hands and files out of the conference room, I lock eyes with Mushu, who grins and winks back. What has my well-meaning cousin roped me into?

CHAPTER SIX

"What have you done?" I moan at Mushu for the sixteenth time.

From behind the changing room curtain, Mushu's voice calls out, "I've saved the buyout for you. You're welcome. How're those jeans looking?"

"Like normal jeans? I'm still not quite understanding why I needed to get a new pair when I own, like, ten pairs of perfectly good jeans at home."

"Mulan, Mulan, Mulan." Then, without checking, Mushu yanks the curtain open dramatically.

"Hey!" I scramble to cover my shirtless top half.

Mushu gasps, her gaze locked on my jeans. "Oh, Mulan, they look so good! Turn around."

"Get out of here," I snap.

Completely ignoring me, Mushu pokes at my hip and says, "Look at the way these Western jeans hug your hips without squeezing your waistline. Which ones are these? The WRESTLE ME LOUDLY COWBOY jeans?"

I pinch the bridge of my nose as Mushu locates the tag attached to the back of the jeans. "That cannot be a real name for a pair of jeans."

"Ah," Mushu says, squinting at the tag. "Nope, this is the ULTIMATE FUN TIME DON'T MESS WITH THIS COWGIRL collection."

"These names have got to be made up," I grumble.

"Well, yes, they are. That's exactly how names come about. You see, when an advertiser falls in love with a product, they get together and make an ad campaign with all sorts of catchy names in it," Mushu says slowly.

I roll my eyes, but can't help smiling. "Shut up. You know what I mean."

"According to this tag, the ULTIMATE FUN TIME DON'T MESS WITH THIS COWGIRL jeans are designed to make your ass pop while also having superfine stitching on the inside leg so your thighs don't chafe when you ride." Mushu grins and wiggles her eyebrows.

"Ew, gross, stop that, I wasn't even thinking of him!"

Mushu's eyebrows knot together. "Who's him? Obviously I meant when you ride a horse. Who did you think I meant?"

Heat blooms in my cheeks and I avoid meeting Mushu's gaze as unwelcome images of Shang float through my traitorous mind. "Uh, nobody. Just, you know, in general. Don't be a perv."

Mushu narrows her eyes. "I don't think I'm the one being perverted here." A slow, horrible grin spreads across her face. "Ooohh."

"Stop that, you look like the Joker."

"I think we know who's been on your mind," Mushu sings.

"Nobody is on my mind!"

Mushu clasps her hands and presses them to her cheek. "Oh, Shang," she trills. "Please sweep me off my feet with those granite-hard arms of yours and carry me into the setting sun!"

"Are you a horny teen?" I snap, but I can't help giggling a little as Mushu swoons dramatically. Plus, Mushu isn't technically wrong; I haven't been able to keep Shang out of my mind ever since our disastrous meeting the day before.

After the meeting, I had gone to visit Baba at the hospital. He was asleep, so I talked to Mama and told her how badly the meeting had gone and how we now had to go to the Wutai Gold ranch and distillery to prove my "manliness."

Mama laughed so hard that she had to grasp my arms to keep from collapsing to the floor. "Oh, Mulan," she cried. "Only Mushu could've wrangled that outcome out of the meeting."

"What do I do, Ma?" I said with all the helplessness of a toddler.

As Mama wiped her tears of mirth away, she said, "Well, you made your bed, now you have to lie in it."

"I didn't make my bed! Mushu did."

"And who chose to go into the meeting pretending to be a managing partner, with Mushu as your associate?" Mama said, ignoring my groan. "You go to this ranch and you show them who's the man."

"I hate it, thanks," I mumbled through my hands.

"You've got this, Daughter."

But now, with my grandma underwear squashed by the tight ULTIMATE FUN TIME DON'T MESS WITH THIS COWGIRL jeans, the only thing I'm sure I have is a wedgie.

"These Western jeans are a winner," Mushu says. "You look very much like a cowgirl, in the best possible way."

Despite myself, I have to agree. The jeans are undeniably flattering, making my hips look curvier and my legs look longer. And, just as advertised, the stitching is smooth, making the material feel comfortable against my skin. All I need to do is lose the grandma undies and this would be the comfiest pair of jeans I've worn. How come I've never thought of getting a pair of Western jeans for myself? "Okay," I say. "Let's go pay."

"Uh, you didn't think we were done, did you?" Mushu says.

I stare at her with growing trepidation. "Um, I kind of did, actually?"

"Mulan, Mulan, Mulan," Mushu says again, this time with an exaggerated sigh. "We're only getting started."

"We are?"

"Oh yes. We didn't drive all this way to Wild Coyote to just get a pair of jeans. We're here for an entire LOOK. We're here to turn you from boring finance bro to Yankee cowgirl."

After that, there's no stopping Mushu. As I stand helplessly in the dressing room, Mushu drapes more and more things over me. First, a push-up bra so aggressive that I swear my breasts are shoved right up below my chin, followed by a tight checkered shirt. Despite the fact that the checkered shirt is long-sleeved and so barely shows any skin, it's so figure-hugging that it leaves nothing to the imagination. I hug myself, feeling oddly naked in the mirror.

"Gosh, look at the lift that bra is giving you," Mushu says. "I'm getting myself one for that Women Entrepreneurs banquet that's happening in about two weeks' time."

"Oh! Did you score an invite?" I say. Mushu has been talking about the banquet for almost half a year now.

"Not yet, but I know a couple of the organizers and I've been dropping hints to them about getting me on the list, so any day now," Mushu says. Although she says this in her trademark flippant way, I sense a trace of insecurity behind her confident mask. I know how much Mushu would love to attend a banquet for women entrepreneurs. I wish there were some way I could help her.

Mushu gives herself a little shake and focuses her attention back on me. "Anyway, you look amazing."

"Are you sure about this? The shirt's so tight I can barely lift my arms."

"Arm movement is so overrated," Mushu says.

I try to lift my arms and get as far as my waist before the fabric threatens to rip. I glare at Mushu.

"Oh, all right, I'll get a shirt that's one size up. But it's not going to make your boobs look as good, though."

"You know what, that's a trade-off I'm willing to make," I call out.

As it turns out, the next size up is still really figure-hugging, but I am at least able to move around freely in this one. "Is it really supposed to hug my curves like that?" I shudder at the thought of walking around in such a revealing outfit. I'm used to straitlaced navy and dark gray suits, clothes that are designed to make finance bros take me seriously, not see me as anything vaguely attractive. This shirt and these jeans are definitely a far cry from my usual office wear. Then Mushu adds a bright red kerchief around my neck and drapes a light blue denim jacket over my shoulders and I breathe a sigh of relief over the extra coverage that the jacket gives me.

"I look ridiculous," I say, staring at my reflection.

"Only because the look isn't complete yet." With that, Mushu plops something heavy on my head.

It's a cowgirl hat, because of course it is. It's eggshell in color and has a brown feather sticking out of the left side, and I'm pretty sure I can't go out in public wearing this outfit. "I—I can't—"

"Wait, wait!" Mushu cries. "It's not ready yet."

"It's not?"

"All right, ready for the pièce de résistance?"

"No," I say earnestly.

In answer, Mushu brandishes a pair of shockingly ornate cowgirl boots. "These are the highest-quality cowgirl boots. Made of calfskin, they are supersoft on the inside but are so strong they'll withstand anything the Wild West can throw at you, including boulders rolling over your feet and snake bites. Assuming the snake's on the outside of the boot, that is. If the snake's inside your boot . . ." Mushu laughs, slapping my back. "Well, gotta check your boots for snakes every morning, okay?"

I swallow. "Snakes?"

Mushu levels a flat gaze at me. "Mulan, we're about to brave the wilderness. Of course there will be snakes. And scorpions, I shouldn't be surprised. As well as loons."

"What's a loon?" I cry.

"You know, I'm not too sure myself. A wild bird would be my guess, but could easily be some kind of fox? Who knows. Ask Google. Now put these boots on."

In somewhat of a daze, I do as Mushu says, stuffing my feet into the boots. "I—I don't know, they feel kind of tough."

"That's because they are. Snake bites, remember? Anyway, you'll break them in soon enough." Mushu stands back, looking me up and down. "You look like a real cowgirl."

I gape at the mirror. Who is this girl staring back at me? "Why is my reflection someone I don't know?"

"Girl, stop being so dramatic. You look like you're ready to ride the bronco."

"I don't even know what a bronco is. Is that a wild cow?"

"Oh dear." Mushu slaps a hand over her forehead. "We need to do a lot of work to get you ready for this trip, don't we?"

"God, this isn't going to work," I moan, taking off the cowgirl hat and facing Mushu. "No one is going to buy that I grew up on a farm or a ranch or whatever it is my dad supposedly grew up on. What is even the difference between the two?"

In answer, Mushu places her hands on my shoulders and turns me back to face the mirror. "It's going to work. You know how I know that? Because you're the most determined human I have ever known. It's honestly annoying as hell."

I laugh. "Thanks, cuz."

"No, but really, do you know what it's like growing up alongside you? My mom's favorite phrase is: 'Why can't you be more like Mulan?'"

I draw in a sharp breath. "Oh, Mushu, I'm sorry."

"Don't be, it's not your fault you're so driven. I mean, did our other cousins and I bitch about you behind your back? Incessantly."

"You need to work on your pep talks."

Mushu gives a wry smile. "My point is, even though it was very stressful for me and probably contributed to my teenage acne, at the end of the day, I'm grateful to have you as a cousin. Because you showed me to work harder and aim higher. God, without you as a cousin, I would probably have been—I don't know—a high school dropout. I mean it," she adds when I open my mouth to protest. "I was so aimless in high school. I didn't know what I wanted to do, I still don't, honestly. But I was so inspired by you because you always knew. You never wavered. From when we were kids, you were like, 'I'm going to work in finance.' Can you imagine how freaking obnoxious that was? You were only eight. I didn't even know what finance was. I thought it was like fortune telling or something."

I laugh. "It kind of is like fortune telling."

"Huh. Yeah, you're right. But anyway, you know what I'm getting at. You inspire me, cuz. And you're going to inspire these people."

I gaze doubtfully at the mirror. "The only thing I'm going to inspire looking like this is laughter."

"Or admiration. And let's face it, who are we kidding? I bet you've done your homework for this trip, haven't you?"

I gnaw on my bottom lip and avoid meeting Mushu's eye. "I don't know what you're talking about."

"How many hours of reading have you done on ranches and distilleries since you found out you're going on this trip?"

"Only the appropriate number of hours."

"If it's anything over one hour, it is not appropriate," Mushu says dryly. "And what resources did you use? Wikipedia?"

I don't answer.

"Great, so knowing you, you've spent at least five hours researching all the technical details of ranches and distilleries on Wikipedia."

"Not just Wikipedia," I grumble.

"God, you nerd," Mushu says. "But that's why I love you, cuz."

I nudge Mushu with my shoulder. "I don't deserve you."

"No, you don't. And yet, here I am."

"Doesn't the whole 'Show them you can be manly, too' thing bother you, though?"

"Nope."

I give her the side-eye. "Not even a little bit?"

"Isn't that what you've been doing this whole time at the firm? So, you don't look like yourself. You know what? I don't even know what the real you looks like. I always see you in the office wearing power suits and talking like a finance bro. Or when you're with your parents, you turn into this perfect Chinese kid and you carry yourself different. You even laugh differently. You're used to playing all these roles, what's one more?"

A lump forms in my throat. "Jeez, Mushu," I joke, trying to hide how much Mushu's words have affected me. "Since when did you become so perceptive?"

"Oh please, I have always been perceptive. I am one of life's quiet observers. Also, I literally heard you out-burp Brian in the lunchroom last Tuesday."

"That was because we were— We'd gotten those giant subs for lunch and were . . ." My voice trails off as I recall what I and the other analysts had been doing.

"And you were having a competition to see who could eat their sub the fastest," Mushu says. "A more dudebro way of spending your lunchtime I have never heard of."

I sigh and look down at my feet.

"Face it, you've spent half your life trying to fit into the finance world, and it's dominated by bros. The worst of bros, actually."

"The quants at hedge funds aren't that bad," I mumble.

"They're the least bad of the bunch, but guess what, we don't work with them."

"It's the only way I can get taken seriously." I haven't felt so miserable, so much like a sellout, in a long time.

"I know," Mushu says, her voice suddenly turning gentle. "I'm not holding it against you. I may not be an associate or an analyst, but I know what it's like to have to work in a man's world. I hate that we can't just be ourselves for these dudebros to take us seriously. It's just a sad fact, and you're doing everything right. Which is why I know you can do this, you can convince the Lis that you're man enough to take their stupid whiskey all the way to the top."

"If you say so. But . . ." I massage my temples. "I don't even have a plan beyond 'Get the deal done.' I mean, what's going to happen if we do get the deal? I don't have a long-term plan in place. Are we going to keep up this charade even after we acquire the company?"

"One step at a time," Mushu says in a reassuring tone of voice. "First of all, you're not the one who usually steps in and runs the companies you guys acquire. You hire someone else to actually run the operation, right?"

I nod. "Wow, Mushu, so you do pay attention to all this 'finance-y stuff' after all."

"I've got hidden layers so deep you don't even know," Mushu says. "So you'll acquire this company, you'll find the right person to help fix whatever's broken in it, and you'll meet with these people, what, twice a year? Or maybe every quarter to look over their performance? That's doable, right?"

It does sound doable, but none of it feels good to me. Why hadn't I foreseen how slimy it would all feel? "I guess so."

"I know so."

Somehow, even though Mushu's pep talk is the most confused pep talk in the history of pep talks, it's having an effect on me. I gaze into the mirror and watch as my face turns from uncertainty to determination, my brows setting low and my mouth pinching grimly. Mushu's right. One step at a time. The most important thing here is to not lose the company that Baba was so excited to acquire. I've had years of experience fighting to be accepted in a heavily male-dominated industry. This trip is going to be nothing compared to everything else I've had to go through to get to where I am in life. So I'll have to herd a few cows, maybe uh, feed a couple of chickens or whatever it is they do at a ranch. Did I not graduate top ten in my class? Did I not wow my Princeton professor with my thesis on game theory models and how to shed light on determining financial offers? Did I not beat out my classmates, many of whom were savants with IQs above 140 and titles like World Chess Champion or World Mathematics Champion? I am Hua Mulan, daughter of Hua Zhou and Hua Li, and the Lis would do well not to underestimate me.

CHAPTER SEVEN

By the time we're through shopping, Mushu has talked me into buying so many things for the trip that I know my suitcase will be filled to bursting.

To make things worse, when Mushu picked me up to drive to the rendezvous point at Uncle Hong's house, she took one look at my giant bag and said, "Jeez, cuz, what did you pack in here, a whole horse?"

"Don't make me put you on probationary leave," I snapped, at which Mushu giggled. It took both of us to lug the suitcase into the trunk.

Uncle Hong's house is a palatial mansion in Atherton with a long, snaking driveway lined with lush trees. Gravel crunches under the tires as Mushu navigates the car through the drive, and I'm more and more intimidated as we get to the end of the driveway and find ourselves staring up at the massive mansion. The Lis are already gathered out front, chatting and carrying their bags to various vehicles—it's a mix of sporty cars and even a humongous, flashy trailer that will take some of the family up to the ranch and distillery.

Mushu parks the car and, with one last deep inhale, I get out. Here we go.

Conversations pause mid-sentence as we climb out, and I have to remind myself not to hunch my shoulders as eyes crawl over us. Oh god, I knew it. I knew I shouldn't have listened to Mushu about the stupid outfit!

It's a scene straight out of my nightmares—not one of the Lis is dressed in a ranch outfit. Sure, a few of them are wearing cowboy boots, but these boots look like proper work boots, dusty and hardy and not at all ornate like mine are. A couple of them are indeed wearing checkered shirts, but none of the shirts are as tight as mine. They look like shirts that the wearers can move around freely in. And no one, not a single one of them, is wearing a cowboy hat. Some are wearing baseball caps, many of the women are wearing aggressively large visors, but there isn't a single cowboy hat to be found in the crowd.

Then I spot Shang talking to his mother, and my heart skitters to a stop. He looks good enough to pounce on and do really bad things with. There's his face, for one, which is so pretty I could just die looking at it. I mean, really, those intense eyes under those thick brows, and that sexy-as-hell bun, which makes me wonder what his hair looks like when it's loose. . . . What's a girl to do? He's wearing a gray sweater with the sleeves rolled up to his elbows, exposing his muscular forearms. And the material is so soft that it shows off the shape of his pecs, which are— Oh god, am I drooling?

As though sensing me staring, Shang lifts his head and turns around. Our gazes meet, and in that split second, his eyes widen as he takes in my ridiculous getup. His lips part, as though he's forgotten himself for just a moment, and I would love nothing more than to believe that he's as enchanted by me as I am by him. But then, gruffly, he looks away, as though completely unimpressed by my outfit. Well, not that I was expecting him to be impressed, but still.

I snatch my cowgirl hat off, mentally cursing Mushu. And myself for listening to Mushu.

"Morning, girls!" James calls out, swaggering toward us.

I can't believe he just called us "girls." But outwardly I smile and say, "Hello, kid."

Behind James, Shang coughs and covers his mouth with his fist. Can he be hiding a smile? Nah, not possible.

James recovers quickly. "You gals ready for some rough wilderness?"

"Oh yeah, totally," I say in as convincing a voice as I can muster. "Can't wait to, uh, shear sheep and, uh, catch wild loons."

Shang coughs again, and I raise my brows at him. "Sorry, did you want to say something?"

"No, not at all. Uh, you look very . . . ranch-y."

"Thanks," Mushu says with unabashed pride. "We make it a point to fit into every situation we're in."

James leers at Mushu's tight checkered shirt, and I thank my lucky stars for the denim jacket, which I now surreptitiously wrap tighter around myself. I notice Shang throwing James a dirty look as his lecherous gaze sweeps over Mushu, who for her part doesn't seem at all bothered by it.

"So we've got the main trailer, that'll be where most of G-one's riding," James says. "I'll be driving Sultry, obviously."

"I'm sorry, Sultry?" I already know I'm going to regret asking.

"His car," Shang mutters, at the same time as James is saying "My Lambo."

"Ah."

"You're welcome to join me and Sultry, of course," James says with what he probably thinks is a suave smile. "The ladies love her."

"Uh . . ." I can feel the grimace taking over my face, but can't quite seem to wrestle it off. "That's very kind of you. . . ."

Shang, who's been watching quietly, says, "There's plenty of room in my car."

Somehow, though the idea of being stuck inside James's car is appalling, the thought of being in Shang's car makes my throat close up.

"Yeah, okay, sounds good," Mushu says. She turns to James. "Sorry, but ain't no woman going inside a car named Sultry. Let's go, cuz." And without waiting for a response, Mushu stalks off in the direction where the cars are parked.

I glance over at Shang and to my consternation, he's studying me with an expectant look. "Sounds good," I say. His expression warms ever so slightly.

"I've got to admire how your cousin just assumed she'll figure out which car's mine," Shang says, holding his hand out.

I look, unmoving, at his outstretched hand. Then, swallowing, I place my hand in his. His palm is big, the skin a little rough, with calluses, but it's warm and solid and comforting. The heat from his hand flows all the way up my arm, warming my entire body.

"Um," Shang says. "I meant to help you with your bag?"

"Oh!" Embarrassment explodes throughout me like a supernova. The bolt of shame is so intense that it feels like it should've blown a crater deep into the ground so I could bury myself in it. I step back, wiping my hand down my jeans as though his touch has burned me and babbling, "Right! Well, there's no need for that! I can take my bag myself."

"Okay, come on."

We walk to the line of cars, where most of the Li family has gathered, chatting and loading bags into their various vehicles. James hurries here and there, telling anyone who will listen that he's waxed Sultry just for this trip. Mushu is leaning against a Volvo.

"There's a bit of a problem," she says when Shang and I get within hearing distance.

"Yes?" Shang says.

"There doesn't seem to be any room in the back seat of your car."

"How did you know this was my car?" Shang says.

Mushu slides her gaze deliberately to the car before saying, "This car, just like its owner, is giving dad vibes."

Shang laughs and says, "Okay. But what do you mean there's no room in the back seat? There's— Oh."

The back seat of his car is stuffed with bags piled on top of one another, plus a huge cooler taking up all the remaining space.

"We ran out of room in the trailer," one of the aunties calls out. "You don't mind, right, Shang?"

"I may have suggested it to them," Mushu says helpfully.

Shang sighs. "You didn't think to suggest they put stuff inside Sultry?"

"James was smart enough to keep his car locked," Mushu says. "Otherwise, yes, it would've gotten filled to the gills with Chinese barbecue pork and frozen wontons."

"Smart guy," Shang says.

"So," Mushu continues, "I'll go ride with the aunties. They all want to matchmake me with their sons, apparently."

I frown. "I'll go in the trailer, too."

"No," Mushu says. "Go with Shang. There's no more space for you in the trailer."

"What?" I say, but already she is walking away, waving a careless hand behind her.

"See you there, cuz!"

I watch her go. It's slowly sinking in that I'm going to be in the car with Shang. Alone. On a five-hour car ride. I gulp, and though we are outdoors and there's a pleasant breeze around us, the gulp is painfully audible. "Um . . ."

"You can put your bag in here," Shang says, popping open the trunk.

"Uh, thanks." I yank my bag next to the car and struggle to lift it.

"Let me help."

"Nope," I snap. I need to show him that I am more than able to handle this entire trip, never mind one stupid bag. One stupid, oversize, overstuffed bag. *I'm normally a light traveler*, I want to wail. I bend my knees, my quads straining as I grasp the bag with shaking hands, and lift. After a lot of very unattractive grunts, I somehow manage to pull it off the ground and onto the lip of the trunk. But as I shove it in, I hear a rip. "Oh no."

Shang winces. "Sounds like it might've gotten caught on something." He reaches over and easily lifts the bag one-handed. "The fabric's a little torn."

"That's okay!" I say, trying not to let my face fall at the thought of my precious Samsonite bag all torn up. Maybe I should've accepted Shang's help. But no, the whole point of this trip is to show them how manly I can be, and haven't I proven that by lifting a bag I can easily fit my whole body into? I open the passenger side door and slide in. *This is a work trip*, I remind myself. *So what if you're alone in a car with the most beautiful man you've ever come across? You are a professional, and this trip means everything to your father. Behave professionally and bring, uh, honor? No. Equity? Yes. Bring equity to the firm.*

Then Shang gets in as well and as soon as the doors shut, the nearness of him is overwhelming. I can feel every molecule of air spinning between us, can hear the sound of his breathing, the rustling of his clothes as he reaches for his seatbelt. He occupies the space in a way that is impossible to ignore, filling all of my senses. When he finally turns the engine on, the sound of a podcast floods the car, and my shoulders unknot a little. Ambient noise, that's good. That way, Shang won't be able to hear the weird, neurotic thoughts speeding through my head. I try not to notice the way he turns the wheel with one hand while the other is—ack!—placed on my headrest as he backs the car out of the parking space. He's totally going to catch me stealing glimpses of his forearm. Why is one-hand steering so freaking sexy?

The thing is, I'm not sure why I'm so nervous around Shang. Sure, he's devastatingly handsome, but so are plenty of other men; we are in California after all, a state teeming with avocados, matcha lattes, and hot guys. Maybe it's because there is so much riding on me impressing him and his family, on striking just the right note with them. Yes, that's it. When it comes to romantic relationships and past boyfriends, I've never had to work hard to impress them or their families, simply because I've never really cared about a guy that deeply. But with Shang, it's about a deal, it's about making and preserving connections—guanxi— and that's so much more important than any romantic relationships.

I force myself to focus on the present moment. The narration coming from the stereo catches my attention. "What podcast is this?"

Shang spares me a quick glance. "It's not a podcast. It's an audio-book." He hits a button and it stops playing.

"An . . . *audiobook*?" The word is so alien to me that it comes out sounding like a foreign language.

"Yeah, you know, like a novel, but in audio format?"

"I know what an audiobook is, I just . . . have not come across an actual person who listens to them."

"That's because you're a finance bro."

My mouth drops open in mock annoyance. "I am not a finance bro!"

"Oh, really?" Shang gives me a skeptical look. "What was the last thing you did on vacation?"

"Ski trip in Aspen."

One of those dark, thick eyebrows rises.

"Okay," I say. "Maybe that is a tad finance bro-y. But that's only because it was a company trip."

"The fact that you even go on company trips just screams finance bro," Shang says.

"I do tai chi! That's, like, the antithesis of finance bro."

Shang side-eyes me as he merges onto the main road.

"Okay, my mom does tai chi and she makes me do it when I go to their house for our weekly meal."

Shang snorts.

"You're not any better," I grumble. "You're a—whiskey bro? Is that a thing?"

"Oh yeah, that is definitely a thing. And I'd like to say I am not a whiskey bro, but I'll leave it up to you to decide."

I ponder this for a bit, a smile working its way over my mouth. "Okay, let's see. What audiobook are you listening to? Let me guess: *How to Be the Manliest Man Who Ever Manned*?"

"You know, I think James is actually listening to that one."

"James probably only listens to podcasts about how to be a good alpha male."

"Okay, you're probably right there. Anyway, I'm listening to a novel, not a nonfiction book."

"A novel?" I narrow my eyes.

"A novel is a work of fiction, usually between seventy to ninety thousand words in length. It has a plot, which consists of a conflict that the protagonist is trying to resolve."

"Okay, smart-ass," I groan. "Wow, thank you for mansplaining what a novel is to me. What would I do without your wisdom?"

"Listen to podcasts about how to be a good alpha male, probably," Shang mutters.

There's a slight pause; then, as one, we both devolve into peals of laughter. What a surprise it is to be laughing with Shang. He's come off so buttoned-up this whole time that I wasn't sure that he even knew how to laugh, but now that he is, I'm realizing what a delightful sound it is, boyish and low, with the slightest tinge of surprise that makes me want to make him laugh again and again.

"The book's called *The Water Outlaws*, by S. L. Huang. It's a gender-swapped reimagining of *Water Margin*, one of the greatest works of Chinese literature. Only instead of the traditional male monks, it follows a group of women who are criminals—or alleged criminals—as they try to live peaceful lives as monks. But they're not very good at it, especially because men keep trying to kill them for simply existing," he says wryly.

"Wow, I would never have guessed," I say, and there are no traces of sarcasm in my voice. I glance over at Shang, and I really cannot make sense of this man who's obviously a sexist alpha male, based on his family and their whole whiskey persona, but who also reads a book about female monks.

By now, we're about to get on the freeway. James pulls up next to us, grinning with his tongue out. He waves, then revs Sultry so the engine screams, before speeding off ahead of us. Shang shakes his head, sighing. "I hate that thing," he says.

"That's not a nice way to talk about your cousin."

Shang laughs again. The corners of his eyes crinkle adorably, and I have to make a conscious effort to drag my gaze from him. I scold myself mentally. *I'm here to do my job. I'm here as Zhou, not as Mulan.* There are about a million reasons why I shouldn't be attracted to this man, not least of which is the fact that it would be highly unethical given my company is trying to acquire his. With no small effort, I envision myself repositioning my work mask back into place.

Okay, time to do a little digging into the family company. "So tell me, what made you decide to meet with my d—my firm?"

For a few moments, Shang looks deep in thought. He adjusts his grip on the wheel and merges onto the freeway before taking a big breath. "Well, like you pointed out at the meeting, our sales are falling, and I thought maybe if we could sell to a firm it would revitalize our numbers."

"Have you tried improving the numbers yourselves?"

"It's . . ." Shang pauses, pursing his lips as he mulls this over. "Thing is, it's kind of tough in my family company to make big changes. Maybe because it's a family company, or maybe because we got used to doing things a certain way, whatever it is, I feel like we've kind of stagnated.

That's why I thought, well, an outside perspective would help."

"That's not uncommon. Actually, I would say that most of the businesses we acquire have similar issues of stagnation, whether it be the management or the production. Whatever it is, I'm confident that our firm has the expertise to shake things up."

"Great," Shang says. "Well, I like change. You might have to work a little harder to convince the rest of my family, though."

"Yeah, I get that. What's it like working for family?"

Is it my imagination or does Shang grip the wheel a little harder? "It's a mixed bag," he says finally.

I wait to see if he'll say more, but a few moments crawl by, and it becomes clear that this topic has come to a close. After a while, he reaches over and taps at the control screen. "I'll start it back at the beginning." He hits play, and the audiobook begins.

The *Water Outlaws* is as riveting as Shang promised, and as I listen to the epic tale of women in ancient China who, through bad luck or bad decisions, find themselves seeking refuge at Liangshan, my curiosity deepens. I can see Shang reading hard-boiled detective thrillers, with some grizzled, chain-smoking ex-addict as the protagonist. At a push, I could also see Shang reading some action spy thriller, with an ultra-buff killing machine as the protagonist. But here he is, listening to what is probably the most feminist story I've heard in years.

I give myself a little shake, trying to focus on the task at hand. The acquisition relies on me getting to the heart of the Li family. And Shang, being the CEO, is the one I need to win over most of all. But the way he clammed up when I asked him about the family company tells me that there's plenty underneath the surface, like land mines that I need to get good at avoiding.

For the next hour or so, we ride in silence, lost in the lush narration of the audiobook. It's easy to be completely immersed in the rich tapestry that Huang has woven, and when Shang's phone rings, I jerk up in my seat with surprise. Shang taps answer, and his mother's voice floats through the speaker.

"We want to break for lunch," she says.

"Okay, Ma. Next exit?"

"Okay. We go to Little Chang's."

"See you."

Shang turns off the audiobook and begins to switch lanes. "What do you think so far?"

I blink at him. It takes a second for me to leave the beautiful, yet heart-wrenching tale of Lin Chong and her sworn sisters. "Brutal" is all I'm able to come up with.

"Yeah, it's pretty heavy stuff, sorry."

"No, I think it's great. I'm going to buy a copy for my dad, actually. I'll play it to him at the ho—" I stop myself in time. Oh my god, I can't believe I almost let that slip, what is wrong with me? "At home," I say quickly.

"Cool. You guys close?"

"Yeah, we are, actually. I'm close to both my parents, but I take after my dad, so he and I have always had this understanding."

The corner of Shang's mouth twitches into a small smile. "Sounds like me and my mom."

"Are you a mama's boy?" I tease.

"Yeah, totally," he says, unabashed. "My dad passed away when I was ten, so it's just been the two of us since."

"Oh, I'm sorry."

"It was a long time ago. My mom's the only daughter in her family—"

"So your uncles and aunts are from your mom's side of the family?"

"Yup. I'm what they call the 'outside nephew.'"

I wince. In Chinese culture, a child that is related to the family through their father is called the "inside child," meaning they are "closer" to the family. And a child who is related through their mother is called the "outside child," because traditionally, when women get married, they are considered to belong to their husband's family. My own parents don't behave that way, but it's a stark reminder that outside of my nuclear family, plenty of families still uphold this tradition.

"Do they treat you very differently?"

Shang shrugs. "Eh. You'll see, I guess."

"How come they voted you in as CEO?"

"Through a lack of choices," Shang says with a rueful smile. "None of my cousins are interested in managing the company; James studied economics in school and is our marketing head, Christopher oversees distribution, Ryan is in accounting . . . I'm the only one who actually wanted to oversee everything."

"That sounds really complicated."

"It can be. Speaking of family, you ready for lunch with them?"

"Yeah, I'm starving."

Shang checks the rearview mirror as he signals to take the exit. "I mean, are you ready to deal with my family? They can be a lot to take in, I know."

"I don't know, aside from James the rest seem okay. But give me pointers."

"Okay. So, the eldest is Uncle Hong. That's James's dad. You have to treat him with the most respect."

"I know that much," I say. Age is a form of hierarchy in Chinese culture, and every year, during the Lunar New Year reunion dinner, I know enough to always wish my oldest aunt Happy New Year before wishing my own father, since he's the second oldest in the family, before wishing Third Uncle, Fourth Uncle, and so on.

"His wife is Auntie Chuang. My second uncle is Uncle Jing, his wife is Auntie Jamie, and their two sons are Christopher and Ryan."

"Are all your cousins male?"

Shang grimaces. "No. I have three female cousins, but they weren't allowed to get involved in the family company. They're all on the East Coast."

Somehow I manage to keep my face straight. I'm not one to judge other people's families—god knows mine is far from perfect—but everything I'm learning about Shang's family sounds so sexist that it's tough to understand why Baba would want to work with them.

"Third Uncle is Uncle Xiaotian, and his wife is Auntie Lulu. Their son is Thomas and their daughters, the ones I mentioned, are Holly, Portia, and Candice."

"Wow, three daughters," I say.

"Yeah, they were trying for another boy before they gave up."

I can't tell what Shang is thinking based on that statement. It sounds so shitty though, the concept of trying for a boy, as though the girls they got along the way are nothing more than a burden they have to discard. No surprise, then, that the sisters left home and flew to the East Coast, as far from the family as they could. I can't help but feel the animosity toward Shang's family bleed out onto him as well. I myself have so much resentment about this subject. Again, I recall my aunt's comment to my mother. *She isn't even a boy!* I give myself a mental shake. It's not my place to judge their family. I'm only here to judge their business. Pure numbers, I remind myself. Nothing more.

"My mom's the youngest. Her name is Jiayi."

I nod. Though I'm curious to know more, I also feel overwhelmed by all of this information and truth be told, I'm dreading learning even more about them than I already know.

When we arrive at Little Chang's, James's ultra-loud race car is already parked alongside Thomas's BMW. The massive trailer holding the rest of the family trundles in just as we get out of the car.

Aunties and uncles spill out and immediately lunge into aggressive stretches.

"Wah, that was long journey," Auntie Chuang says, bending over with her legs spread out and grunting until she touches the tops of her shoes. She looks up and glowers at the cousins. "Eh, you all better stretch, too! Otherwise you will have back pain later."

"Ma," James whines, "can you not do that at a literal parking lot?"

Auntie Lulu, who is in the middle of a lunge, shoots him a glare. "James, you want your mother to have back pain?"

"Never mind," James mutters.

I stand aside and watch as Shang goes up to his mom, wrapping an arm around her shoulders and talking to her softly. His entire demeanor changes when he interacts with his mother, turning soft. To my surprise, Shang's mother glances over at me and smiles, as though Shang has just said something nice about me. Then she pats him on the arm and gestures at him to do some stretches, too. Looking pained, Shang obliges, and I bite back a grin as he does a few stretches. When I crane my neck, I'm unsurprised to see that Mushu is behind him, hands on waist, lunging with one foot, then the next.

"Hey, Zhou!" Mushu calls out. "Come on, you don't want a stiff back, do you?"

With a sigh of defeat, I do as I'm told and go into a deep stretch. After all, as Baba has always told me, when doing due diligence for a company we're looking into buying, it's good to walk a mile in the board of directors' shoes.

CHAPTER EIGHT

The owner of Little Chang's is, in fact, named Gary Lin. As Shang's mother patiently explains, Gary didn't think that "Little Gary's" or "Little Lin's" would go over well as a restaurant name, and so he chose Chang's. I have to agree with that. Gary, who seems to know the Li family well, greets them warmly, with many arm and shoulder pats and much loud exclaiming over who's gained/lost weight, hair, and wrinkles. He shouts merrily at us to go to the "usual table" and the big group makes its way over to a massive round table at the center of the room.

To my dismay, I'm seated between James and his mother, Auntie Chuang. I shoot Mushu a look of panic and Mushu shrugs with an *Oh well* expression. Easy for Mushu to be all chill; she is fortunate enough to be seated next to Shang's mom and Thomas, whose gaze hasn't left his cell phone.

"Now, Zhou, how old did you say you are again?" Auntie Chuang says.

"Oh, um, twenty-eight."

"Oh, my dear, you are getting so old!" Auntie Chuang exclaims.

"Um. Thanks?"

"Twenty-eight is not old, Chuangling," Auntie Jiayi says. She gives me an encouraging smile. "Why, I didn't have Shang until I was thirty."

"Yes, and look where it get you. Just one child only," Auntie Chuang snaps.

Auntie Jiayi's smile disappears. My stomach knots. Auntie Jiayi was just trying to make me feel better, and she got smacked down for it. I scramble for something to say to take the attention away from Auntie Jiayi. "Oh well, I don't plan on having kids anytime soon, so."

Auntie Chuang turns her attention back to me. "You don't? Why not? You are too busy working? Aiya, this is what is wrong with your generation now. You children are too selfish, only thinking of yourselves, not your families."

"*Mommm*," James groans. "Do we have to?"

"You are not getting any younger either, James," Auntie Chuang snaps. "How about you stop fooling around and find a nice girl like Zhou to settle down with?"

I choke on my oolong. "Uh . . ." From the corner of my eye, I catch Shang watching me with yet another unreadable expression. With those thick eyebrows of his, he always looks slightly angry.

Auntie Lulu, Thomas's mother, pipes up. "Oh yes, Zhou, tell us, what is your ideal man? Maybe someone like Thomas? Well-educated," she says with a pointed look at James, "loves cooking, don't you, Thomas?" She elbows Thomas viciously.

He looks up from his phone, says "Sure," and dips his head once more.

What would Baba say in this situation? Of course, the answer is he wouldn't even be in this situation to begin with, because he's a man. Still, I do my best to channel my inner baba. "I am very flattered by your concern. Thank you. I will take your comments into consideration." There. That is a very Zhou answer. The aunties smile, looking mollified for now.

Fortunately, the food arrives then, even though there hasn't been, as far as I know, any ordering. The Li family must have stopped over at Gary's enough for him to know exactly what they like, and soon, the table is positively groaning under the weight of various Chinese dishes, all of them steaming hot. There's beef cooked in a numbing spicy Szechuan sauce, a platter heaped high with honeyed roast pork buns, two whole deep-fried fish covered in sticky sweet-and-sour sauce, a large pot of pork rib and winter melon soup, a plate of spicy cucumber and chicken salad, and a giant pot of rice. Everyone calls out, "Chi fan!" which directly translates to *eat rice* but means *dig in*, and so we do.

I've been raised well enough to know that I must serve my elders first. Since I'm sitting next to Auntie Chuang, I serve her first, ladling generous portions of the fish and chicken salad onto her plate.

"Aiya, don't bother yourself," Auntie Chuang scolds in a merry sort of voice, clearly enjoying my attention.

Shang picks up a spoon as well and takes a portion of braised tofu for his mother, but Uncle Hong snaps, "What kind of man serves the food?"

At the sharp tone of voice, there is a momentary silence around the table. Shang looks like he's about to protest, but his mother places a hand on his arm and he lowers the spoon, looking down at his plate.

"Shang is a filial son," Auntie Jiayi says with an apologetic smile.

The other aunties, uncles, and cousins resume their conversation hurriedly, as though to cover up the awkward atmosphere. I turn my attention to Uncle Hong, who merely grunts his thanks as I serve him. A look around the table tells me that the only other person serving their elders is Mushu. She is moving as quickly as a Chipotle line server, slapping spoonfuls of food down on everybody's plate while calling out, "Don't get up, Auntie, I'll get it for you, there you go, don't even think about moving, Uncle, you want the fish? I'll get you the fish, and there's an extra-large pork bun for you."

The aunties and uncles seem impressed by this show of respect, all of them smiling and nodding. Auntie Chuang gives James a pointed look. "You see, Son? You see the value of having a good wife?"

I fight back the grimace that's threatening to take over my face. Growing up, I was always taught to serve my elders at meals, something I've done well to remember while working at Eighty-Eight Capital; we always serve our guests first. I've never really thought of it as something a dutiful wife would do, but now it seems obvious, and all of a sudden, I'm filled with resentment. Did my parents mean to instill this sexist practice in me? I wish I could stop, and yet it is so ingrained in me that I can't bear to see any uncle's or auntie's plate remain unfilled, and so I continue serving everyone until their plates are piled high with food before serving myself the remnants of the meal. And obviously Uncle Hong and the rest of the Lis agree that this is a woman's job. I can't remember the last time I've had to do something purely because of my sex. By the time I spear a piece of fish with my chopsticks, I've lost the bulk of my appetite.

I can't help noticing how Shang is eating with abandon, chatting and laughing with the others, and at the sight of him, I'm once again reminded that I'm here to play a role. How easily Shang shrugged off that awkward moment back there. Now he seems completely at ease to sit back and let Mushu and me serve the food. He's different from the guy listening to a feminist story in the privacy of his car, because in front of his family, he's playing a different role, just like me. *What would Baba do?* Well, since he would be trying to put the Lis at ease, he would serve the food regardless of his gender. So I've played my role well as Zhou. It's all right, everything is the way it should be. Damn it, I'm so off-kilter because of this new role I'm having to play and also because of whatever hormone-driven attraction I have toward Shang. I really need to get a grip.

Halfway through the meal, I signal to Mushu to go to the restroom. As soon as we're out of earshot from the main group, I pull her close.

"Switch with me," I say.

Mushu stares. "Uh. No thanks? My outfits are all carefully curated to form one cohesive look with my hair and makeup. No offense, but I don't think you can carry it off."

"How is that at all inoffensive?" I shake my head. "Anyway, never mind that. I didn't mean switch outfits, I meant switch seats with me so you go in Shang's car and I go in the trailer."

"Oh!" Mushu frowns. "Why? I thought I was doing you a favor by leaving you alone with that hottie." She cranes her neck, leering at Shang in the distance. "I mean, whoo boy. Look at that bod."

"Mushu, focus." I grab her shoulders and give her a little shake. How do I explain to Mushu that I feel this incredible attraction to Shang and I need to put some distance between the two of us to focus on what I actually came here to do? "I just . . . think it would be good for me to have a chance to talk to the aunties and uncles. Try to get a feel of the business from them," I say finally.

"Sounds legit," Mushu says.

Thank god. "So you'll do it?"

"Sure thing, cuz. Anything for the fam." With that, Mushu traipses back to the table, jumping into the conversation seamlessly.

When the meal ends, Mushu jumps up and calls out, "Yo, Shang, I'm going to be your road trip buddy."

Shang's eyebrows knot together in confusion. He looks over at me, but I steadfastly avoid his gaze. I can feel his curious stare burning a hole in the back of my head, but finally, he says, "Cool."

Relief and disappointment course through my veins in equal measure. I follow the big group of aunties and uncles and climb inside the trailer. It's a behemoth of a vehicle, the inside resembling a fully furnished apartment. There are snacks and fruits piled onto every surface, and the noise level inside is overwhelming as the aunties and uncles shout over one another. Ryan takes the wheel, yelling at everyone to sit down as he starts the engine.

"Zhou, you come sit next to me," Auntie Chuang calls out. "I will tell you all about James's golfing trophies."

Oh no. But before I can acquiesce, Shang's mother Jiayi pats my arm.

"Sorry, Chuangling, she's with me," she says.

Auntie Chuang glowers but doesn't say anything.

"Don't worry, she'll get over it," Auntie Jiayi says.

"Thank you," I say.

"Oh, I was saving myself as well as you. Who wants to hear about James's golfing trophies? Come, I will tell you about Shang's martial arts medals."

I pride myself on having a good poker face, but I must've shown a flicker of dismay, because Auntie Jiayi roars with laughter.

"Oh, my dear!" she cries. "I am just messing with you. Oh, your expression! No, don't you worry, I won't bore you with all that. And Shang would kill me if I did. Speaking of bore, was he very boring in his car? Is that why you choose to sit with us old folk?"

"No," I say quickly. "He was great. We listened to an audiobook and I really enjoyed it. But I wanted to spend more time with the rest of the family."

"Ah." Auntie Jiayi smiles. She gazes around the trailer, her expression tender. "Well, you've met everyone. You know Uncle Hong is my big brother."

Uncle Hong has a Chinese paperback open in his hands, but his head keeps lolling forward as he dozes off. Even when he sleeps he somehow manages to look stern.

"He is a tough nut. But he is how we manage to survive. He was always the one who took care of all of us, even back home in China."

Auntie Jiayi's words wash over me, bringing with them a warm glow. They're familiar words, words of a story I've heard many times over from other immigrant families. How there's always a sibling—usually the eldest—who took on the burden of looking after the younger siblings while the parents worked two or three different jobs. I'd thought of Uncle Hong as nothing more than a chauvinist, but of course there are so many more layers to him. No one is ever just one thing.

"Now, Uncle Jing is my second brother, and he is the brains of the family. He was the one who thought of all the ways to put us through school, which grants to apply for and this and that."

I smile and let myself be absorbed into the rich tapestry of the Li family history, and by the time we arrive at the ranch, I see them all in a new light. Maybe this is the first step to understanding why Baba wanted to acquire the company.

But when the trailer comes to a stop, Uncle Hong jerks awake and says, "Ah! We are here! Now, listen, ladies. No complaining, no moaning, let us men do our job at the ranch, eh?"

And I suppress an inward sigh. Like Baba always tells me, people are complex, and Uncle Hong can be both a wonderful older brother and, unfortunately, also a chauvinist.

Outside, Mushu waves wildly to me. "Zhou, over here!" she calls out. "How was your ride?"

I avoid meeting Shang's eye. "It was good. Yours?"

"Could be better. No offense, Shang," Mushu says in her usual jovial tone.

"Really? What was so bad about it?" Shang says.

"Well, the audiobook—what was it again? *The Water Pirates*? It was good, but we skipped the first nine chapters, so I was a bit lost, to be honest with you. I thought they were in San Gabriel Valley the entire time until you told me they were in ancient China, *whaaat?*"

"I asked if you wanted me to start at the beginning!" Shang protests.

"Oh I can't be bothered with beginnings," Mushu says flippantly. "Jump in right where the action starts, that's what I always say."

Shang pinches the bridge of his nose; then, taking a deep breath, he says, "I'll help you with your bags."

Would Baba allow Shang to take his bags? No way. "Don't bother," I say, jumping in front of him and yanking at my overstuffed bag. My back twinges in protest, but I ignore it and give a savage wrench. My bag slides out of the trunk and thuds to the ground with a loud *thunk* and a cloud of dust.

"You sure?" Shang says.

"Yep!" It was supposed to come out cheery, but ends up coming out with a lot more bite to it than I meant. Shang's brow furrows for a moment; then he shrugs and goes to help his mother with her luggage.

"Is there something going on between you and Shang?" Mushu says as I struggle with the bag.

"I need to show these people that just because I'm a woman, doesn't mean I can't handle my own crap. We need to build confidence in them, remember?"

"Hmm." Mushu doesn't look convinced, but luckily she chooses not to dig further.

The Li family ranch and distillery is located in a massive plot of land, almost one thousand acres in size, and the beauty of the land is breathtaking. When we enter the ranch, I see a barn and stables and farmlands, and as we go deeper, the farmhouse comes into view. It's an expansive farmhouse, a gorgeous structure that is a mix of modern and traditional, with an exterior made from a mix of natural stone and cedar and tons of picture windows letting in pools of golden sunlight. Framing the house are two enormous oak trees, offering plenty of shade from the unforgiving Californian sun.

Not exactly what I had in mind when I thought of a farmhouse. This house looks more like the elegant older sibling of the traditional farmhouse. I look down at my ridiculous outfit. It feels even more ridiculous in this setting. This modern farmhouse calls for simple silk dresses and Hermès sandals, not the ULTIMATE FUN TIME DON'T MESS WITH THIS COWGIRL jeans and cowgirl boots. I shoot Mushu a glare, but Mushu is too busy staring in open wonderment at the house.

"Dang, this is nice!" she says.

"I know," James says proudly, as though he built it with his own two hands. "It's our little jewel."

"Did your family build this?" I say.

"Yeah," James says.

I guess his pride makes sense.

"Uh," Shang interjects, "not unless you count hiring an architect and a contractor as 'building this ourselves.'"

James throws him a dirty look. "We came up with the design ourselves."

"Actually, my mom came up with the bulk of the design," Shang says.

"Oh, are you two arguing about silly things again?" Auntie Jiayi says. "Come on, Zhou and Mushu, I show you to your room while the boys bicker as usual."

The inside of the farmhouse is even more beautiful than the exterior, which I hadn't thought was possible. But it's somehow cozy and airy, modern and traditional at the same time. The space is large and filled with sunlight streaming in through the large picture windows everywhere, and the natural stone walls lend it a welcoming warmth. There is an open-plan living room furnished with overstuffed couches and a massive kitchen boasting a gorgeous granite island. The dining room is surrounded by windows on all sides, and I can just imagine the numerous loud, merry meals they've had there.

The bedrooms are on the second floor of the house. Auntie Jiayi leads us to the second room on the right and says, "I hope this is okay for you?"

It's more than okay. Large enough to hold two queen beds with ample closet space, and with its own en suite to boot. There is a makeup table near the window with a pot of fresh wildflowers on it.

"We hire cleaners to prep the house for our arrival," Auntie Jiayi explains when she sees me looking curiously at the flowers. "We also have farmhands and workers all over the ranch and the distillery, of course. Now, I will let you two rest a bit and then we will go on a tour of the place, okay? Oh, and I will bring by your sleeping bags for our overnight camping trip in two days' time."

"Overnight camping trip?" I say, trying not to look too horrified.

"Oh yes, we do every year. You'll love it."

"I'm sure I will," I say, then add "Thank you, Auntie" with genuine affection. Auntie Jiayi, with her kindness and her honesty, has grown on me.

The door closes gently behind Auntie Jiayi, and Mushu and I fall onto our respective beds with sighs of relief.

"Phew, this place, man!" Mushu says. "I wasn't expecting it to be quite so large. This is amazing. It's like Disneyland, but for ranchers."

"Yeah, it is pretty incredible."

"Hey, so," Mushu says, "while I was riding in the trailer with the elders, I kind of got the feeling that they don't want to sell."

The back of my neck prickles. "What? How's that possible? They invited us here."

Mushu shrugs. "I don't know, it's kind of a vibe I got from them. Also, I heard Uncle Hong say, 'I don't want to sell the company.' "

A pit opens up in my stomach. I try to make sense of the situation, and fail. "But why would they go along with this if they didn't want to sell in the first place?"

Mushu chews on her lip as she ponders this. "Maybe it has to do with Shang? He's the CEO, right?"

I think about the friction between Shang and James. I'd assumed it's just regular stuff between cousins, but maybe there's more to it than that. Annoyance bubbles up inside me. What kind of game is Shang playing?

"Well, I'm not here to have my time wasted," I say after a while. "They brought us here, and I'm going to do my job, and if their company is really worth buying, then I'm going to make a good case for it."

"Attagirl." Mushu props herself up on her elbow and gazes out the window at the expanse. "So all this is owned by the company?"

"Well, the distillery is, and parts of the land, but the farmhouse is owned separately by the family."

She whispers, "I bet it's worth a lot of money."

"Yeah, it's a large part of their valuation, the land. We need to evaluate how much it's worth."

"How do we do that?"

"Mushu, how do you still not know this stuff after working at the firm for as long as you have?"

"Okay, well, this sounds like a you problem," she says.

I can't help smiling at this. "Mushu, never change."

CHAPTER NINE

I badly need to change out of my ridiculous clothes, but as I'm about to open up my bag, there is a knock at the door.

James's voice pierces it. "Yo, ladies! You ready for some outdoor activity?"

Everything inside me shrivels up and shrinks away. God, what I wouldn't give to be able to say no. But I'm here to do due diligence, and part of that is learning everything I can about their ranch and how it operates. What good would it be to hide away in the guest bedroom? Even if it is the nicest guest bedroom I've ever been in, more five-star hotel than guest bedroom, really. I take a deep breath and envision a new mask. Not quite Work Mulan, but Ranch Mulan. Right. A persona that Baba apparently has that I never knew about. Anyway, what would Ranch Mulan say right now?

"Sounds great!" I call out with much more confidence than I actually feel. I can do this. I've researched all that can be researched about ranches and distilleries, after all.

"All right, well, don't keep everybody waiting. You two are beautiful already, you don't need to put any more makeup on." James snickers like he's said something funny and walks away.

I make a face at Mushu that conveys: *What an ass*.

"What an ass," she says.

"Shh! He might be able to hear us!" I hiss.

"Good, then he'll know what an ass he's being."

"Oh my god, Mushu." But despite myself, I snort with laughter. "Well, I guess we'd better go. I was hoping I'd be able to change into something more sensible, but whatever."

"I told you, your outfit is perfect for ranching."

I give her a flat look before turning and walking out of the room.

As James said, many of the uncles, aunts, and cousins are already gathered downstairs. There's a grazing table set out with a mix of Chinese and Western snacks, and when Mushu and I join them, Auntie Jiayi calls out to us and pushes a mandarin orange into each of our hands. Shang is in the far corner of the dining room, looking on at the crowd without saying much. I try not to notice how good he looks, leaning against the wall with his hands in his pockets. He's so tall and broad-shouldered, though, that it's impossible not to steal glances as I mingle with the family. Before long, Uncle Hong directs the group out of the house.

"Come, Zhou," he says, and I hurry forward so I'm walking next to him. "I want you to see our family's land."

They walk down a pathway that leads from the house toward the ranch. The beauty of the land is impossible to ignore. My eyes roam the soft, rolling hills and the vast expanse of grass. There is a slight breeze in the air and it smells sweet somehow, like fruits and fresh spring water.

"Our father bought the land," Uncle Hong says. "We all grew up here, and when we earned more money, we bought more land. This place is not just a family company, it is a family legacy."

"It's beautiful," I say, and I mean it.

Uncle Hong looks at me for a moment, the expression on his face unreadable, and then he nods. "Yes, it is. Here we have our geese. We just got them three years ago, not too long. Where are they from again, Jing?"

Uncle Jing puffs up his chest with obvious pride. "We bought them from Chaoshan, which is in the Guangdong province in China. They are known for breeding the best geese. Chaoshan geese rival the French foie gras. They are not bred to sell, we breed them for ourselves, to have during our Lunar New Year meal. They are the most delicious geese you will ever eat. Shang will cook the yummiest dish out of them."

I look at the gaggle of honking geese. I have mixed feelings about this, though I know I'm being a hypocrite; I'm an omnivore, so the thought of animals being butchered for the table shouldn't make me squeamish, and yet it does. The thought of Shang cooking, too, somehow doesn't really compute with what little I know of him. I look over my shoulder at Shang and try to envision him cooking. I think of how he would look utterly focused, how his square jaw might clench a little as he works, and the thought of it makes my face turn red. Of course, he happens to glance over at me at that very moment, catching me staring at him. I snap my head back and hurry to keep up with Uncle Hong, my cheeks burning.

"And here we have our pigs. Now these are from Zhejiang province," Uncle Hong says. "These are Jinhua pigs."

Uncle Jing pipes up: "Jinhua pigs have the most tender meat. Auntie Jiayi makes the best roast pork, you will see for yourself later."

"Does Auntie Jiayi do all the cooking around here?" I'm somewhat surprised at that; I'd assumed that they'd have a private chef to do that.

"Oh yes. Well, she used to before her arthritis started to bother her." As Uncle Hong says this, he gives a flippant wave of his hand, illustrating how unimportant he thinks things like cooking are.

I swallow the lump of irritation in my throat, focusing instead on the large pigs rooting around in the trough. The smell of manure is unexpected in its intensity, almost like a punch to the nose. They're much bigger than I expected, though of course I have no idea what the standard size of a pig is, and unlike pigs in cartoons, none of them are pink. They're white, in fact, with black coloring on their heads and rumps, and surprisingly hairy, and the sounds they make are disturbingly guttural. It strikes me again how different real life is, being here in the flesh with live animals as opposed to seeing them on the screen—

My thoughts are interrupted by a loud squelch, and I look down to see that I've stepped right in a pile of—*argh*, of something really thick and sticky and *argh, argh*. When I lift my leg, my cowgirl boot comes free from the pile with a sucking sound. Somehow, I manage to swallow the cry crawling up my throat and merely utter a small, "Oh."

"You'll get used to it," Uncle Hong says.

I nod slowly, trying to ignore the muck that now encrusts my new boots. *Focus on the ranch, focus on the ranch* . . .

A loud, monstrous sound wrenches my attention away from my boot. Contrary to popular belief, cows do not, in fact, moo. The sound that they make is closer to *Mrrroggrrrrhhh*: a deep rumble that comes straight from the depths of their bellies and sounds closer to something a sleeping dragon might make than an animal whose favorite pastime is grazing on grass.

"Oh my—" I manage to stop myself, but it takes quite an effort, as I look up and find myself right next to a massive cow's head.

When did the cow sneak up on me? It's so close that I can feel its warm, gusty breath on my cheek. Once again, the smell overpowers me. When I read up on ranches and what to expect, I hadn't spared a single thought for how they might smell. The only way I can describe it is: *It smells very much like a large, warm, living beast.* I step quickly away from the monstrous thing, and Uncle Hong says, "A beaut, isn't she? This is our Qinchuan cow. She is very prized; her milk is like liquid gold. And all our cows are grass-fed only, and range freely, so they are super healthy. This one is named Xingxing."

"Star," I say weakly, taking another step away from the cow.

"Yes. Star, because she is a star," Uncle Hong says. "Oh, watch out behind you."

I jump as a shockingly wet snout nudges the back of my head. It's another cow, and its touch is so solid, so real, and so powerful, even in its casualness, I can't help the small squeak from escaping my mouth, but manage to keep it from turning into a scream.

"This one is called Tiantian."

"Sweet," I say, backing away from the cows.

"Yes, because her milk is sweet as candy."

More cows have appeared, seemingly out of nowhere. I am now stuck in a horror film, probably one named *The Silence of the Cows*. They are all massive, every step they take makes their bodies judder a little, and the closeness of them is overwhelming. They're so incredibly loud, too. I don't understand how children are taught that cows go *moo* when it really sounds nothing like that. Every time one of them goes *Mmrrrrrruuurgghhh*, the sound reverberates through my eardrums and down the length of my body.

Uncle Hong studies me from the corner of his eye. "You are familiar with cows, yes? You said you have them in your family farm back in China?"

"Oh yes!" I give a vigorous nod. "Yes, plenty of cows back home." I fight to keep the confident smile on my face. "There's, uh, Daisy, of course. And Maisie. And ah, Hazey."

Uncle Hong tilts his head to one side. "You gave them Western names? Interesting."

Damn it. Of course they wouldn't have been given Western names. "Only personally," I say. "I mean, their real names were, you know, things like Diyi, Dier, Disan . . . um, yeah. We just numbered them, we didn't really name them."

"Ah, you didn't want to get attached before they were slaughtered? Smart thinking." Uncle Hong's eyes never leave mine as he speaks. "You told Shang you miss your farm a lot."

Shang has caught up with us and is standing a few paces away, stroking one of the cows' sides while listening to our conversation.

I try hard not to look at Shang as I say, "Yup, I did. I do miss it a lot."

"You grew up herding the cattle back home, right?" Uncle Hong says.

"Um . . . sure. Sometimes, yes." *Please, universe, please do not let this lead to where I think it's leading to. . . .*

"Would you like to herd our cattle? It is time they go back to the barn. There are coyotes here, you know."

"Oh." The word comes out as a half gasp, half squeak. My gaze scrabbles frantically from Uncle Hong, to the cows, to Shang, who is watching with his usual stern expression. "That . . ."

"Sounds excellent!" Mushu cries, popping out of nowhere. She claps me on the back before squeezing my shoulder. "You can totally do that, can't you?" She glares meaningfully at me. "I mean, it's just cows. They're such peaceful animals, aren't they?"

"Uh, yeah. Of course." I nod slowly at first, then more convincingly as I digest Mushu's words. Yes, what could possibly go wrong? Cows are known for being calm, slow creatures. I am a vice president at a private equity firm. I know how to put my foot down, how to protect my territory, how to make my way in a male-dominated profession. And I have, after all, read up on ranching, and one of the many ranch duties I've read about is herding cows. I want to laugh when I think of how I'd brushed it off as "an easy task" when I was doing my research. Nothing about it seems easy now. *Okay, stop it. You are Ranch Mulan, remember? You can do this. What would Baba say?* "It would be my honor."

Soon, the Li family, along with Mushu, is gathered to one side, watching me as I approach Xingxing.

"This is gonna be good," James says nastily.

"Tsk," Auntie Jiayi says, glaring at James. Then she turns her attention back to me and calls out, "It's all right, Zhou, she looks big, Xingxing does, but she's a softie, really."

"She gives very good milk," Auntie Chuang says, to the agreement of Auntie Jamie and Auntie Lulu.

"Oh yes, very creamy," Auntie Lulu says. "If you let it sit for a while, the fat will separate and you can skim it off the top—"

I try my best to shut the chattering out as I scramble my memory for what I've read up on just a day ago, but now that I'm actually here and needing the information, what crams my mind instead are random useless facts about cows. They, um, they sleep standing up and pranksters would sometimes try to tip them over. That's not information that's useful for me right now, brain. Right. Um, they taste really good? Yet another useless fact. Right, well, I have to, ah, I have to take the bull by the horns. After all, that's an actual saying, so it's got to come from ancient wisdom, right? Except these are cows, not bulls, and they seem to be missing actual horns. Well, never mind, I don't need to take it quite so literally. I just have to establish that I am the alpha of the herd. Now, finally, bits and pieces of my prior reading come back to me. I need to be in the right frame of mind—calm and confident.

I stand up straight, lifting my chin, and stare Xingxing right in the eyes. Well, in one eye, since Xingxing's eyes are on either side of her head and I can only really glare into one at a time.

"Well, hello, Xingxing," I say in a firm voice. "I am Hua Zhou, and I'm here to herd you." Hmm, that might have come out wrong. "Not 'hurt,' but herd. Just to clarify." I'm officially talking to a cow. Then again, people talk to their dogs and cats, so is talking to a cow really much worse than that?

95

Xingxing doesn't give any indication of having heard anything I just said. She chews on her mouthful of grass placidly, and again it strikes me how real it is, how large a cow's head is, and how huge its tongue is and how loud the grass-chewing is. I can actually hear the rustle of the grass in Xingxing's mouth, and somehow this fact is really disturbing. I need to just do this. *Just do it*, like Nike says.

With a slightly trembling hand, I reach out and pat Xingxing gingerly on the side. Well, that was the intention, anyway. What ends up happening is as soon as my fingertips touch the warm solidity of the cow, my survival instincts kick in and I hurriedly jerk my hand back. I didn't expect the cow to feel so . . . cow-y. The fur is a lot bristlier than I expected, and it's just so solid and so there. *Stop this right now. Everyone is watching. You need to do this now.* I reach out again, ignoring every instinct inside me that's screaming: *Argh, run away!* This time, I steel myself and lay my whole palm on Xingxing. I release my breath. There, that wasn't so bad.

Xingxing raises her enormous head and nudges my arm.

"Good, Xingxing," I say, patting her shoulder. Or the back of her neck? I'm not entirely sure what part of the cow I'm touching. "Um, let's get you back to your bedroom. Uh, barn."

I could get used to this. Xingxing's gently nudging my arm and it's kind of cute in a way. A gentle bovine way. Hah, this is easy. Don't know why I was so scared before.

Then from the corner of my eye, I see James move so he's behind Xingxing. Before I can ask what he's doing, James raises his hand and does something to the cow's back.

Xingxing utters a monstrous bellow—a sound so deep and guttural that my bones shudder with the resonance—and charges. Part of my brain manages to think: *She's not charging, she's just walking.* But it hardly matters; Xingxing is surprisingly fast, and she was standing right in front of me, so whether she's walking or charging, it's terrifying in its suddenness. With a yelp, I leap backward—or did Xingxing shove me, that stupid cow?—something catches the back of my legs, and before I know it, the sky is tipping, and I'm falling, falling—

There is a thick splash and cold muck envelops me. Spatters of mud rain down on me, splatting my face, some of it going into my open mouth. The breath is knocked out of me and for a second, I wonder if I've fallen straight into the depths of hell. The only sounds I hear are my own ragged breaths.

Then noise floods back in. People are shouting. People are laughing. People are going "Aiya!" and "Are you okay?" and "Xingxing, come back!"

Mushu appears, looking down at me. "Hey, cuz, how you doing?"

"Help," I manage to choke out of my mud-filled mouth.

She leans down, grabs my arms, and lifts. With a groan, I scramble back up to a standing position. I spit out as much mud as I can and wipe my face before blinking at Mushu and trying to not think of how the stench of everything is now clinging to me. "Tell me how bad this is," I whisper.

"You remember that time in college when we went to that house party and I drank all those Jäegerbombs and got sick in the back of the Uber and the smell was so bad it made you puke, too? This is worse. I mean, you're literally covered in cow poop."

"Oh god. I thought it was mud."

Mushu looks at me with pity. "Sure, let's go with that."

James, Shang, and a handful of other people come toward us. James and the other cousins are doubled over laughing, slapping each other on the arm. Shang is staring at me, his thick brows heavy and knotted.

"Damn, Zhou, what happened?" James says. "Did you get bull-ied?" He cackles with laughter at his own joke.

"She got bull-dozed," Thomas says, and he and James give each other a fist bump.

"What did you do to Xingxing?" I snap.

James's eyes widen in a show of innocence. "No idea what you're talking about."

"I saw you, you got behind her and—"

"Did you hit your head?" James says with mock concern. "I think you're confused."

"Aiya, stop it, you kids," Auntie Jiayi says, bustling over. "Oh, Zhou, are you okay? Are you hurt? Okay, come here, I'll clean you up."

I let Auntie Jiayi lead me toward a nearby barn, where she hands me a garden hose. "You hose yourself down first, then you can go inside the house to have shower. Don't track cow dung all over the house."

"Of course not," I mumble, and douse myself in freezing-cold water. This is it. This is the lowest of lows. I have hit rock bottom. There is no possible way I can get lower than this. At least the others have stopped crowding around me, instead dispersing around the ranch to check on various things.

After I've washed off most of the dung, I trudge back toward the farmhouse, dripping wet and shivering violently. Halfway there, Shang calls out to me. I keep walking, pretending not to hear him.

"Hey." He hurries over and tosses something at me. It's a blanket. "Got this from the barn. It's a horse blanket."

He got me a blanket? I can barely look him in the eye. He's all handsome and clean, his skin fresh and not covered in cow dung like mine is. I wrap the blanket around myself. It's scratchy and so stiff it might as well be made of cardboard, but I'm still grateful for the warmth it offers me. "Thanks," I mutter.

"So you grew up herding cows, huh?" he says.

I glower at him. Did he give me the blanket as a way to get in an interrogation? "American cows are different from Chinese cows."

"Oh?" Shang's eyebrows rise, making him look slightly less stern than usual. God, but he's attractive. "But you heard what Uncle Hong said, these are Chinese cows."

Unfortunately, he's right. "Well, then you guys haven't raised them right. They are belligerent."

Shang nods, and says dryly, "Hooligans, they are."

"Exactly. You need to discipline them."

"Mm. And I'm guessing the cows you have back home are not like Xingxing?"

Is he teasing me? I can't tell, partly because my head is a mess, and partly because I'm so painfully aware that nothing can develop between the two of us. He's forbidden fruit, I remind myself. The CEO of a company I'm trying to acquire. Not allowed. Out of bounds. "No, actually. They are very respectful and filial and they go where I tell them to."

"Wow, respectful and filial cows, this I have got to see."

"Maybe one day," I mumble. Okay, I need to put a stop to this. Somber, buttoned-up Shang is already distracting enough. Chatty Shang is damn near irresistible, and I need to keep things very professional. "Look, Shang, I would love to continue this witty repartee we've got going on, but—"

"It's hard keeping up banter when you're covered in shit?"

"Yes. I would like to walk in silence now. Thank you for your understanding and cooperation."

CHAPTER TEN

The garden hose has washed away most of the mess, but I take an extra-long, particularly hot shower because, well, no amount of water can wash away the memory of that *squelch* as I landed in the pile of dung, not to mention the stench and feel of it. I'm in the middle of toweling dry my hair when the bedroom door opens and Mushu calls out, "Zhou? You in there?"

Thick, fluffy, white terry-cloth robes have been prepared for every room, and I gratefully wrap myself in one before stepping out of the bathroom.

"How we doing?" Mushu says.

"Well, considering I was covered in cow pats less than an hour ago, I think we're recovering just fine."

"Good, because we really need to step it up, and by *we*, I mean you."

I glance at Mushu's reflection in the mirror as I continue drying my hair. "What do you mean?"

Mushu steps closer and lowers her voice. "I overheard some pretty disturbing things."

"Oh? Like what?"

"Well, for one thing, Shang said it's really weird that you didn't know how to herd cattle when your emails said you grew up with cows on a farm. Apparently you'd told him over email that the cows were practically your brothers and sisters growing up?"

I suck in a breath through my teeth, thinking of my father telling Shang that. I can just imagine it, my dad's happiness at having cows; in China, most farmers would rear only pigs since they were lower maintenance, so having cattle would've been a point of pride for Baba. The thought of him makes my heart ache. "There's more than a ten-year gap between my dad and his older sibling, so he was alone for most of his childhood."

"Aww, poor Uncle Zhou," Mushu says. "Well, anyway, so you can see why Shang would find your incompetence when it comes to herding cattle somewhat sus."

Is it possible for an entire human body to cringe? Because that's certainly what this feels like. But even as I shrivel up with embarrassment, part of me rears up in anger, because screw Shang and his flawless outfits and neat haircut and his stupid utter perfection. I'd like to push him into a pile of cow dung and see how unruffled he manages to remain. "James did something to the cow. I saw him move behind her and I think he shocked her or something."

"Maybe he did, but no point dwelling on it. Even if we did manage to prove it, it'll just make you look petty."

I groan. I'm so ashamed of myself. I thought I was prepared for this just because I studied for it? And now I'm realizing that unlike school, this isn't something I can prepare for just by studying. Intellectual understanding does nothing when I find myself in the middle of the real, actual thing itself. I do need to step it up. "You're right."

"As always. Anyway, then Shang said something like 'I don't know about selling anymore. It does seem . . .'"

I continue staring at Mushu as her voice trails off. After a beat, I realize she isn't going to finish the sentence. "Does seem what?"

"I don't know, they walked out of earshot."

I groan.

"Hey, I tried my best. Channeled my inner auntie and eavesdropped to the best of my ability. Our ancestors would be proud."

I gaze forlornly at my reflection. "Our ancestors would definitely not be proud of me right now."

"Well, yeah, you're a different story." Mushu pats my shoulder.

"So what does this mean? They don't want to sell anymore because I didn't manage to herd their friggin' cow?"

Mushu places both hands on my shoulders and turns me so we're facing each other. "I know you think you're great at studying. Me, on the other hand? Not so great at tests or studying, but it's okay because I've got my incredible looks and personality to rely on. You can't study in the traditional sense to prepare yourself for ranch life, Mulan. You need to embrace social media."

"I'm not sure I follow what you're trying to say," I respond.

In answer, Mushu whips out her phone and taps the screen before brandishing it at me.

I squint at the screen. "How to hog-tie a man—"

"Whoops, wrong app," Mushu says, snatching the phone away. She swipes at it. "Okay, here we go."

When she brandishes the screen this time, it's showing a TikTok instead. Sure enough, it's a video of a short-haired woman shearing sheep, and the sheep is sitting on its rump, its belly exposed and its legs sticking up in the air.

I watch with wide eyes as the woman makes short work of the shearing, working the electric shears down in long, confident strokes. "This is kind of therapeutic to watch."

"Heck yeah!" she says. "I'm only on TikTok to watch her and that hot lady woodchopper."

"I'm not even going to ask." I study the video intently. At the end of it, the sheep shearer holds up a thick wool blanket, which she rolls up, and the sheep is looking happy after its haircut. "I can do that."

"Heck yeah! That's the right attitude. Now come on, get dressed and we're going to shear the hell out of some sheep."

"Thanks, Mushu. You're saving my ass here."

Mushu pauses, seemingly caught off guard by the sincerity in my voice. She clears her throat. "It's nothing."

"It's not nothing," I insist. "I was so wrapped up in studying about ranches and distilleries in the traditional sense. I didn't know there are TikToks about shearing sheep. You don't give yourself enough credit for all of your creativity and entrepreneurial spirit, so I am telling you now, you are a talent, Mushu."

Mushu grunts, her face red. "If only I can get a job using my talent."

"You'll find your calling." I reach out and give Mushu's hand a squeeze. Then, sensing her discomfort at the sudden earnest conversation, I turn away to give her a moment to herself. I focus on finding a tank top to layer underneath my checkered shirt.

As I brush my hair, I level a stern gaze at myself in the mirror. Ranch mask is coming back on. I point at the mirror and snarl, "You need to do this. Get it done." No sheep is going to get in the way of this deal.

I stride out of the bedroom with newfound purpose and almost walk right into Shang, who's standing in front of the door with his hand raised.

"Oh," he says. "Hey. How's it going?"

No losing focus now, no matter how hot he is. *You are Ranch Mulan. You are a different person. You've watched a TikTok.* I raise my chin and look him squarely in the eye. "Hey, buddy!" *Buddy? Oh god. This is not going well.* "It's going really well, actually. How are you? Good? Good. I'm glad."

"Uh. Great. So um, we were thinking of—"

"Shearing sheep, right?" I'm vaguely aware that my voice is coming out louder than necessary, but there's no stopping me now.

"Oh," Shang says, visibly taken aback. "I didn't think—"

"That I'd be up for that?" I say. "I am very much down for sheepshearing."

"Yeah," Mushu says, her head popping up from behind my shoulder. "Back home in Yunnan, she was champion sheepshearer in the county."

I try to elbow Mushu while still keeping my eyes on Shang, but my elbow hits nothing but air.

"Wow," Shang says.

"Yes, and back home in Yunnan, she was also the village's best horse rider. Any horses that the neighbors got that needed breaking in, they'd take it to Zhou here. Isn't that right, Zhou?" Mushu says.

It is now a huge challenge to keep the confident smile on my face. In fact, it feels more like a grimace than anything. Through gritted teeth, I manage to say, "Sure, Mushu. Anyway, shall we?" Without waiting for a reply, I walk past Shang and stride out of the house, where I find James standing on the porch, talking to someone on the phone.

"—thing will come of it," he says.

My ears prick up because James isn't using his usual patronizing tone, but a deferential one. Too late though, as James notices my arrival and quickly says, "I have to go. I will update you later."

Hmm. I don't think it was a significant other he was talking to, because saying "update you later" sounds too sterile. Maybe some business deal?

"Washed all the cow dung off you?" James says by way of greeting.

"Well, I tried to, anyway."

Shang and Mushu come out of the front door, and James's face lights up. "Ah, we're all here. Shall we?" he says.

Shang's eyes are on me. "Why don't we just have a nice, easy tour of the place—"

"What?" James says. "*Borrrring*. Nobody wants that."

I shrug. "I hear there might be some sheep that need shearing?"

"Yes!" James says.

"All right, let's not waste any time," I say, steadfastly ignoring Shang's concerned look.

When we finally reach the barn and I see the sheep, my confidence wilts. My god, these are sheep? They're massive! Are they secretly dwarf cows? Are they genetically modified sheep who have been injected with steroids every morning? I give myself a mental shake. *Stop it. You've watched a whole video on how to shear sheep. You'll be fine.* Yeah, an online tutorial is totally sufficient to prepare you for the actual thing.

Confidence, I remind myself. Animals can sense fear. Though how they can sense fear is up for debate. Dogs can smell it, but what about sheep? Is their sense of smell as keen as a dog's? Are my pores even now opening up and releasing the funky odor of fear? I try to will my pores to close up as I approach. I take a deep breath the way that snipers do before squeezing the trigger, but quickly realize taking deep breaths isn't the best thing to do inside a barn full of animals. It's fine. This is totally par for the course. I'm just going to relax and—and introduce myself. Yes.

Because that went so well last time.

Maybe I shouldn't bother introducing myself this time. Maybe I should just get in there and take the sheep by the horn . . . the fur . . . the *wool*, and show it who's boss, the way that I often have to with the finance bros of the world.

But it feels wrong to do that, and so I decide that regardless of my bad experience with the cow, I'm not about to forget my manners.

"Good afternoon," I say to the sheep. "I am Zhou, and I am here to shear you."

The sheep does nothing to indicate it heard me. I reach out to pat it. Like the cow, the sheep feels far sturdier than I am prepared for, but this time I'm not as shocked as before. I turn around to see Shang standing there looking concerned, flanked by James and Mushu. Behind them is a gaggle of aunties and uncles. Auntie Jiayi has her hands clasped under her chin, looking worried. Auntie Lulu is shamelessly holding up her phone, recording me.

"Shears, please." I hold my hand out to Shang.

He hesitates. "If you don't do this right, you could nick Geraldine."

It takes me a second to realize that Geraldine is the large black sheep I'm supposed to shear. "Geraldine is in fine hands," I say with a lot more confidence than I feel. I've shaved my legs plenty of times, probably thousands of times by now, and I've only nicked myself a handful of times. I can totally do this. I reach out and pluck the electric shears smartly from Shang's hands. "Thank you."

Then, before I can chicken out of this, I put my hands on Geraldine's shoulders and lift. To my surprise, Geraldine doesn't fight it, instead letting herself be lifted up, so she's standing on her hind legs, and then held against my legs. Geraldine's unexpectedly heavy, but I've braced for it, planting my feet firmly on the ground to support the sheep's weight. For a moment, I blink in surprise. I've somehow maneuvered Geraldine into the correct position.

"Very good, Zhou!" Auntie Jiayi calls out. There are murmurs of agreement from the others.

There is a half breath where I swear I lock eyes with Geraldine and a look of understanding passes from the sheep. It's a look that says: *You got this, girl.* Or maybe I'm losing my marbles.

I grip the electric shears tight and turn them on. Steadfastly ignoring the stares on me, I bend over and begin, starting from Geraldine's chest and moving the shears down toward the lower belly region. To my complete and utter surprise, the shears move easily, slicing through the soft wool. It leaves behind a path of smooth, short wool. A shot of pure endorphins floods my senses and I very nearly jump up and whoop. Fortunately, I stop myself in time and keep going, doing another neat path down to the belly. Recalling the TikTok, I make sure to cover

Geraldine's teats with my free hand to avoid nicking them.

It doesn't take too long before Geraldine's entire belly is shaven. I stare in wonderment at my handiwork.

"Very smoothly done," one of the uncles murmurs.

The others nod at me with expressions of approval. I catch Shang's eye and let a smirk take over my mouth. In response, he tries—and fails—to fight back a smile. *Don't lose focus now.* I force myself to turn back to Geraldine.

Now comes the tricky part. I have to shift Geraldine to her side so that I can begin shearing her sides. Moving my right foot a step back, I maneuver Geraldine, who acquiesces quite happily, flopping to her side and staying there. My breath comes out in a wobbly laugh. Channeling the TikTok video, I begin to run the shears up Geraldine's hind leg, from the hoof up to the butt. The wool is far thicker on this side than on the belly, and I can feel more resistance. I push harder on the shears to keep them going, and before long, the effort begins to cramp my hand.

James crouches next to me. "You okay?" he says.

I don't spare him a glance. "Yep." I keep my focus on Geraldine.

"Only it looks like you're struggling a little."

"Nope" is all I manage to huff out. Geraldine's weight, in addition to the friction of the thick wool, are adding up.

"James," Shang says in a warning tone.

"I just don't want her to nick the sheep, is all. It'll get skittish if she does."

Do not lose focus, I tell myself again. I keep going, watching in satisfaction as Geraldine's hind leg comes free from its thick, matted wool.

"You need help," James says, and without warning, reaches out and grabs Geraldine's hoof.

The movement knocks the shears askew, and I experience the next two seconds in horrified slow motion as my tired, stiff hand loses

107

control of the shears. As the shears swerve, I see the whirring blades bite into Geraldine's skin. Geraldine jerks, her entire body bucking up, and knocks into my legs. "Sh—" I cry out as I lose my balance and topple over backward, straight onto a bucket of dirty water. Freezing water sloshes over my neck, shoulders, and back. "Not again!"

Laughter. They're laughing. Anger shoots through me, hot and fast. I cough out spatters of dirty water and when I open my eyes, Shang is leaning over me, his arm outstretched toward me. My pulse is thrumming so furiously it's more like a whir than any discernible rhythm. They're laughing at me after making me hurt poor, sweet Geraldine. I don't think twice before reaching up and accepting Shang's hand. Then, before he can pull me up, I yank, hard.

I'm rewarded by a glimpse of pure shock taking over Shang's features as he loses his balance, then he lands on top of me. He manages to break his fall with his arms, but enough of his weight lands on me to make me feel winded. His body is solid, rock-hard, and incredibly warm. For a moment, we both forget to breathe as our eyes meet, mere inches apart, and it's only then that I question the wisdom of yanking this ridiculously hot guy down on top of me. Close up, he should look less attractive. He should. His pores should be grossly visible, perhaps I'll find blackheads on his nose, or an errant nose hair or two. But no, defying all laws of nature, Shang is even more captivating up close. His scent envelops me, a mix of something leafy, like rosemary, and a subtle hint of cologne. I could lose myself in that smell forever.

Or not.

Because the next second, it hits me that Shang is braced on his forearms on top of me and his family is all around us, some of them squawking, "Are you okay?" and the rest of them guffawing and slapping their legs.

I place a hand on Shang's chest to push him off (my traitorous mind goes: *Pecs! Pecs!*) and he springs away like he's just been burned. Oh well, I can hardly blame him for that reaction, given I'm the one who pulled him down. With fluid grace, Shang hops back up to his feet. I clamber up as well, immediately scanning the barn for poor Geraldine. She's a few paces away, huddling close to Auntie Jiayi, who is murmuring softly in her ear. Guilt pierces my chest. I've hurt that lovely animal.

"James, what the hell?" Shang says in a low voice.

"I was just trying to help, man," James says. "Not my fault that Zhou here freaked out and nicked the sheep."

"I had it under control," I say, fighting to keep my voice even. Damn it, what am I doing, arguing with our potential partners? Baba would most definitely never do anything like that. I rein my temper in and add, "But I appreciate you trying to help."

James looks smug. Shang narrows his eyes, probably wondering what I'm up to.

"I think I would like to take a second shower now," I say. "Excuse me, gentlemen."

I march off toward the farmhouse once more, holding my head high, but once I'm out of sight, I veer away before going inside to give myself time away from everyone else. It's not just the fact that James sabotaged the whole thing that infuriates me, but also the fact that before he interfered, I had been doing fine. Great, even, especially given that it was my first time shearing sheep. Not to mention poor Geraldine. I cringe as I recall how Geraldine had jerked in my arms. At the end of the day, it was my fault. I hurt Geraldine through my inexperience. I take a few deep breaths, fortifying myself mentally, and head toward the house.

When I get inside, I find the bathroom locked. "I'm going to be quite a while," Mushu says from behind the door.

"Oh! Sorry, yeah, okay!" I hurry away, hugging a set of clean clothes to my chest.

Should I look for another bathroom? The farmhouse is massive;

surely there would be a different bathroom I can use. I wander down the hallways until I locate a different bathroom, but find this one occupied by Uncle Jing.

I am about to give up and just change into dry clothes without showering when Auntie Jiayi spots me.

"Ah, Zhou," Auntie Jiayi says, eyeing my disheveled state and the change of clothes in my arms. "Are the bathrooms all taken up?"

I nod.

Auntie Jiayi shakes her head. "At our age, everything takes an extra-long time to process, including digestion."

"Uh . . . okay. That makes sense." I have no idea what else to say to that, and begin inching away, desperate to get out of my wet clothes.

"Ah, why don't you use the outdoors shower? It's very pleasant. We keep it clean."

"Oh?" The thought of an outdoors shower doesn't particularly appeal to me, but then again, I don't have much of a choice.

"It's nicer than you think," Auntie Jiayi says, reading my mind. "I would have suggested it after you got covered in cow dung, but I didn't want cow poop all over the shower floor. Out the back door and to the right." She smiles and ushers me away. Is it my imagination or did Auntie Jiayi's smile look more cunning than usual?

I don't have a choice but to trudge out through the back door, as suggested. Outside, I let out a long, heavy sigh before making my way along the path. I'm exhausted. It isn't so much the disastrous activities of the day, though they certainly didn't help, but mostly the way that I have had to play a role. Even though I've been doing it for as long as I can remember, having Shang's mother call me Zhou still feels really bad, a reminder of my deceit.

Lost in my gloomy thoughts, I fail to notice the outdoor shower until I am standing right in front of it. I also fail to notice that the shower is turned on, and that there is someone standing underneath it.

What I do manage to notice is the fact that the outdoor shower is basically a large cubicle with a very small door. A door that barely covers the upper half of anyone inside and leaves very little to the imagination. A door that is doing the bare minimum to cover Shang as he stands under the showerhead with his head tilted back and his eyes closed.

For a second, I freeze. Is it possible to do anything but freeze in this situation? After all, my mind has been torn apart, with one side shrieking: *Oh my* god, *naked man, get out of here!* And the other side shouting: *Oh my god,* gorgeous *naked man, stay here!* And he truly is gorgeous. Clearly, he is one of god's favorites. That face of his, those eyebrows and those cheeks and that straight nose. And his hair! This is the first time I'm seeing his hair down. It's long enough to graze his shoulders, and draws the eye to his ripped shoulders and huge pecs. His body looks like it's been sculpted lovingly out of marble, and the sight of the water sluicing down his dark hair, dripping down those high cheekbones and that strong jaw before sliding down his muscular chest—

Then my senses slam back into place and I duck out of sight, practically leaping away before Shang can see me. I move with the kind of speed I never knew I had, landing on hands and knees before going into a roll. Fortunately, the soft grass stops me from hurting myself. I'm clambering up to my feet to sprint off when Shang's voice slices through the air.

"You dropped this."

Oh god. A pit has opened in my stomach and all my insides are falling through it. Slowly, painfully so, I turn around, my eyes shut so I won't see anything I'm not supposed to see.

"You can open your eyes, I'm decent." There is no denying the hint of amusement in Shang's voice.

I do so. "Decent" is clearly up for debate. Shang has a towel wrapped around his waist, which means his abs and pecs and shoulders and arms are very, very bare. And very, very wet. And very, very—

111

Damn it, focus! Focus on the thing he's holding out to you. Which is . . .

My bra. Because of course it would be my bra. And of course it would be the most unflattering bra I own, because the universe is clearly punishing me for deceiving his family. My toxic trait is keeping comfortable underwear for years beyond their lifespan, and this bra is one of my ancient treasures, a cotton bra I'd bought my sophomore year at Princeton. It had fit me so well and been so comfy that wearing it felt like I wasn't wearing a bra at all. And now, years later, this same bra, graying and tattered on the edges, a sad piece of underwear clearly past its prime and begging to be retired, is in Shang's outstretched hand.

I get it, universe. You are giving me a sign. Start refreshing my wardrobe. Okay. Message received, loud and clear.

I reach out and snatch the bra from him. My scalp feels like it's grown way too tight for the rest of my head. Somehow, I manage to bite out a terse "Thank you."

"Shower's all yours," Shang says, stepping out and standing in front of me. He's so close to me that I can see each individual water droplet on his tanned skin. Why is he standing right in front of me, just staring down into my eyes?

I swallow, and the sound is painfully loud between us. "Um—"

"Do you mind?" Shang says.

"Oh!" With a start, I realize that the reason Shang's been standing inches away from me for the past two seconds is because I'm blocking the pathway. My god, just when I thought I couldn't possibly be more mortified. I hop to one side quickly and open my mouth to apologize, then close it again. *Do not apologize. He is a potential business partner and he needs to see you as his equal.* Argh. Honestly, there should be a law of nature that prevents business partners from being so hot.

"Thank you," Shang says, walking past me. He pauses, then turns around. "You did well with the sheepshearing."

"Oh." I wasn't expecting that. "I wouldn't call what happened doing well—"

"That was James's fault. You were doing well up until then." There's a new expression I haven't noticed on Shang's face before. It almost looks like . . . respect?

I've learned enough in school to know when to accept a compliment. Even though every part of me wants to bat away his kind words and diminish myself, I make myself nod and say, "Thank you. I really appreciate it."

Shang nods. "Want me to stand guard so no one walks in on you showering?"

"No!" I yelp.

To my surprise, color blooms in Shang's cheeks. "I didn't mean— Uh, I'd obviously wait on the other side of the wall. I wouldn't, like, look or anything."

"Oh, I didn't mean you'd look, I just—"

Welp. Now we're both flustered. At least it's no longer just me. "Anyway. See you around." With that, I step into the shower and quickly shut the door.

Shang gets the hint and walks off. After making sure no one else is in the vicinity, I whip off my clothes and take the quickest shower, slapping soap all over myself before washing it all off and toweling myself dry in record time. Now that I'm clean once again, I can't wait to tackle whatever else the Li family has in store for me. No doubt that whatever it is, I'll end up dirty and humiliated once again.

CHAPTER ELEVEN

If there is anything I am good at, it's sheer dogged determination. When I was little, I once got into a fight with the schoolyard bully. He was twice my size and easily bested me, grabbing my hair in one fist and yanking it until tears rushed into my eyes and streamed down my cheeks. *Say you were wrong!* he'd yelled, but even though I was trapped, I resolutely kept silent, even as tears ran down my face in rivulets and snot dripped down my chin from the burning pain in my scalp. I'd stayed like that until he lost patience and shoved me to the ground. And though anyone who'd witnessed this would say that I got the shit kicked out of me that day, I felt like I'd also won, in a way. I'd managed to hold back from saying I was wrong. The tears and snot had been a physiological reaction I couldn't control, but the words were something I could hold back, and I did, despite the excruciating pain. And ever since then, I have known I have what it takes to make it in a world that doesn't want me to succeed.

This is the thought I cling to that evening, after my shower. Though my body, bruised and exhausted, begs me to stop and crawl inside my room to hide, I force myself to get back out as soon as I'm dressed. Thankfully, the Li family seems to have dispersed all over the ranch. It seems they have given up on our tour for now. Mushu is probably out there somewhere, taking a million selfies with the animals. This is my chance to have an undisturbed look at the ranch and distillery. I've learned by now that no amount of reading or analyzing can replace actually going around the physical space and learning more about it through observation.

The Li family ranch is beautiful and maintained with care and love, there's no doubt about it. As I walk past the barnyard, I notice how healthy the animals look, how several of them approach me with a curious friendliness. None of them shies away, which means they're used to being treated by humans with kindness. I smile and pet a nearby sheep. I'm getting used to them now, their bucolic movements, their guttural noises, and their earthy smells.

"Having a moment with Geraldine?" a voice says.

I look up to find Shang there, watching me with yet another one of his unreadable expressions. "Yeah," I say. "Thought I'd come by and apologize to her for nicking her earlier."

"That's nice of you. Except that's Sheldon. Geraldine's over there."

I roll my eyes. "Obviously I knew that. I was just getting Sheldon here to pass the message to Geraldine." Why am I speaking with such abandon? This isn't Ranch Mulan, nor Work Mulan, and it definitely is not Zhou. I need to focus. There's something about Shang that encourages me to take off my masks, and I can't let that happen, not when there's so much at stake.

The smallest hint of a smile cracks Shang's face. "When you're done talking to Sheldon, what say you to a tour around the distillery?"

It's all I can do to say, in as casual a voice as possible, "Sounds good. Just give me another moment with Sheldon." I turn back to the sheep and close my eyes, drawing in a deep breath to recenter myself. I can do this. I can tour the distillery with Shang. I am not attracted to him or his dark brown eyes and that warm olive skin of his or those extremely kissable lips—damn it. I am not attracted to him. Nope. Not at all. Okay. I can do this. "Okay, ready!" I say brightly.

Like the ranch, the distillery is carefully maintained. Shang pushes a tall, heavy door open and we walk inside, escaping the fierce glow of the late afternoon Californian sun, into the large building. The distillery might as well be a whole other universe. As soon as I step inside, I become distinctly aware of the rich history behind this family-run whiskey company. It's impossible not to when all of my senses are enveloped by everything whiskey-related, from fermented barley to smoke from the kiln to the impressive copper stills that look as though they were built way back in the industrial era.

It's a humbling space to be in, because every part of it is so unfamiliar to me. It's a completely different space than the one I'm used to; I'm used to cold, hard numbers, so far removed from their sources that by the time they get to me, the product itself has become an abstract concept, less tangible than the numbers they generate. But now I am standing in the product's territory.

As though reading my mind, Shang says, "This is one of my favorite places in the world. It's where the numbers cease and the art begins. In here, nothing else matters. The market, or the shifting supply and demand, none of it matters. This is where the barley is soaked, malted, and fermented. The farmer doesn't care about marketing or packaging; here it's all down to pure farming for the love of it."

I nod, absorbing the rich history of the art of whiskey-making through his words. As we walk deeper inside, I begin to understand why Baba might want to acquire the company. It's obvious that everything here has been built and maintained with love. *Maybe he attended one of their public tours once and hasn't been able to forget it since?* I smile at the thought. I can just see it. Baba is a hopeless romantic after all. And none of the reading I've done on the science of whiskey distillation can compare to actually being here, taking in the massive copper stills that tower over me and smelling the rich, sweet scent of roasting barley blanketing the space.

"Come here," Shang calls out. "This is a kiln," he says. "It's where we dry the barley. It's also where we introduce flavors by using peat smoke during kilning. We can also get different flavors by altering the temperature within the kiln."

"Oh yes," I reply, glad that some of my reading is finally coming into good use. "Like how high-nitrogen barley is steeped and then cooked with no airflow to create a caramel flavor."

Shang pauses, studying me with a curious expression. "You've done your homework."

I allow myself to give him a lingering look before shrugging and turning away. I haven't missed the way a muscle works on the side of his jaw, as though he's thinking something he shouldn't when he looks at me. The same exact way I'm thinking things I shouldn't be when I look at him. "It's just a bit of general reading," I say casually.

After a moment, Shang says, "Would you like to put your hands inside the kiln? It's not too hot right now."

"Oh, sure!" I step forward, feeling the warmth emanating from the kiln, and, gingerly, I reach out and touch the drying barley. "Oh my gosh." I breathe in. An odd sense of peace overwhelms my entire being as I bury my hands in the smooth granules.

Shang steps close to me and does the same, breathing in deeply as he does so. "When I was a kid, this used to be my favorite place. I'd just come here and touch everything. Burned my hands pretty badly once."

The way he describes it makes me realize how much more there is to this place than just pure numbers. I see Shang as a little boy, wandering around the distillery, touching everything with curious little hands. I think of him burning his palms and my heart aches with the need to comfort him. *Oh, Baba, I think I'm starting to understand what you saw in this company.*

I'm about to reply when my right hand, buried in the barley, bumps against something solid and warm. Shang's hand. We both tense at once, but neither of us moves our hand away. Oh my god. All my senses have focused, laser-sharp, onto the electric sensation shooting up my arm from the sliver of skin-on-skin contact. The attraction I feel toward Shang right now is so irresistible, so magnetic, that it scares me a little. What is happening? This can't happen. This is so unprofessional! And with that, I use the last vestiges of my self-restraint and pull my hand away. Shang does the same just a split second later while clearing his throat.

"It's getting late," he says gruffly. "I need to help prep for dinner."

"Oh, right! Of course." I hurry after him and we both walk out of the distillery in thick silence.

Outside, the sun is slowly setting, limning everything gold. I stop to admire the gorgeous land, loving the way the breeze makes the leaves sway. Farmhands are guiding the animals back into the barn, and a sort of peace is settling over the land. When I glance up, I find Shang watching me with an intense gaze. He opens his mouth, as though to say something, then seems to think better of it and walks on ahead of me.

"I'll see you at dinner," he says.

"Yep, see you."

I hurry back toward the farmhouse, wincing as my new boots bite into my feet. I've been able to ignore the pinch of the tough boots this whole time, but after wearing them for so many hours, I can no longer pretend not to notice the way my poor feet are blistering inside this torture device. Inside the house, I yank off the boots with a grateful sigh and steal a precious few minutes just submerging my aching feet in a shallow bath before dinner.

Dinner that night is a feast, a collection of steaming dishes, each one worthy of a restaurant. When Shang said he had to help prep for dinner, surely he didn't mean he cooked all of this? He probably helped with the simple things like washing the rice or chopping the vegetables. I'm so tired by now that I can barely keep up with the multiple conversations going around the table, but thankfully, Mushu is in her usual fine form, regaling this uncle and that auntie with funny stories and as always making everyone fall in love with her. I chew my green beans (which, like everything else on the table, have come from the farm) and smile and nod, smile and nod. A couple of times, I catch Shang's eyes on me, and when I look over at him, he quickly breaks eye contact. This can't happen, I remind myself.

By the time dinner is over, I'm all ready for bed. Mushu opts to stay in the living room, where the cousins are gathered to play poker, but I bid everyone good night and retire to my bedroom. But once I'm in bed, I don't go to sleep. Instead, I grab my phone and open up TikTok. By tomorrow morning, I am going to know everything there is to know about ranch living, and I'm going to wipe the smug looks off everybody's faces.

When I wake up the next morning, Mushu is sprawled across the other bed, her mouth hanging open as she snores. Soft, dim light streams in through the gap in the curtains. I peep through the gap and see gentle, golden sunlight blanketing the fields. I'm so used to waking up at dawn that I no longer need an alarm to rouse me. I get up slowly, careful not to wake Mushu, wondering what time she finally climbed into bed last night. After brushing my teeth, I shrug on a pair of jeans and a sweater and pad down the stairs.

Having the whole house to myself, if only for a bit, sounds like heaven. Yesterday, I wasn't able to enjoy the beautiful house because I'd been overwhelmed by the sheer number of people in it. Right now, I would like nothing more than to make myself a nice hot mug of coffee and settle down on the porch and take in the bucolic surroundings.

But as I near the kitchen, I hear the clanging of pots and pans. I groan inwardly. Clearly I won't get the kitchen all to myself after all.

Still, one can hope that perhaps it's the housekeeper cleaning up after last night's feast, or maybe a stray raccoon that I can just let out through the back door? Anything would be less intimidating than a member of the Li family, come to think of it.

No such luck. When I go inside the kitchen, I come face-to-face with Shang, wearing an apron and wielding a wooden rolling pin. The sight is so unexpected that I freeze, staring at him. I've never had a thing for men wearing aprons before. But now, seeing Shang wearing one, I'm realizing how incredibly sexy it is. He's somehow more masculine in an apron, his broad shoulders accentuated by the apron strings. Unbidden, the thought of him buck naked, wearing only an apron, flashes through my mind. My god, what is wrong with me?

"Something on my face?" he says by way of greeting. "Only you're kind of staring."

I break eye contact and clear my throat, trying to hide how flustered I am. "I wasn't expecting anyone down here this early in the morning."

"Me neither," he says. He flours the roller, picks up a small piece of dough from the counter, and begins to roll it out into a circle.

The sight is incongruous—Shang wearing an apron with a nectarine print, his hands floury, rolling out dough with expert ease, and meanwhile his biceps are bulging as he works and he's got an expression of intense focus that makes me sweat a little bit.

"Can I help you get something?" he says, glancing up for a second before turning his focus back to the dough.

"It's okay," I say hurriedly. "I'll just— I'll make some coffee and get out of your way."

Of course, as soon as I say that, I notice the professional barista-style espresso machine on the kitchen counter. No easy-use Nespresso machines around here. Maybe they might have an instant coffee mix that I can simply add water to?

Shang must've seen the hesitation on my face, because he wipes his hands on a towel and says, "I'll make you a coffee. Latte? Cappuccino? Americano?"

"Uh. Latte." I lean against the counter and watch as Shang picks out a jar of beans and pours them into the grinder. He measures out the ground coffee carefully, obviously comfortable with the espresso machine. "Where did you learn to make coffee like that?" I say, watching him fiddle with the pressure controls.

"Instagram," he says, so simply and so straightforwardly that it takes a second for the answer to sink in.

I laugh. "Really?"

"Yup. That's also where I learned how to cook most of my dishes."

"Seriously? My Instagram algorithm only pushes parodies of finance bros. I'm not complaining, they are funny as hell, but they don't exactly teach me anything I don't already know."

Shang presses a lever and the machine hisses as foamy coffee begins to pour into a mug. "Nothing wrong with that. Your job sounds very high pressure and it's probably good to have something that lets you blow off some steam."

I frown at him, wondering if there's a secret jab hidden in his words, but Shang is now walking to the fridge, where he takes out a jug of milk. "Fresh from our cows," he says, grinning. "There's nothing better than our cows' milk." He pours some into a small cup and slides it over to me.

"The last time I had milk on its own must've been when I was eight," I say.

"Don't knock it till you try it."

I sip the milk, and Shang was right: There really is nothing better than their cows' milk. It's so creamy it almost tastes like I'm drinking heavy cream, but with a lightness to it that keeps it from being too cloying. There is no aftertaste; everything about it is refreshing and clean. "Wow. Okay. You were right."

"Sorry, what was that again?" Shang grins, showing those deep dimples of his, and I roll my eyes.

He steams the milk, then pours it carefully into the mug with espresso in it. When he brings over the latte, I see that he's drawn a leaf on it. Is there anything this guy does not excel at? And of course the latte is one of the best ones I've ever tasted, if not the best. The first sip makes me groan, its rich nutty flavors making my muscles relax even as the caffeine wakes me up.

"Quit your job and open up a café," I mutter.

Shang chuckles. "Yeah, let me get right on that."

I watch him roll out the dough. "Are those . . . pancakes?"

Shang cocks an eyebrow. "And just from that one question alone, I can tell you have never set foot in the kitchen."

"Nope. My mom sends me food regularly and the rest of the time I subsist on Postmates." I say this without shame, and in fact with a tad of pride because I am truly so sick of finance bros who tell me in many different, exhaustive ways that my place is in the kitchen.

"Fair enough. No one can beat Mom's cooking. These are not pancakes. You don't roll out pancake dough. These are dumpling skins."

"Oh! Wait, you're making dumplings from scratch? Don't they sell dumpling skin at the supermarket?"

Those dimples appear once more in his cheeks. "They do, but I like making my own. I started making them when my mom's arthritis flared up, but over time I realized I liked working with dough. It's therapeutic. Wanna try making one?"

Not wanting to seem like a grump (which I kind of am), I agree. I hop off the barstool and stand in front of the kitchen island. Shang sprinkles more flour on the counter and puts a ball of dough on the prepared surface before handing me the rolling pin. "Hold it like this," he says, standing behind me and reaching out to show me the proper grip.

His hands are on either side of me! my mind squeaks. And indeed, they are. The nearness of him is impossible to ignore. If I lean back, even a little, I'd feel his hard chest against my back. His scent envelops me—a clean, woody musk that fills my senses and clouds my mind. I want to nuzzle my nose into his neck inhale deeply. I blink rapidly, forcing my mind to concentrate on the rolling pin. I place my hands on either end and press down on the dough.

"Not like that," Shang says, and leans in closer. His chest pressing against my back is so solid I want to simply melt against him. Gently, he lays his fingertips on the back of my hands, and it takes all of my will not to react. "A soft touch," he says.

My mind goes to very, very NSFW places. *Stop it, you pervert.*

"You want to start from the edges and go in. The edges of the skin should be thinner than the center, so when you fold it you'll get a uniform thickness all around."

My god. That is so sexual. No, wait. Is it sexual? Or is my perverted mind just turning everything into an innuendo?

To be fair, Shang's hands are still over mine, so he must be aware of the sexual tension sparkling in the air.

Or not.

Technically speaking, it's only his fingertips, and very, very technically speaking, they are just barely grazing my skin.

But grazing of the skin is a well-known sexual practice! Is it?

Okay, enough of this.

I jerk up and Shang, startled, steps back. "You okay?"

"I think the coffee's just kicked in," I say, sidestepping so I'm now a very safe arm's length distance from him. To place emphasis on the coffee, I take a big gulp of it and go "Mmm." Shang looks like he's about to say something, so I hurriedly say, "Hey, do you need chores doing around the house? I feel like I should pitch in."

"Uh—"

"How about firewood? You got enough of that?"

"Well—"

"Do you guys chop your own firewood around here? You know what? I love chopping firewood and I'm going to chop some up for you."

Shang stops rolling out dough. "Really?"

"Yeah, chopping firewood is like my favorite hobby." I spent nearly a whole hour last night watching female woodchoppers on TikTok and by god I am not about to let that go to waste.

"Cool, well, sure, we always need firewood around here. Come on, I'll show you where the chopping block is." Shang wipes his hands on the hand towel again (is there anything hotter than a guy with his sleeves rolled up to the elbows, wiping flour from his hands?) and gestures at me to follow him.

We walk out the back door. Outside, the air is biting cold and the grass is dewy. I shiver as we make our way down a small path. I take another sip of the latte, relishing the way it warms me up from the inside. It's setting up to be yet another flawless Northern Californian autumn day, the air carrying with it the sweet smell of apples, and wispy white clouds dabbed here and there across the endless blue sky.

When we get to the chopping block, I don't give myself any time to hesitate or marvel at the realness of the situation like before. I spot an axe resting against the block and grab it. My mind goes: *It's heav—*

I shut the thought down. Of course it's heavy, it's a real axe, not a TikTok axe. I even throw a confident smile at Shang as I strut past him, heaving up a log and settling it on the chopping block. Feet apart, strong stance. I grip the axe handle tight, letting it hang for a second, then swing it up over my head the way I've watched people do on TikTok before slamming it down onto the log, drawing power from my abs. The axe bites into the log with a satisfying thud. It doesn't go all the way through, but no matter. I've seen this happen plenty of times on TikTok and merely lift it again, this time carrying the log up along with the axe, and then swing it down again and again until the log is completely sliced in half. Then I step back, looking at the split log in disbelief.

I did it. Joy rushes through my veins like sparkling wine and I toss the axe down and jump up with a whoop.

"Nicely done," Shang says.

I bow. "Thank you, I agree." I puff out my chest. "Throw me another. I will chop up a bunch of these before you know it."

Shang smiles as he places another log on the chopping block. "All right, chop your heart out. I'll be back at the house making dumplings."

I do exactly that, chopping log after log before I realize that I am, in fact, famished.

"Zhou!" Mushu calls out from a distance. "How's it going?" She jogs down the path. "What the— When Shang said you were out here chopping wood, I thought he meant you were taking a dump."

I lift my eyebrows. "Why would 'chopping wood' mean taking a dump? And why would I do that out here when we have perfectly good working toilets indoors?"

"I don't know," she says with a shrug. "I ain't judging."

I laugh. "I think I'm just about done. Chopping wood is fun, but it's also pretty tiring. You know, I bet this is even better than Pilates."

As we walk back toward the house, Mushu fills me in on the night before.

"They brought out their best whiskey."

"Ooh, sounds like I missed a good time," I say.

"You really did. These people are actually pretty fun to spend time with."

"When they're not trying to sabotage your sheepshearing moment," I mutter.

Mushu laughs. "Well, James is . . . not the best dude, but once you get a couple glasses of whiskey in him . . ." She hesitates, then says, "He's even worse."

Now it's my turn to laugh.

"But you'll be glad to know that I took the chance to talk you up."

My laugh shrivels up and dies in my throat. "Um. You mean about how brilliant of a managing partner I am?"

"What? No!" Mushu cries. "Mulan, these people are ranchers and distiller— What are people who make whiskey called? Whiskey-ers? Whatever, my point is, they are about as far removed from finance as you can get. They're not going to appreciate your skill with numbers. They have this attitude that's almost, like, anti-money."

"I can't even begin to comprehend that," I say dryly.

"You and me both, cuz. I'm all about that hustle. But the Li family is more concerned about their image. Their brand. Their legacy. That's what I got from them last night. They really want the company who buys their whiskey brand to know what the company stands for," she says.

I sigh. "I know what it stands for. Toxic masculinity."

"Exactly!" she says. "So anyway, I talked you up with that in mind. Told them of your prowess when it comes to anything even vaguely masculine."

"Uh-oh." Dread is beginning to bubble up from deep inside my guts. "Um, what exactly did you say about me?"

"Oh, nothing much. Just how good of a hunter you are—"

"Hunter? I have literally never held a weapon in my hands."

She waves that away as though it were hardly important. "How deadly of a fighter you are—"

"Are we talking, like, fighting on the internet? 'Cause I am pretty good at taking down Chads online."

"And when they mentioned that overnight horseback camping trip we're going on, I told them back in China, you were known as Zhou the Horse Whisperer."

I stop walking and gape at Mushu in horror. "Mushu, I like

horses as much as the next person, but I am no horse whisperer, you know this."

"What do you mean?" Mushu looks genuinely surprised. "Don't you remember our Disney trip when we were kids? You went on that pony ride and you had so much fun, whereas I puked all over my pony and then jumped off and cried?"

"First of all, you'd had three churros, one whole turkey leg, and a bucket of soda, so I'm not surprised you ended up puking. Second of all, you said it: It was a pony. They're half the size of actual horses, and there was a—a pony dude holding on to it at all times."

"Potayto-potahto," Mushu says. "You're going to do great."

"Oh god," I moan.

"They said they have just the perfect horse for you," she says cheerfully.

I pat my cheeks. "This is a nightmare. I need to wake up now."

"Oh, Mulan, you're such a drama queen. Come on, I'm famished. Shang's made dumplings."

The rest of the morning passes by peacefully. Shang's dumplings are delicious and plentiful, and when James heckles Shang about cooking, Shang merely laughs it off. By the time breakfast is done, everyone is stuffed. The Lis show Mushu and me to the distillery, where Uncle Hong takes us carefully through each step of the whiskey-making process.

"The first step to making whiskey is malting," Uncle Hong says. "You know what malting is?"

To everyone's surprise, I say, "Malting is when you take grains of barley or whatever and soak them before spreading them out so they germinate."

"Impressive," Shang says, with a small wink. A wave of pleasure trails down my spine. I think back to the private tour that Shang gave me yesterday and have to hide my smile.

I turn back to Uncle Hong. "Back at my family farm, we used to make everything from scratch, even our own candies. There's this malted candy that we made from wheat and then mulch with glutinous rice—"

Uncle Hong's face breaks into a joyous grin. "Mai ya tang! Ah, my favorite candy growing up. You know how to make mai ya tang?" He sounds so excited it makes my heart twist a little.

If by "know" he means, have I memorized every step I've watched on TikTok? I tamp down my guilt as I say, "Sure, yeah."

"My mother used to make it from scratch," Uncle Hong says, and the enthusiasm on his face makes the years melt away. "She'd boil the syrup for hours and hours, until it was brown and thick and gooey, and my brothers and I, we would sneak little spoonfuls here and there when she wasn't looking. Ah, the smell of the boiling syrup was so good." He closes his eyes and takes a deep breath in, then, seeming to remember himself, straightens his back and says, "Okay, so you know all about malting, very good. Now, over here is where we have our tuns. We mash our dried malt and then mix with hot water in the mash tun. We have to be very careful with the water. We add it in separate stages and each stage has a different temperature—" Uncle Hong turns his head and barks, "James!"

James, who's been sauntering along behind us while scrolling on his phone, lifts his head. "What?" he says irritably.

"What are the proper temperatures for the water?" Uncle Hong says.

All eyes turn to James, who groans and says, "Seriously? Not this again."

"Aiya, Er zi," Auntie Chuang says, "how can you boast about our family distillery when you know nothing about the process?"

"That's why we have employees," James snaps. "So we can delegate."

"The first stage is sixty-seven degrees Celsius," I say helpfully, "the

128

second stage is seventy-two degrees Celsius, and for the third water, you want it to be between eighty and eighty-five degrees Celsius."

There is silence as they all turn to look at me. I secretly thank the gods of the internet. Herding cattle? Not so much. But numbers? All I have to do is glance at them once and they will be imprinted in my memory.

The aunties and uncles nod solemnly. Uncle Hong smacks me on the back and laughs. "Ah, good girl!"

Shang is studying me with something approaching admiration on his face, and the sight of it does funny things to my stomach. Funny, warm, nice things.

Uncle Hong goes through the fermentation process, and again, I am happy to share my knowledge of fermentation, based on a combination of me reading up on the whiskey-making process, what Shang told me yesterday, and my one and only disastrous experience making sourdough (I named my starter Breadley Cooper, but it was all downhill from there).

I could swear that Uncle Hong is looking markedly less annoyed by my presence by now. He brings me to the pot stills. "Every distillery has its own distinct pot stills," he says. "And ours are unique. We use the same shape from the first day we start the distillery. It's what gives our whiskey its incomparable taste and smell."

"How did you come by this particular shape?"

"Trial and error, of course," Uncle Hong says. "We tried different shapes—wider stills and narrow ones. The wide ones will produce more refined spirit, same with tall ones. The shorter and narrower ones will have heavier whiskey. We like our whiskey to be heavy flavored, have more oomph, so we knew we wanted a shorter still."

Though I've read up all I could about the process of making whiskey, seeing it in person—being surrounded by these huge pots and stills, hearing the whir and thuds and steaming of the machines, and smelling the rich scents of fermentation—is entirely different. I feel the gravity of the place, the echoes of its past years, of the trials and errors that the uncles and aunties went through.

"How did your family decide to go into the whiskey-making business?" I say.

At this, Uncle Hong gives a little roar and gestures at Uncle Jing and Uncle Xiaotian. "Ah, we three came up with it, didn't we?"

Uncle Jing and Uncle Xiaotian both grin and nod, but I notice that Auntie Jiayi's eyebrows are raised so high that they've practically disappeared into her hairline. I meet Auntie Jiayi's eye and cock my head to one side, but she gives a small shake of the head and smiles in a *Oh well, what are you gonna do?* way.

"When we moved to America, we were all doing odd jobs," Uncle Hong says. "I worked in a shoe factory."

"I worked in a noodle factory," Uncle Jing says.

"And I worked as a cleaner in an office building," Uncle Xiaotian says.

"Pah!" Uncle Hong says. "You were hopping from job to job, like a rabbit." He turns back to me. "And then one day, when we were eating dinner, we said, 'We used to make our own baijiu. Let's make it again to sell.' But nobody in America knew what baijiu is at the time, so we decided to make an American drink. First we considered making beer, but we didn't know much about beer making, you see. So then we decided, ah, whiskey. Yes. And it turns out there are many similarities in the process of making the whiskey. We started in our own garage, you know. Only after we saved up enough money were we able to buy this space to turn into a proper distillery."

I gaze around the expansive building with newfound respect and awe. I know how hard immigrant lives are from my own parents' struggle, and whenever I comes across a new story, I treat it as a priceless gift handed to me and tuck it in a safe place in the endless tapestry of my memories, something to be cherished in quiet moments.

By the time we end the tour of the distillery, it's past lunchtime. We file out, going back to the farmhouse, where there is steamed mantou stuffed with roast duck that Shang made earlier. We eat outside, soaking in the sunlight and drinking refreshing mint juleps. The drinks are purposely made weak since it's so early in the day, and I think about how much Baba would've enjoyed this trip. He would've fit in as easily as a fish slipping into water, and he would be delighted by the food, the drinks, and the stories. The thought strengthens my hope of securing the deal. Once we buy the company, there will surely be more of these trips, and another chance for me to drink in the sight of my parents laughing in the golden sunlight, mint juleps in hand. Of course, given the fact that I'm impersonating my father, I have no idea how this daydream will ever come to pass, but one can hope.

CHAPTER TWELVE

I n the afternoon, we pack for the camping trip the next day.

"I don't know about the wisdom of sleeping in tents," Mushu grouses. "What if we get ambushed?"

I'm comfortable with the idea of camping, having done it several times growing up and a couple times in college, but the thought of doing it with Shang's family admittedly makes it a tad more intimidating. Still, camping is camping is camping. "And who would ambush us?"

Mushu gestures vaguely. "I don't know, fellow whiskey competitors? Or something in the wilderness? We are kind of off the grid here, in case you haven't noticed."

I laugh. "We've got 5G internet and fifty people working the ranch and distillery. I'd hardly call us off-grid."

"Yeah, but we're going to go even deeper into the wilderness, so then we're going to definitely be off-grid. If I were a whiskey competitor, that is when I'd choose to strike."

"Why would you choose to strike at all— You know what? Never mind. It's fine." I zip up my overnight bag and brush my hands off. "Done! I'm gonna go for a walk."

"You're not going to help me pack?" Mushu whines.

I eye the mountain of stuff she has laid out on the bed. "Why are you taking like five different serums with you?"

"Mulan, we are going to be in the sun the entire day. I need skin protection."

"It's an overnight trip. We're literally only going to be gone one night."

"Just because you're okay with getting age spots this early in life doesn't mean I am." She glowers at me. "If you're going to stand there judging my very sensible choices, then off you go. I don't need your help." She puts both hands on my back and nudges me out of the room.

"Okay, okay." I laugh. "Let me know if you change your mind."

As I walk down the hallway, I see that the various uncles and aunties are also packing. "Zhou!" Auntie Jiayi calls out. "Are you done packing?"

"Yup. Just going to go on a w—"

"Maybe you can help Shang out with dinner," Auntie Jiayi says. She straightens up and smiles at me with eyebrows raised.

"Uh." *Do I have to?* But Auntie Jiayi has been the only member of the Li family who's been consistently kind toward me, and I find it impossible to say no to her. "Sure."

"Oh, good. I feel guilty because he didn't let me help him, you know. You go to the backyard, he is prepping the meats there."

My stomach turns. Oh no. Does that mean he's butchering them? "What is it with your family and killing your food?"

Shang barely looks up, but he smiles and says, "What do you think?"

"Some kind of alpha male thing? To prove that you're the alpha-est of the alphas?"

Shang chuckles. "Why are you obsessed with this alpha male thing?"

"Ask James that question," I mutter, at which Shang laughs out loud.

He pauses and finally glances up at me, wiping his brow with his arm. It's a move that is way hotter than I would ever admit. "Did you just come here to judge me, or did you want to help? I mean, I'd be happy either way."

My mouth stretches into a thin, flat line. "Aside from a sudden, and very brief, interest in making sourdough bread, the most elaborate meal

I've made was a peanut butter and jelly sandwich, and it was a failure."

"How does one mess up PB and J?"

"I didn't have grape jelly, so I used leftover cranberry jelly from Thanksgiving."

"That sounds like it would be a nice combination, actu—"

"And what I thought was peanut butter turned out to be leftover gravy."

For a moment, Shang falls quiet. Then he opens his mouth, throws his head back, and laughs. It's the best laugh that I have heard, pure and filled with so much unadulterated joy, I can easily picture him as a little kid. I drink in the way his eyes turn into crescent moons, his entire face going soft and tender when he laughs, and the way he places one large hand on his chest. My god, I am in so much trouble.

When Shang next meets my eye, I get the sense that something has changed between us. Just a small shift, but I can feel it. He's looking at me in a new way, like he's seeing me properly for the first time.

"Slide some leftover turkey in there and you've got yourself a great sandwich," he says finally.

"Agreed, but I'd been expecting a PB and J, and when I bit into it and my brain registered that *Hey, this isn't peanut butter*, it was so disconcerting. Ruined the entire thing."

"Tell you what," Shang says, "I'll make sure to guide you every step of the way."

"Ah!" I squeal, clapping both hands to my cheeks. "You mean," I say breathlessly, "you're going to mansplain everything to me? I can't wait!"

Shang levels a flat gaze at me. "I sense sarcasm."

"Good, because I meant to be sarcastic."

Shang flips the cleaver in his hand and holds it out to me, handle first. "Here you go. Start with something simple—finish descaling this carp."

I take the cleaver, then look with open distaste at the fish on the chopping block. I place my fingertips on it, resisting the full-body shudder that threatens to run through my entire being.

"Hold the blade at an angle, like this," Shang says, putting a hand over mine for just a second before letting go. "Now hold the fish firmly—"

Nothing for it. I grip the fish, biting back my grimace, and hold it fast.

"Now slide the blade down—"

I do so, and a shower of silvery scales flies up, spattering across my face. I sputter and drop the fish. I look at Shang and he, too, is covered in scales. Wordlessly, Shang reaches out and his thumb and forefinger graze my cheek, leaving a fiery trail where they touched. My mouth parts, but when Shang pulls his hand back, there is a scale caught between his thumb and forefinger.

"I forgot to tell you to angle the fish this way," he says finally.

It's a strain to bite back my laughter. I drag my attention back to the fish and this time, make sure to angle it down so that when I slide the cleaver down, the scales fly away from me and Shang. It takes a surprisingly long time to get rid of all the scales, and by the time I'm done, my hands are aching from the effort. I stretch them and try not to make a disgusted face as I watch Shang deftly gut the fish.

"What got you into this?" I say.

"By 'this' do you mean cooking, or . . ."

I shake my head. "Plenty of people are into cooking. Not so many people would kill their own ingredients first, though."

Shang smiles, and it strikes me that this is perhaps the most relaxed I've seen him. "Well, what got me into butchering was cooking, believe it or not. When I was growing up, my mom would cook for the both of us. She made the most amazing dishes, and I spent all of my free time in the kitchen with her. But then she developed arthritis in her hands, so I slowly took over. We spent most of our time together in the kitchen, with her guiding me while I cooked."

Damn it, how dare he have such a sweet backstory. It's become a real struggle to keep my Zhou mask on around him. "That's really nice, but plenty of people cook without feeling the need to butcher?" I wonder if perhaps that came out sharper than intended, but Shang doesn't seem to mind.

"Funny you say that," he says. "My mom's always complaining about how sterile everything is here. She'd tell me how back in China, her family butchered their own meats, and so it made them more thoughtful and careful about what they ate. They didn't have meat most days; maybe only once or twice a week. Of course, that's not the case in the big cities, but my family, like yours, isn't from a big city. It got me thinking about how over here, we get our meats in these neat packages. My nephew didn't even know that beef comes from cows. He was like, 'It's beef, it's from a hamburger!' "

We both laugh, and he continues: "It's really cute, but it's also sort of sad in a way. I resolved to learn more about food, about where it comes from and about being a responsible consumer. I visited meat factories, and what I saw"—he grimaces—"it made me not want to eat factory meats. Back in the city I usually eat vegetarian, and it's only when we come out here to the ranch that I eat meat, and even then, I want to make sure that I'm respecting the meal by not sterilizing myself from it. I hate killing these animals, just so you know. It makes me lose my appetite a little bit, but better that than pretending that I'm not eating what used to be a live animal."

Shang speaks with so much compassion, without any traces of judgment in his voice. After a while, all I can say is "Wow."

Shang grins. "Sorry, did that sound as obnoxious to you as it did to me?"

"No, not at all. It makes sense, actually." I think of the many rows of neatly packaged meats at the supermarkets I go to and how I've never once thought about how far removed we are from the food we're eating. How I, too, haven't thought of the fact that beef comes from cows; I know it on an intellectual level of course, but haven't taken the time to really consider what that means.

"So," Shang says, "would you like to do the honors? The fam has requested roast goose."

My mouth drops open in horror as excuses ram through my head. Baba would agree to do it. But this is where I draw the line. "I—don't—uh—"

Shang laughs again. "I was just teasing. I wouldn't ask you to butcher a whole goose as your first time. That would be animal cruelty."

"Not to mention Zhou cruelty."

"Yes, that too. But you could help me pluck the goose feathers."

I can't find a good enough reason not to help with that, and so I do. It's an exhausting, disturbing affair, and my hands are cramping by the time I'm done. Also, I have zero appetite for goose meat now. I watch Shang clean the goose and prep it for the oven.

"We need to make sure the skin is really dry so it gets extra crispy when we roast it," he says.

"How do you know all this?"

"How do you know which companies are worth acquiring?" he says.

"Through careful market research and meticulous due diligence," I answer smartly.

"Okay, mine's a little bit less clinical than that." Shang laughs. "If you must know, I mostly learned through watching YouTube videos. And from my mom."

"Honestly, I'm grateful that I was mostly raised by my mom. What little I remember of my dad was okay, but not amazing. He reminded me a lot of my uncles. You know, with all that 'You must be a man's man' bullshit."

My eyebrows knot. Everything I thought I knew about Shang pointed to him being the biggest man's man. And yet here he is, soft and vulnerable in an utterly disarming way. Could it be that he's been wearing a mask of his own and I'm only now seeing it slip?

"Okay, I think this is ready to go in the oven." Shang lifts the goose and carries it to a huge pizza oven that he's warmed up in advance. He sticks the goose inside and closes the door before turning back to me. "Now let's do the fish."

While I chop up various vegetables, Shang deep-fries the fish, filling the air with an incredibly savory smell. He places the cooked fish onto huge metal platters, then whips up a mouthwatering Szechuan chili sauce, which he pours over the fish. To finish it off, he puts fresh Szechuan peppers, chopped chilies, and cilantro on top before dousing it with boiling hot oil. The oil sizzles as it hits the garnish, and I find that I'm practically drooling. He takes the vegetables from me and throws them into a pot of half-cooked rice, then asks if I could do the salad, before going back to whipping up yet another delectable dish.

Before long, the outdoor dining table is groaning under the weight of at least ten amazing dishes, each one more delicious than the last. Everyone gathers, and glasses are filled to the brim and plates loaded up with steaming-hot food.

"Zhou, you eat more," Auntie Chuang says, piling huge scoops of rice and sweet braised soy sauce pork onto my plate. "You are so skinny, you need to gain more weight to get good baby-bearing hips."

My parents have never said such things to me, but I've grown up around enough immigrant families to not be taken aback by it. I thank Auntie Chuang and return the favor by spooning food onto the elders' plates.

"Zhou, what is your astrology?" Auntie Chuang says.

"She told you before, she is a dragon," Auntie Jiayi says.

"Oh yes!" Auntie Chuang claps. "James here is a rooster, very good match for dragon."

I'm also not a stranger to these avenues of conversation, but the fact that it's James who's being pushed on me makes it that much more awkward. I try to keep a straight face as I heap more food onto Auntie Lulu's plate.

"Pah, you are speaking rubbish. We've settled this a long time ago," Auntie Lulu says to Auntie Chuang. "My Thomas is a rat, a rat is the best match for dragon. The rat is the smartest animal in the Chinese horoscope, it is fast and thinks outside the box. It will lead the dragon to big success."

"Hah!" Auntie Jamie says. "You two don't know what you talking. The best match for dragon is my Ryan. He is also a dragon. Two dragons, oh my, can you imagine what fire?" She grins meaningfully at Ryan and me, and just in case we didn't get the message, she adds, "There will be much passion."

"Mom!" Ryan moans.

"Oh god," I mutter. I scoop more food onto Auntie Lulu's plate, only to find that I've filled her plate to overflowing. "Sorry!" I cry, grabbing napkins.

The aunties all laugh. "Oh dear, Jamie, you and your dirty mind have embarrassed poor Zhou!" Auntie Chuang says. Then she turns to me and says, "Zhou, don't be so shy, we know you young people are filled with the hormones. It is nothing to be ashamed of, it's what leads to grandbabies."

"*Stoppp,*" James groans. "If you guys don't behave, we're going to go eat at a separate table."

"What about me, aunties?" Mushu chirps. "I'm a monkey, who's a good match for me?"

139

"Ah, you are a monkey!" Auntie Jamie cries. "Christopher is a snake, you two are the perfect match! Your babies will be so intelligent, will definitely get into Harvard."

Mushu eyes Christopher, who sips his whiskey sour quietly, his cheeks burning red. "Why not?" she says cheerfully, and, picking up her plate, she goes and sits next to him. The aunties and uncles burst out laughing and cheering.

"Wah, Jamie, maybe you will have a daughter-in-law by next year, eh?" Uncle Hong calls out.

Despite how embarrassed I'm feeling, I can't help laughing along with them. My family is on the quieter side, and I relish the light-hearted raucousness of the Li family. I pick up my plate and find an empty seat, which happens to be next to Shang. On Shang's other side is his mother, and he's cutting up her food into bite-size pieces.

"Zhou, are you doing okay?" Auntie Jiayi says. "Shang says you help him out a lot with the cooking."

"Oh, I wouldn't say I helped out 'a lot.' I mostly just stood there and watched."

"She helped descale the fish and clean the goose," Shang says.

"Hence why I'm not having any of the goose," I say, gesturing to my plate.

Auntie Jiayi laughs. "I remember when I was little, I saw my mother kill chicken for the first time. There was so much blood! I didn't eat chicken for a whole year after that."

I laugh, too. "Yep, exactly."

"There you go, Ma," Shang says, pushing the plate of neatly sliced up food toward her.

"Thank you, Er zi." Auntie Jiayi gazes at him with obvious fondness. "He is a very good boy, he cuts up food for me because of my arthritis, you know."

My heart swells. The thing with mama's boys is that they're known to be spoiled and self-centered, never thinking of anyone other than themselves. But Shang is a mama's boy in the best possible sense of the term, looking after his mom with such understated kindness, never once calling attention to the way he takes care of her. Maybe I was wrong to judge him as a toxic alpha male. I watch him for a bit and notice the way he subtly does this and that to make things easier for Auntie Jiayi, like placing extra napkins next to her plate and moving her drink closer to her. He does all of it without saying a word, giving his mother the dignity of feeding herself but making her aware that he's there to help if she needs it. Okay, I should definitely not be noticing such things about my potential business partner. Pretending to be Baba is already so unethical. Going down the romance route with Shang would only make everything worse. I force myself to drag my gaze away from him.

The food is, as always, sumptuous. I have second and third servings and by the time we're done, everyone is leaning back in their chairs and rubbing their stomachs while groaning happily.

"Shang, you'll make someone a lovely wife," James calls out.

"It's the twenty-first century," I snap, "are you really still stuck with such old-fashioned gender roles?"

"Aw, come on, loosen up," James says. "I'm just kidding. Good job cooking, Shang. Whatever girl I marry, I hope she cooks as well as you do."

"Thanks," Shang says, and gives me a quick wink. He's obviously unbothered by James's heckling.

After a few more minutes of chatting, the uncles and aunties get up, stretching, and start shuffling back into the house, leaving the cousins and Mushu and me behind.

"All right, boys, saddle up, we're off to the Squealing Pig," James says. Then he seems to remember our presence, and adds, "And girls."

I look warily at James. "Um, don't we have an early start tomorrow?"

"We do," James says. "But who cares? Who needs sleep when they're young, am I right?"

"I think I'll sit this one out," I say. "As fun as the Squealing Pig sounds."

"Uh-uh," James says. "No can do. It's part of our ritual. Come on, touch up your makeup or whatever you girls need to do and meet out front in ten."

Is he humanly capable of saying anything that does not make him sound like a complete douche? I walk toward Mushu, who is deep in conversation with Christopher. "Sorry, Christopher, I just need to borrow my cousin for a sec."

The two of us walk to the far side of the backyard. "What's up?" Mushu says.

"Did you hear what James said? We're going to a place called the Squealing Pig?"

"Oh yeah, Chris told me about it. Sounds fun. They've got one of those mechanical bulls. I've always wanted to ride one."

"Oh my god, you're not in college anymore, Mushu," I groan. "A mechanical bull? Seriously?"

"What's wrong with that? Sounds fun to me."

"Oof." I pinch the bridge of my nose. "We're setting off early in the morning tomorrow, so let's not stay out too late."

"We're trying to win over clients," she points out. "What would your father do?" And to that, I have nothing to say.

The Squealing Pig is about as bad as I was expecting. It's a bar in the middle of the town center, and even from a block away, I can hear music blaring out of the space. And once we get inside, the thumping bass is so loud that it reverberates all the way through my bones. I can feel my teeth chattering to the stomping rhythm. It seems to be a cross between a Western-style bar and a nightclub, and the patrons here are probably mostly people from the city who stay at nearby ranches and have come to have the full ranch experience—there are plenty of cowboy hats and cowboy boots being worn. Still, Zhou, or Ranch Mulan, would plunge into this whole thing headfirst in the name of pleasing her potential business partner. I give my head a little shake, trying to perk myself up. I can do this. I am Ranch Mulan. Ranch Mulan does things like chop firewood and shear sheep. What's a little romp through a nightclub?

The group makes its way through the crowd to the bar, where James orders everyone except Shang and Thomas, the designated drivers, a shot of tequila. The last time I had a shot was in senior year of college, and my roommate and I had ended the night taking turns puking, so I take the shot slowly instead of downing it like everyone else does. Even so, the drink burns a fiery trail down my throat, making me cough.

"To the ranch life!" James hoots.

The others cheer along, Mushu loudest of them all. James orders another round, and Shang says, "Take it easy, man, we've got a full day of riding tomorrow."

"Some of us want to actually live while we're young," James says, and passes around the second shot.

I look down at my half-full shot glass in one hand and a newly filled glass in the other. I meet Shang's eye and he shrugs at me, as though to say I shouldn't drink it if I don't want to, but then James claps me on the shoulder and says, "What the hell? She hasn't even finished her first drink! And you think you've got what it takes to run a whiskey company?"

"James—" Shang says in a warning tone, but I shake my head.

"You're right," I say, and in one smooth motion, I down the full shot glass and chase it with the half-full one.

143

James cheers as I try hard not to gag. Someone thrusts a glass of ice water into my hand. Shang. I nod at him with gratitude and chug the water. It feels as though the tequila is rushing through my veins, and the next moment, I feel my limbs relaxing as the drink takes effect. Maybe it's not so bad after all, taking shots. A warm glow rises from my belly and fills the rest of me with a relaxed, quiet joy. I ease into the music, letting my body sway along to it. We all snake onto the dance floor, joining the crowd and for the next hour or so, I lose myself in the music. It's been a long time since I've gone out dancing, and I've forgotten how much I enjoy it. The only reason I stop dancing after a while is because my feet, inside the new boots, are absolutely killing me. I hobble off the dance floor, only to be yanked to one side by Mushu.

"Mechanical bull time!" she hollers.

Mushu is first to go on, and she manages to last ten whole seconds before being flung off, at which point James hops on and is unceremoniously tossed off within two seconds. Mushu nudges me forward, and I take a deep breath and step toward the bull. I don't meet Shang's eye, but I can feel his gaze on me as I climb on. Back in high school, I did gymnastics. I wasn't good enough to compete at the regional level, but I was decent, and as I settle on the bull, my reflexes kick in, my thighs tightening around it, my core strong, but the rest of me relaxed and fluid. The bull starts up and I move along with it, taking controlled breaths and imagining myself as a bamboo stalk whipping around in a gale. Strong core, flexible upper body. The crowd gets louder the longer I stay on, and the bull bucks harder and harder, until it becomes almost humanly impossible to cling on. Just before I lose my grip, the bull winds down and I climb off, my entire body buzzing with adrenaline, and bow to the wild cheering of the crowd. When I straighten up, I lock eyes with Shang. There's that look again, like he's half-surprised, half-amused. His eyes linger on mine before trailing down to my parted lips.

"Woo! That was awesome!" Mushu cries, grabbing me and leading me past Shang back to the bar.

I'm out of breath and my cheeks feel hot and I don't remember when was the last time I've had so much fun. What with the endorphins coursing through me, I almost forget about how much pain my feet are in. Almost.

"Damn, you were amazing up there!" Mushu cries.

I grin and take a huge gulp of ice water. Shang slips through the crowd, coming to my side. He stands close enough to me that I can see each ridiculously long eyelash of his.

"Nice job on the bull," he says.

Before I can reply, James, Christopher, Thomas, and Ryan stumble to the bar. "Dang, Zhou!" Christopher shouts. "Who would've thought you had it in you?"

I cock my head to one side and say, "What, like it's hard?"

"We have Elle Woods in the house!" James crows.

There's a presence behind me. I turn around and see a tall, well-built man standing uncomfortably close to me. I consider taking a step back, but I was here first and he's kind of encroaching on my personal space.

"Saw you up there on the bull," he says in a low voice.

"Okay," I say. I turn away from him.

"The way you rode it, phew." He whistles.

The hair on the back of my neck rises.

"I always knew you Asian girls were wild, but man." He shakes his head and leers at me.

I begin inching away from him, but Mushu is suddenly behind me, whispering, "Everyone's watching, you can't just walk away from this. You gotta show them you're strong enough to stand up to this shit."

"What?" I hiss.

"Oh, hey, there's two of you," the man says, his grin growing wider. "What're you two ladies whispering about?"

I glance around us. Sure enough, James, Christopher, Ryan, and Thomas are watching with interest, while Shang looks about ready to murder the guy. Oh god, against all that is sensible in the universe, somehow Mushu is right. If I were to back down right now, no doubt James would report back to the uncles and aunties and let them know that I am too weak to take over their company. Ranch Mulan would definitely not be backing down. Fighting every instinct of mine, I raise my eyes to meet the man's leering gaze and glare at him.

"Ooh, she's a fighter, this one," he says. "I like it when they fight." He glances over his shoulder and to my dismay, this guy has friends with him, and they all look as ready for trouble as he does.

I pick my words carefully. "We don't want any trouble, so why don't we forget this happened and go our separate ways, yeah?"

"Or why don't you let me buy you and your doppelgänger here a drink?"

I grit my teeth. Mushu and I look nothing alike, but of course to him we're "doppelgängers." "No, thanks."

"Listen, bitch—"

"Damn it, she said no!" Mushu snaps, hopping forward. She trips, slamming into me, and I experience the next moment in slow motion as I stumble. I watch my drink smash into the man's chest. Icy water splashes all across his face. I watch his face contort in a picture of rage, the veins in his neck bulging, his teeth gritting, his forehead turning red. His hand shoots up to grab me, and my survival instincts kick in and I lift my hand, palm up. The heel of my palm meets his nose. It's not hard enough to break anything, but it's a healthy bop on the nose, a sensitive place, and he screams in pain.

Everything happens in a rush. Shang is suddenly in between me and the man, and his friends are clambering forward, fists are being swung, and Mushu has picked up a chair and is holding it over my head while bellowing, and what the hell is happening? I duck under

146

someone's fist and hold out my foot. Someone else trips over it. When I look up, I meet Shang's eye and he raises his eyebrows, apparently impressed by me.

"All right, that's enough!" the bartender bellows, and a group of burly men appear, plucking people off each other as easily as though they were mother bears yanking their cubs away.

One of them pulls me up by the elbow. Shang is immediately there, holding off the guy and saying, "Easy there. We're leaving." He places a gentle hand on my back and together, we weave through the crowd and spill out into the cold night air.

Outside, I brace my palms on my thighs, trying to catch my breath. Shang hurries me along. "Come on, before those guys come out and look for more trouble."

"Mushu—"

"She's with the others."

Sure enough, a few paces away, Mushu calls out, "See you back at the house, homies!" She waves to me.

"Let's go," Shang says, and I stumble after him. We get inside his car and lock the doors. The silence buzzes in my ears.

I clap my hands to my cheeks. They're numb. "Oh my god, what happened in there? Did we really just get into a bar fight? A literal bar fight?"

Shang glances at me, amused, as he backs the car out of its parking spot. "Yep, I believe that was what we were in."

"Oh my god," I gasp. "I can't believe it. I don't get into bar fights. I—I drink matcha lattes."

Shang snorts. "People who drink matcha lattes don't get into bar fights?"

"No!" I cry. "Especially not those who order theirs with oat milk," I add.

Shang throws his head back and laughs. "Oh wow, definitely not bar fight material then. But you know what? For someone who drinks oat milk matcha lattes, you did really well. You took out, like, two guys back there."

Somehow, despite the ridiculousness of our night, joy, sparkling like champagne, is bubbling through my limbs. A slow smile spreads across my face, taking over my entire expression. "I did," I say, softly at first, then louder. "I really did, didn't I? Did you see the way I tripped that guy over? He was twice my size and I took him down just like that." The pride and joy I feel right now are real. Nothing to do with the Ranch Mulan persona, or the Zhou persona, or any of it. For the first time in a long while, I don't think: *What would Baba do?* I don't care, not in this moment. I want to be carried away with the giddiness of what just happened.

"Power move," Shang says, still laughing.

"And the way I punched that guy in the nose—"

"Hmm, I don't know that I would call it a punch," Shang says. "It was more like a smack. But was it really a smack? I saw your face when you did it, you looked more shocked than he did."

"That's because I *was* shocked!" I cry, gasping with laughter. "I didn't— I wasn't even thinking, I just raised my hand—I remember reading that you shouldn't punch with your fist, because you run the risk of breaking your thumb, so you should do it with the heel of your palm, and I just— I just did it." I stare at Shang for a second, mouth agape. "All these years I thought I was meant to be in finance, but what if I missed my calling as an MMA fighter?"

"Oh yeah, the UFC missed out there." Shang grins at me. Then his grin fades and he gazes at me with a new expression. "Jokes aside, what you did back there . . . I really did not see that coming."

My chest turns warm. Self-doubt begins to creep in. Did I completely misjudge the situation back at the bar? But when I glance back at him, he's shaking his head in awe.

"I mean, that was— It was pretty amazing," he says. "You are unexpected in so many ways."

"In a good way?" I tease.

"Very much so," he says, and the seriousness in his voice makes the back of my neck break out into a sweat. I sneak another glance at him, but he seems content to stare down the road, so I tell myself to resume breathing normally and try to forget the sudden intense moment.

For a while, we drive in comfortable silence, enjoying the deserted, long road. I look through the windshield and am surprised by the sheer amount of stars glittering in the dark sky. Back in the city, the stars are never quite so visible due to the light pollution, but now here they are, shining in all their glory. We stop at a red light. "I've never seen anything quite so beautiful," I say.

"Yeah," Shang replies.

I glance over at him and catch him looking at me. It only lasts a split second before he tears his eyes away from me and focuses on the road.

And because I'm buzzing off adrenaline and alcohol, I say, "That was a total romance novel moment, you know."

Shang keeps his eyes steadfastly on the road, waiting patiently for the light to turn green. "What was?"

"When I said I've never seen anything so, uh . . ." My voice falters. Am I really about to explain the whole thing about something being beautiful and him saying yes while looking at me? My entire face burns. I'm not quite as drunk as I need to be to have this conversation with him right now. "Never mind."

Shang turns to look at me, and I spot the playful smirk he's wearing. I narrow my eyes at him. "You totally knew what I was talking about!"

"No idea," he says, full-on grinning now.

"You're about as convincing as my cousin's toddler when he swears he doesn't know where all the cookies went."

Shang laughs. "That obvious, huh?" He glances over at me again, and this time, his smile is so soft that I can no longer deny it. That change in him. No, not in him, but between us. We're no longer employees from two companies. We're two people whose masks are slipping despite our best efforts.

What would B—

I shush the voice in my head. I'm so tired of wondering what other people would do. I know exactly what I want to do, and maybe it's time to stop pretending. Slowly, achingly slow, I lean over toward Shang. His eyes widen for a split second, then he leans over toward me, too. In the silence of the car, the rhythms of our breathing are so loud. Our lips are mere inches away when there's a sudden honk behind us. We jump, jerking back.

"Light's green," I blurt out, my entire head burning with embarrassment.

"Yeah," Shang mutters. We drive some way in painful silence before he says, "You should get some rest. I'm driving pretty slowly because it's so dark out here, so it'll take a while before we get home."

"Good idea," I say. My heart feels like it's no longer in my chest but thumping somewhere inside my skull. Did I really almost kiss Shang? I'm definitely blaming that on the tequila. Okay, I can't dwell on that right now because if I think about it even for a second longer, I am going to implode. Instead, I settle back in my seat and replay the bar fight in my mind. I've never done anything even remotely close to that ever, in my lifetime. And though it's something I never want to do again, it's certainly a memory I'll treasure for a long, long time. And, despite the strange almost-kiss, I feel so warm and safe now, in the car with Shang, driving into the darkness, where it feels as though we are the only two people in the whole world. I never expected to feel quite so safe with him. When my eyes drift shut and I start to doze off, I do so with a small smile on my lips.

CHAPTER THIRTEEN

I barely remember getting back to the ranch. I was only vaguely conscious of Shang giving me a gentle shake and me snorting awake and finding a dried trail of drool down my chin. I then remember bits and pieces of the rest of the night: me and Mushu staggering into the house and crawling—literally crawling—up the stairs before collapsing into our beds.

Morning comes all too quickly. We'd forgotten to close the curtains the night before, so sunlight blares through the windows without mercy, piercing through my eyelids like a golden knife.

I squeeze my eyes shut tighter, but I become more and more aware each second of a flurry of movement in the rest of the house. Footsteps stomping up and down the stairs, people chattering, calling out for this and that, more footsteps, and *argh*, why is this household so alive when it's barely even dawn yet?

A groan from the next bed tells me that Mushu is rousing. I push myself up into a sitting position, wincing at the way my skull feels like it's two sizes too small. My mouth is so dry that my lips are stuck to my teeth. The last thing I want to do is get out of bed, but at the sight of the tall glasses of water on the makeup table, I crawl out of bed and make my way to the table, where I chug the entire glass. Then I take the other glass to Mushu.

"Drink," I tell her.

Mushu groans and says something that sounds like "Fugoff."

151

"Come on." I help her up and push the glass in front of her face.

She drinks obediently before flopping back onto the bed. The water revives me a little and I go to the en suite and splash some cold water onto my face before brushing my teeth. There's a knock at the bedroom door. When I open it, Shang is standing there, looking as fresh as ever and carrying a tray of food and drinks.

"Eggs, toast, coffee, and a Virgin Mary," he says.

"Virgin Mary?" I say, my nose wrinkling.

"Trust me, it's the best thing for a hangover. All that vitamin C and salts are just what your body needs after a night out."

I step aside and watch as he comes in and sets the tray down on the makeup table.

At the sound of clinking cutlery, Mushu leaps up in bed. Her hair is all mussed up and pointing to the left, and she blinks blearily at us. "Food?" she says.

"Yep," Shang says.

"Gimme." Mushu makes grabby hands and Shang hands her a plate of sunny-side-up eggs.

I accept the glass of Virgin Mary and sip it slowly. Shang was right; it really is good. The salty, tangy, and slightly spicy mix is exactly what my body needed. I take a long gulp and feel my senses coming back to life. "Did you put glasses of water on the makeup table last night?"

"Yeah, I thought you guys might need it." Shang glances at the empty glasses.

"Thank you," I say, suddenly feeling awkward. Bits and pieces of last night are only now whizzing into my mind, and I want to curl up into a tiny ball and hide from the world. Am I imagining it or did Shang and I almost kiss last night? "Um, about last night—"

One corner of Shang's mouth quivers up. "You kicked ass. Literally."

"Oh god. Please try to forget everything that happened—"

"Sorry, but James has been telling everyone this morning about how you got us into a brawl."

"No!" I gasp, horrified. "Oh my god, all your uncles and aunties are going to think the worst of me."

"Actually, they're really impressed so far. They didn't think you had it in you to start a bar fight."

"Not to interrupt," Mushu interrupts, "but technically I think I started the fight?"

"Yeah!" I say.

Shang cocks his head to one side. "That's not how I remember it. Well, regardless of who started it, I'd say you guys did well. I'll see you downstairs in a bit. We're going to head off soon."

As soon as Shang leaves, I sag against the wall. "I can't believe we got into a literal fight last night."

"Yeah, it was awesome. We can all learn a thing or two from Fake Zhou," Mushu says.

I stare in stupefied terror at the beast that the stable hands are leading to me. It's a huge black horse who looks really bad-tempered. I wasn't even aware that horses could have resting bitch face, but this one definitely does. Or maybe I'm just really freaking nervous about riding a horse, and this one seems more gigantic than the usual horse.

"Only the best mare for Zhou the horse-riding champion," Uncle Hong announces with pride.

The rest of the Li family nods with approval, smiling at the sight of the snorting horse.

"Uh . . ." I begin to say, then falter when Mushu pulls my arm.

"Can I talk to you real quick?" Mushu says.

I let myself be pulled some distance away before rounding on

Mushu. "I can't ride that thing. It's going to kill me. I'm going to get thrown off, and I'll either break every bone in my body or it'll—oh, I know what it'll do—it'll trample my skull into pieces."

Mushu stares at me. "Okay, first of all, that is really grim. Your mind goes to some pretty dark places, cuz. Second of all, you have to ride it. Because, uh, I don't know if you remember, but I mentioned to them that you're a champion horse rider? I kind of maybe, uh, sort of really drilled down on that fact."

"What fact?" I hiss, trying hard not to explode at her. "The fact that I have never ridden a horse before in my life?"

"Not true. You said it yourself, pony rides at Disneyland," Mushu says. "It's the same thing," she continues, though when she glances back at the beast, she looks somewhat hesitant herself. "Come on, Mulan, you rode the mechanical bull last night and you were amazing at it. Same concept, right?"

I don't even deign to give this one a reply. I merely glare at Mushu until she looks down guiltily. Then Mushu looks up again. "And you're the badass who started a bar fight, remember?"

"I thought you started it."

"Come on, let's go, people!" James calls out.

I take a deep breath. "Damn it." I narrow my eyes at Mushu. "You need to stop talking me up."

"Copy that."

With that, the two of us rejoin the group. From what little I know about horses, most of which I've learned from TikTok, I've gathered they're sensitive, highly intelligent creatures and that I would do well to treat them with the utmost respect. So when I get to within touching distance of the mare, I stop and say in a gentle tone, "Hello, beautiful. What's your name?"

"This is Slugger," Uncle Hong says. He's holding on to the reins of his own horse, a docile-looking one the color of sand.

"Slugger?" I say incredulously. I catch myself. God, what with my hangover and the anxiety crashing into me in waves, it's next to impossible to keep the Zhou/Ranch Mulan persona up. "Okay, cool. Hi, Slugger."

Slugger snorts, and I have to stop myself from stepping back. Swallowing, I raise my hand slowly, making sure that Slugger can see it. "Can I touch you, Slugger?" Of course, Slugger doesn't answer, but she tips her head toward my hand, which I take as an invitation to pet her. The moment my palm meets Slugger's neck, the knots in my shoulders release. Slugger is warm, her hide smooth, but underneath that she is pure muscle. Touching her is a privilege, and I stroke her gently. I can't quite describe it, but I trust this creature. And the way that Slugger leans into me makes it clear that she trusts me as well.

Could it be this easy? That Slugger and I just so happen to have that one-in-a-million connection that you only ever read about in stories?

The answer is of course: Nope.

Slugger hasn't decided to murder me then and there, which is a relief, but she also hasn't decided to let me ride her. As soon as I climb up—or rather, try to climb up—Slugger turns so that her butt is in my face.

"Come on, Slugger," I mutter, walking around to Slugger's side. "Work with me here."

Around me, everyone else has climbed up onto their horses. Even Mushu is happily sitting on top of a dark brown horse and asking the stable hand if her horse responds to "Giddyap."

I give a soft tug on Slugger's reins, not enough to actually turn her head or anything, just enough to get her attention. "Listen here, Slugger, I'm not in a good place right now. I'm kind of struggling, and I really need everything to just work out, you know? Especially in front of him." I nod toward Shang, who's climbed onto his horse with fluid grace and is looking as regal as a prince. Slugger exhales, and I swear the horse understood me and is going: *Girl, fine.*

This time, Slugger allows me to climb up. There is half a second of relief—I'm up!—before I look down at the ground and panic claws at my throat. I'm up! I am very, very much up. This is really high up: Is this a normal height to be at when horseback riding? The ground looks like it's twenty feet away. Slugger clops forward and my torso sways backward with the momentum. I haven't even started into a trot or—god forbid—a gallop.

"Do not go fast, do not go fast," I mutter. I'm gripping the reins so tight that my knuckles have turned white.

"Everybody ready?" Uncle Hong calls out.

No, my mind squeaks. Everyone else hoots and cheers. Shang looks over at me, his eyebrows raised. I manage a weak smile. Uncle Hong lifts his reins enthusiastically and his horse starts trotting down the pathway. Everyone else follows suit. Everyone, that is, except for Slugger. Because of course.

"Come on, baby," I coax. I try to remember the advice I've learned online on how to make the horse go forward. I tighten my thighs around Slugger and feel the animal shudder to life. Then, as though by magic, Slugger starts walking forward. Jogging. Trotting? "Too fast, too fast," I squawk, pulling back the reins, and Slugger slows down her pace. "Okay. This is okay. It's fine." My mouth is a desert, and though I've only ridden for about twenty seconds, my bum is tired and my hands are cramped.

Much, much later, I wish my bum were tired instead of whatever it is now—swinging back and forth between numb and painful. My feet aren't just killing me, they are slaughtering me. And my hands are definitely not okay. I stretch them open, but the reins jerk in my hands and instinctively my fingers claw back around them again. The others are some distance ahead of me. Several times, Slugger started increasing her pace, and my heart just about jumped out of my mouth and I quickly pulled back on the reins to slow her down. As a result, I've fallen way behind and, in fact, I've sort of lost sight of the group altogether. But as long as I follow the trail, I'll get to the campsite. Right?

"Right," I say out loud.

"What's right?" someone calls out, and I look up to see Shang riding toward me.

I swear inwardly, but then, against all odds, I'm also kind of really glad to see him here. "Hi," I say when he stops next to me. "Fancy seeing you here."

Shang smiles, and it strikes me how easily his smiles are coming the past couple of days. And I have to admit that I don't hate it. "How're you coming along?"

"Oh, you know, taking it easy, just kind of bonding with my girl Slugger over here."

"Cool. You mind if I ride with you?"

"You didn't want to gallop ahead with the wind?"

Shang laughs. "I swear you think I'm actually the guy from our ads. It's the long hair, isn't it?"

"That sounds about right." I can't quite understand the change that's happened to reveal this Shang—silly and relaxed and teasing. It's such a marked change from the Shang I first came across, all buttoned-up and stiff. "But really, though, wouldn't it be boring riding at my pace?"

Shang shrugs, pursing his lips. "Cloud here got a stone in his shoe and it took me a while to remove it. The rest rode on ahead, so I was getting kind of lonely."

"Oh. Then sure, I would be glad to have your company," I say. As soon as I say it, I half wonder if that was too eager. But then I realize I don't really care; somehow, over the past couple of days, Shang and I have gotten to a sort of easy camaraderie, almost as though we were friends instead of this weird business relationship that we started off with. I feel my own mask slipping, and for the first time, I don't care enough to put it back on. And anyway, it doesn't hurt to ride with Shang, especially given how gorgeous he looks atop his horse. He may kid about looking like the guy from the Wutai Gold ads, but he really isn't that far off, all muscled chest and shapely arms and those thighs that have obviously never missed a leg day. And the way he directs his horse so easily, moving his arms with casual grace . . . I can't remember the last time I was this attracted to someone.

"So, uh, this whole horseback riding champion thing . . ." Shang says. His voice trails away and he gives a meaningful sideways glance at me.

A million excuses crowd my head, and I'm about to make up some story about some traumatic experience during a riding competition, but when I open my mouth, what comes out is: "Yeah, that might've been a slight exaggeration."

Shang chuckles. "Okay. Still, I was impressed that Slugger even let you on. James has been trying to ride her for months now, and she still keeps giving him her hind legs."

I break into a huge grin. "Really? I would've loved to see that."

"Yeah, he kept threatening to sell her to a glue factory."

I roll my eyes. "Sounds like James." I pat Slugger. "Don't worry, Slugger. James is all talk and no action. Slugger's a really good judge of character."

"Yeah, most horses are. But why did you lie about being a horse-back riding champion?"

"Oh." I bite my lower lip, wondering how honest I should be with him. I'm so tired of pretending, and somehow, Shang feels like the one person I can be honest with, which is ironic since he's the one person I shouldn't be honest with. But somehow, I sense that he would be okay with the truth, and after days of playing a role, all I want to do is pry my mask open, just a crack, and let a tiny sliver of truth out, and so I say, "It seemed like the sort of thing your family would appreciate in a business partner."

"Ah." Shang frowns and doesn't speak for a while. My mind chases its own tail in circles, wondering if I've said the wrong thing.

"I didn't mean—" I begin.

"You're right," Shang says. "It is the kind of thing they like. My uncles and aunties, they've got this whole image of the American man that's basically the Marlboro Man. You know, the stoic cowboy who is strong and does things like ride into the sunset and hunt for his food and loves whiskey and guns."

I nod slowly.

"When they first moved here from China, they were seen as outsiders and they were outcasts, and at the time, there were all these Marlboro ads everywhere. And I think they felt like in order to fit in, they had to become the Marlboro Man."

"Is that why they've got this chip on their shoulder about being hypermasculine?" I say.

"Yeah. Especially with the media doing everything it could to emasculate Asian men, I think my uncles felt like they had to go to the extreme, be the most toxic alpha males they could be. I mean, I'm not telling you all this to excuse their behavior, I just . . ."

"I get it." And I do. Even though the portrayal of Asian people in the media has improved over the years, I'm not so young that I don't remember the stereotypical characters that Asian actors were often forced to play. The way the male actors would be stuck with the harmful "Chinaman" role with high-pitched voices and silly antics, and meanwhile, Asian actresses would be given hypersexualized roles with awful, dehumanizing lines that made them sound more like sex bots than anything human.

"How did your parents deal with it when they moved here?" Shang asks.

I take some time to ponder this. "Their whole philosophy in life is *Keep your head down and don't make a fuss.* So I think whatever abuse came their way, they just kept their heads down and chugged along." My words weigh heavily on my chest as I say them. I think of Baba and Mama when they were my age, young and full of vibrancy, living in a new place where they weren't necessarily welcome and telling themselves that they needed to make themselves smaller, to take up less space so nobody made a fuss about their presence.

"Yeah, I'm familiar with that mindset. A lot of my friends' parents were that way, too. I guess our families kind of went to different extremes, huh?"

I nod.

"Um, to tell you the truth, I had an ulterior motive coming back here to talk to you," Shang says.

"Oh?"

"I wanted to apologize."

"Oh?" I say again. What could he possibly have to apologize for? This entire time, it's been me making all the mistakes.

"That day at Little Chang's," Shang says, "I hated how my uncle said it's the woman's job to serve the food. When it comes to my family, I've gotten used to biting my tongue and keeping my head down, but I should've spoken up that day. I'm sorry."

Flames lick up the sides of my face. "It's okay, it's not your . . ." As soon as I say it, of course, I realize that actually I appreciate the apology and that the only reason I'm waving it off is because I've gotten used to thinking that I don't deserve apologies. But I do. And so I take a breath and say, simply, "Thank you. That means a lot to me."

"I'll do better next time," Shang promises.

I bite my lip, unsure what to say, but there is a warmth spreading out from my belly down my arms and I feel so incredibly safe right now, as though I can let down my guard. When was the last time I've felt this way? Even with Mushu, I've always felt a slight distance, a divide because we are such different people with such different values in life. God, what am I thinking? Shang is part of the Wutai Gold clan, a company I'm actively trying to acquire, so I most definitely cannot let my guard down around him. Not to mention I have no idea what would happen if we do acquire Wutai Gold. Why have I so foolishly thought that this charade was a good idea? Oh right, I assumed that once I took care of the acquisitions, I could hand the account back to my dad and wash my hands of it. But now the thought of that seems laughable, especially given how much time I'm spending with the Lis. *Not just the Lis*, my mind whispers, *but a very specific Li.* A horrible realization begins to dawn on me. I might have to tell Shang the truth eventually. The thought is so dreadful that I shove it deep, deep down as soon as it arises. I give myself a little shake and force a polite smile at Shang but don't say anything else.

With Shang riding next to me, it seems as though he and his horse have set a steady pace and Slugger is no longer trying to go too fast or too slow. I loosen my stranglehold on the reins, wincing as I stretch my fingers.

For the next hour or so, we spend the ride chatting easily about everything from our families to our hobbies (mine: SoulCycle and painting; his: anything that has to do with cooking). Once in a while, we lapse into a comfortable silence, and it feels as though we've known each other for years instead of mere days. For the first time, I'm not thinking: *What would Baba say?* or *What should I say in this situation?* My mouth is forming words without checking in with my brain, and the feeling is so joyous, like fireworks going off inside me.

We're riding through what feels like a whole enchanted forest, complete with winding trails and tall, majestic redwoods, with sunlight streaming through the leaves in dappled golden spots. The air is sparkling cold and refreshing and above us are various birdsong and insect chirps. It's the most beautiful place I can remember seeing, and I can't get enough of it. For the first time in years, I feel like I can really put everything, all of the petty worries and the bullshit of the finance world, behind me. Because I have to focus so fully on not falling off Slugger, it's almost a meditative state where my mind is forced to not wander back to the everyday concerns of the real world.

I'm feeling extra optimistic and happy when Shang reins his horse to a stop. I do the same, pulling Slugger's reins back. "What's up?" I say.

Shang nods to the distance, where a river has come into view. Light reflects off its surface like a million diamonds, and the sight is so beautiful that I sigh appreciatively.

"So gorgeous. Is this where we camp? Next to the river?" I say.

"Um, sort of. Campsite's on the other side of the river."

"Oh, okay." I'm not sure why he looks so worried. "Is the bridge not entirely sound or something? You look kind of concerned."

"Um, more like there isn't a bridge," Shang says.

I blink. "No bridge." I narrow my eyes. "I don't— So how do we get across?"

"We gotta go in the water and ride to the other side."

I laugh. "Very funny."

Shang's expression doesn't change.

All the easy, pleasant feelings I've been experiencing evaporate. "Shit, you're not kidding."

"Nope."

I look at Shang, then at the river, then back at Shang. "People literally drown in kiddie pools."

"Can you swim?"

"Yes."

"Then you'll likely be okay."

I'll *likely* be okay? But then I think better of saying it. After all, I am here to make a good impression on him and his family, and just because we've bonded for a bit doesn't mean that Shang isn't going to be unimpressed if I fail to do this one thing. As much as I hate this, it's time for me to start asking *What would Baba do?* again. Fighting every survival instinct inside me that's going *Noooo*, I summon up a confident smile and say, "Okay, great."

We ride up to the riverbank. Up close, the water looks a lot faster and deeper than it did from a distance. I can't believe that just moments ago, I'd been admiring how beautiful the river looks. Right about now, it looks anything but beautiful. A better adjective would be *fierce* or more likely *deadly*.

Shang gets off his horse and comes round to mine. For a second, I wonder if he's about to tell me it was a joke after all and that of course there is a bridge, but instead, he takes his horse's reins and ties them to Slugger's reins. "There you go, all you have to do is follow me."

"Great," I manage to say. I take in a breath. I can do this. I am not the kind of person to shy away from things like these. I'm here because I charged headfirst into this situation, assuming my father's identity, and I need to see it through. It's not brave if you're not afraid.

"Ready?" Shang says, once he's back on his horse.

"Yup."

Shang signals to his horse to start going forward and they descend slowly into the water. I urge Slugger forward, but there's no need as the reins between the two horses pull Slugger and we head for the river. Unlike me, Slugger seems to have no fear of the water, trotting in quite happily. Within moments, I find my legs submerged in freezing cold river water. It's so piercingly cold that the breath is knocked out of me in a gasp.

"Refreshing, isn't it?" Shang calls back behind his shoulder.

"Yep," I manage to gasp out. I force myself to take a deep inhale and hold it for a few seconds before letting it out. At least this seems to be as deep as it goes—nope, as we near the middle of the river, the

163

water rises until it laps over my thighs. *Is this normal? What if it's been an exceptionally wet year and the waterline is deeper than Shang expected and we get washed away and—*

To my utter surprise, though, despite all the whirling, screaming thoughts going through my head, a part of me is having fun. I can't remember the last time I felt so alive. Every part of me is present in this moment. In my day-to-day life, I spend so much of my time staring at my computer screen, and when I'm not doing that, I'm having to play a role, whether it be Finance Bro Mulan or Filial Daughter Mulan, in order to survive my days. But right now, no piece of me is distracted. All my senses are concentrated on this pinpoint in time, where I'm traversing across an actual river on horseback, with shockingly cold water swirling all around me. I look up at the endless blue sky and laugh.

Shang looks back at me and grins, as though he knows exactly what's going through my mind. There's so much understanding between us. Then his eyes widen and his mouth falls open. I'm about to ask him what's wrong, when I feel it. Slugger's legs giving way, getting caught in the drag. There is a momentary sensation of floating, terror flooding in from all sides. From the corner of my eye, I see something bright blue bobbing in the water, rushing away from us. My overnight bag, washed away just like that, without me even realizing it. The sight of it makes an ugly pit open in the base of my stomach. We're going to get washed down the river. We'll drown, and we'll drag Shang and his horse along with us, so Shang and his horse will also drown. Four lives wiped out, just like that. The horror of it is overwhelming. Then my instincts kick in and I squeeze Slugger and cry, "Go! Hyah!"

Slugger kicks in the water, and her hooves hit river rocks beneath, pushing us up and forward. The water still pushes us down, but once again, I urge Slugger forward. "You can do it, baby, come on, go!" Ahead of me Shang is doing the same, leaning forward and getting his horse to go faster. And somehow, Slugger's hooves find purchase and I feel gravity catching hold as we scramble up, over more and more rocks until we're in shallow waters.

Only then does my breath release, and I sag in the saddle. "Good job, Slugger," I say, and the last word comes out in a half sob. Slugger gives a little whicker, like she knows that I'm this close to bursting into tears. "You saved us," I say, patting Slugger's side. The horse is breathing hard, and I feel a stab of guilt. Shang rushes over as we climb out of the river and helps me down.

"You okay?" he says.

"Yeah." Not. I can barely meet his eye, turning instead to give Slugger a hug. "You saved us, you amazing thing."

Slugger turns her head and nibbles my ear, making me laugh. A tear slips down my cheek, followed by another, and I wipe them quickly away, not wanting Shang to see. I need to compose myself. I need to put my mask back on. But when I finally meet his eye, he's looking as pale and shaky as I feel.

"I think I pooped myself," he says, and I can't help it: I collapse to the ground and laugh and cry.

Shang sits down next to me. "Sorry, I should've—I don't know, been more careful."

"There's been a lot of rainfall this year," I say.

"Yeah. I guess I underestimated how much rain there'd been."

"Do you think the others made it okay?" I say. I don't even want to consider the possibility that they might not have.

"Yeah," Shang says without any hesitation. "Uncle Hong and Uncle Jing are used to camping. They'll know better than I do about safe water levels and they would've chosen to go a different route."

I nod. Although the last thing I want to do is get up, I force myself back to my feet. I can't wait to reach the campsite and change out of my wet clothes—though of course as soon as I think that, I recall with painful clarity my overnight bag getting washed away.

"My bag," I moan.

"Yeah," Shang says with a grimace. "That was a bad stroke of luck. But don't worry, we'll all share our supplies with you."

I nod miserably, mentally going over everything I've packed in there. Good thing they'd told me to leave my cell phone behind at the farmhouse since there would be no cell service here. Gotta be grateful for small favors. We climb back up onto our horses and this time, we ride in exhausted silence.

By the time we arrive at the campsite, the sun is just about to dip below the horizon and the air has gone from refreshingly cool to unpleasantly cold. Everyone cheers as we turn the corner.

"Where have you two been?" James calls out. "We've been here for, like, an hour."

"Shang's usually the fastest rider out of all of us," Christopher says.

They all gather around, chatting and smiling. Mushu helps me off my horse and Uncle Jing leads Slugger to where the other horses are and gives her some feed.

"My horse got a stone in her shoe," Shang mutters. "And I miscalculated the river. We nearly got carried away. Zhou lost her bag."

Gasps all around. Auntie Jiayi rushes to me and says, "Zhou, are you okay?"

"Yeah, I'm fine."

"Your teeth are chattering!" Auntie Jiayi says. "Come on, you change into dry clothes now."

"I'll get my clothes," Mushu says, hurrying away to her tent.

I'm surrounded by aunties clucking away worriedly at me and I don't resist as they lead me to one of the bigger tents. In fact, I find their overbearing concern reassuring. For the first time that day, I feel like I don't have to put up a brave front with them. I've done my part, I've braved the river, and now I'm ready to be fussed over. Mushu comes back with clean, dry clothes, and the aunties hand me a towel and wait outside to give me some privacy. I pull off my soaking wet, hateful boots with relief, wrinkling my nose at the smell of my dripping socks. I peel off my freezing jeans and wrap myself in the towel. With the horribly wet clothes off me, I immediately feel in a better mood, and shrugging on Mushu's warm clothes feels like heaven.

"Zhou, you need help in there?" Auntie Lulu's voice calls from outside.

"No, I'm fine," I say, quickly buttoning up my shirt.

I come out carrying my wet clothes and Auntie Lulu grabs them out of my hands. "I will dry these for you," she says.

"Oh, um, thank you."

"Come," Auntie Jiayi says, putting her arm around my shoulders. "You sit by the fire. Oh, poor girl, you are so cold you're shaking."

Shang is outside setting up his tent next to the others. As we walk past, Auntie Jiayi reaches out to Shang and yanks his ear.

"Ow! Ma, what?"

"You let this poor girl freeze!" Auntie Jiayi snaps. "What kind of gentleman are you? Very bad, I am very disappointed."

Shang's mouth opens, but no words come out. I bite down on my lip to keep from laughing at his half-lost, half-affronted expression. I settle down in front of the fire with a long sigh of relief. It's so warm and cozy here, to be right in front of a crackling fire. I hold out my hands and revel in the heat coursing through my freezing palms.

Shaking his head, Shang goes back to setting up his tent.

"Shang, because you lost Zhou's tent, she will use yours tonight," Auntie Jiayi says.

Shang pauses, looking like he's about to protest, then shrugs. "Okay. I guess I'll share yours, James."

"Nope. Thomas and I are sharing."

"Okay." Shang turns to Christopher. "Can I share yours?"

"We're sharing," Ryan says, pointing to Christopher with his thumb.

Shang looks around, obviously making a calculation in his head. The rest of the group are already paired up—the uncles and the aunties—leaving Mushu and Auntie Jiayi.

"Sorry, my tent is too small," Auntie Jiayi says. "And I am disappointed in you, Shang. I think you should sleep outside."

"Yeah," Mushu says, "my tent's a one-woman tent, sorry."

Shang sighs and says, "Okay." He turns back to finish setting up the tent for me, and I feel a twinge of guilt. Even though Shang blames himself for what happened at the river, I can't bring myself to completely place the blame on him. I get up and walk over to him.

"Need any help?" I say.

Shang glances at me. "Sure. You can get the thingy."

"The thingy," I say flatly.

"You know, the thing that goes inside this thing."

"Haven't you done this a million times before?"

Shang pauses and looks up from screwing in one of the tent poles. "Yes? What's your point?"

"Well, I would've thought that by now you'd have learned the proper names of all these parts."

"Or I would've learned that there's no need to learn the proper names of the parts as long as you can put them together." He smirks at me and gets back to work.

"Okay, well, I will get your thingy." I reach over, grab a random pole, and hand it to him. "Here's your thingy."

"That just doesn't sound right," Shang mutters. His eyes light up. "Hey, you actually grabbed the right thing!"

"Really?"

"No."

I can't help laughing at this. Oh no. All this time I've thought serious Work Shang was handsome. But this Shang, jokey and openhearted and armor-less, is gosh-darned irresistible. Shang grins, rolling his eyes.

"How about this? You hold this pole, yep, and I'll grab the stuff."

I grab hold of the pole and continue screwing it in like Shang was doing, and in a short while, the tent is up. I look at it in wonderment. "I helped build this."

"Yep."

I unzip the front and duck my head to go inside. It's a spacious tent, with enough room for two people. Shang pops his head in. "You like it?"

I hesitate only a second; after all, Shang was forced to give this tent up because of me, and I'm pretty sure that sleeping outside would be massively unpleasant for him. "Um, you know, this could fit the both of us."

Shang frowns, bending over and walking inside. He looks around at the space. "I don't know. . . ."

"I don't snore, and I feel bad about you sleeping outside because my pack got washed away."

"If you're sure? But don't feel like you have to." Shang's eyes burn into mine and I feel a tingle going down my spine.

What was I thinking? I've been so overwhelmed by the events of the day that, honestly, I wasn't really thinking anything when I offered space in the tent, but of course, now it hits me that it means we'd be sleeping together, side by side. My insides turn molten and I swallow, the sound loud and clear in the enclosed space. Which version of me had thought to offer to share the tent? Ranch Mulan? Work Mulan? Would my dad have said that? A small voice inside me whispers: *I think that might've just been Horny Mulan.* I smack the voice down viciously.

"Yeah," I manage to say after an eternity. "As long as you keep to your side of the tent."

"I don't think this space is big enough to have 'sides,' " Shang says dryly. "But yeah, thank you, I'll take you up on your offer because it'll be freezing cold outside. Uh, and another thing—"

"Yeah?" I say, my voice tight.

"I don't imagine you have an extra sleeping bag somewhere on you?"

My mouth falls open. Damn it! I haven't even thought of sleeping bags. *Argh.*

Shang reads the expression of dismay on my face and sighs. "I thought so. It's fine, mine's pretty large and we can unzip it to use it as a blanket and maybe borrow some towels to use as a sleeping pad." He gets out of the tent, leaving me to sink to my knees, pinching the bridge of my nose.

What is happening to me out here? This morning, I would've said the wildest thing I've ever done was to get into a bar fight. But now the day isn't even over and I've just invited Shang into my bed. I shudder to think what else might happen before night's end.

CHAPTER FOURTEEN

There is nothing better than hot food after a whole day of riding. I realize this as I sit down near the campfire and Auntie Jiayi hands me a steaming bowl of ramen. The aunties have fortified the instant ramen with napa cabbage, shiitake mushrooms, crabsticks, and eggs, and it's the most delicious thing I've ever eaten, boiling hot and spicy and savory and utterly *slurpable*.

There is more than enough for everyone, and the mood is merry and lighthearted as we all sit around the fire and slurp at our noodles. At some point, Uncle Hong opens his cooler and passes around cans of beer to everyone. The switching back and forth between steaming-hot noodle soup and sparkling cold beer is heavenly. Even James fails to annoy me with his annoying jokes.

"To family," Uncle Hong says, raising his beer can.

"To family," we chorus, and I meet Shang's eye and feel a warmth that has nothing to do with the hot food or alcohol coursing down to the depths of my stomach.

"You girls have impressed us on this trip," Uncle Hong says.

"Thanks, you've impressed us, too," Mushu says.

Everyone laughs.

"Ah, but really," Uncle Hong says. "To tell you the truth, I was thinking before the trip that you definitely won't be able to cut it out here. Two city girls coming all the way out here? Hah!" He smiles at me. "But you have been such a good sport about everything. To Zhou and Mushu."

The mention of Zhou's name turns the beer bitter in my mouth, but I swallow it with a forced smile, anyway. "Thanks," I say. "It's been a true pleasure being here with all of you, getting to see your beautiful ranch and distillery. I see the love and care you've put into every part of the place, and I really admire it."

Uncle Hong smiles and nods at the other uncles, who nod sagely in return. It feels like there's been an unspoken conversation between the brothers, and I get the feeling that against all odds, I've passed the test. The cousins, too, look satisfied. All of them except James, who's scowling at me, but James has been such a thorn in my side that, honestly, the thought of pissing him off delights me.

"Yes, I like you, Zhou," Auntie Jiayi says. "I think you will give many good ideas for the company."

"But we will still have creative control," Uncle Hong says.

"Definitely," I say. "Our company believes in working together very closely with our business partners, especially when it comes to creative decisions."

James snorts. "That sounds like corporate bullshit for *You don't get a say in anything, suckers.*"

"Not at all," I say with a patient smile. I've watched my father reassure skittish clients enough times to know exactly what he would say in this situation. "A company that isn't happy is not going to be profitable for long, so we take satisfaction very seriously."

"Ah, very good," Uncle Hong says. "You know, over the years, we have had many offers to buy our company. But this is the first time we seriously considered it, because I think it's important to get along with whoever acquires us. I like you, Zhou. Here is to a bright future ahead!" He raises his beer can and everyone, except James, reaches out and clinks their cans together. I try my best to ignore the guilt and anxiety writhing in my guts at the thought of a "bright future ahead." For the hundredth time, I curse myself for coming up with this harebrained idea to fool them into thinking I'm Zhou. I will never be able to face the Lis again once the deal goes through.

Once the ramen is all slurped up, dessert is brought out—Chinese Rice Krispies. Instead of melted marshmallow as the binder, they've used maltose syrup and also added roasted sesame seeds to the puffed rice to give it a rich, nutty flavor. I have two big pieces before I feel like my stomach is about to burst, then I settle back with a mug of hot milk tea. There is a comfortable lull in the conversation as everyone slips into a food coma, and for a while, the only sounds in the air are the crackling of the fire and the occasional hoot of some animal deep in the wilderness. When I look up into the sky, I'm lost in thousands of stars. There are so many of them, and each one shining so brilliantly that they form a river. I can't remember the last time I've felt so at peace.

"When we start working together," Auntie Jiayi says, "that is, if we do go ahead with it, I would love to tell you some of my ideas, Zhou."

I perk up. "I would love—"

"Pah, what ideas do you have for the Wutai brand?" Uncle Hong snaps. "Let the professionals handle it."

My stomach knots up. *What would Zhou*— But then I realize that, actually, I don't care what my dad might say in this situation. My mouth opens, and words flow out before I can stop them. "Actually, Auntie Jiayi, I would love to hear any ideas you might have. Some of the best ideas we've received have come from the most unexpected sources." I smile warmly at Auntie Jiayi, who nods at me with gratitude.

"Welp, this is gonna be a disaster," James mutters, just loud enough for me to hear.

I turn to him and give him a smile as sweet as arsenic. "I would love

173

to hear any ideas you might have as well, James."

From the corner of my eye, I notice Shang coughing. It looks suspiciously like Shang is trying to hide his grin.

"Ooh," Auntie Chuang says, "do I spy a hint of romance between you and James?"

I gape at her. Could Auntie Chuang be any more clueless?

"James, she said she would love to hear any ideas you might have," Auntie Chuang says enthusiastically. "When a girl says that, she means—"

"I meant I would love to hear any ideas anyone here might have," I cut in. There. That should resolve that.

Thankfully, the conversation moves on to other things, and I nod at Auntie Jiayi, who is gazing at me with a curious expression. For the first time, I find myself wondering about Auntie Jiayi's backstory. I know from Shang that her husband has passed away, and I wonder how that has affected Auntie Jiayi's life. It's obvious to me that Auntie Jiayi is a treasure trove of good ideas, especially because Auntie Jiayi is one of life's observers, like myself. She isn't loud or showy like her brothers. She prefers to stay in the background, observing, and I would love to know what it is that Auntie Jiayi has observed and what conclusions she's come to.

After a while, Uncle Hong gets up, stretching and yawning. The other uncles, aunties, and cousins follow suit, yawning loudly and saying good night all around. Even Mushu leaves as well, telling everyone who would listen that it takes nine hours of sleep to wake up looking as fabulous as she does.

Not wanting to leave the comfort of the fire and still lost in the sea of stars, I stay put, calling out good night to everyone else. When I next look down from watching the night sky, I find that only Shang remains, gazing at me with an expression so soft and full of tenderness that my heart, going at a steady pace just moments ago, suddenly slams itself into my rib cage.

"Hey," I say. "Sorry, were you waiting for me to go to, uh . . ." I falter. I was about to say bed when it hit me how intimate that sounded. "To, um, the tent?" I say finally.

"Sort of, yeah. I mean, it's a small space and I wanted to make sure, uh, everything's okay before . . . you know."

Heat rises in my cheeks, and it has nothing to do with the campfire. But I'm also realizing that Shang is nervous, and this knowledge makes me bite my lower lip with glee. Part of me wants to bury my face in a pillow and squeal. Clearly, the part of me that failed to go through puberty.

"Right, sure. Of course." I stand up and my foot knocks over my half-full cup. Tea spills onto the ground. "Oops." I pick it up and notice my hand is trembling ever so slightly.

Shang doesn't seem to notice, walking toward our tent with his hands in his pockets. But once we're both inside, he turns to me and says, "Zhou, I just want you to know that—"

"Yeah?" We are so close, so painfully near each other right now. So close that I can hear the brush of his sweater sleeve against his torso, can hear every breath he takes. My own heartbeat sounds as clear as a drum.

"I uh—I won't try anything funny tonight," Shang says, and he looks so solemn, so earnest, that I snort. Then, before I know it, I'm doubling over, laughing my ass off. "What?" Shang says, looking mystified.

"Sorry. I just— You looked so sincere."

"That's because I was being sincere. Is that a bad thing?"

I can only shake my head as I bend over, trying to stifle my giggles. "No," I wheeze finally. "It's not a bad thing. Thank you for the reassurance. I wasn't worried about that, by the way."

"Okay, great." Shang gets on his knees and unzips his backpack. He

175

takes out a small baggie and pauses. "Um, I only have one toothbrush."

"Oh no. Are we going to have to share a toothbrush?"

"You can have it. It's new." He hands it to me.

I stare at it. "But then I'll have to deal with you having bad breath the whole night. You have it."

"Well, I don't want to be spending the rest of the night smelling your unbrushed teeth."

We narrow our eyes at each other, then I say, "I'll use my wet clothes as a toothbrush. Just give me some toothpaste, it'll be fine."

"Huh. I never would've thought of that. That's pretty smart."

"Yeah, I'm not just a pretty face," I joke.

"No, you're not." Something in Shang's voice makes my chest tighten in that way it so often does when he's around.

The back of my neck prickles and I have to force myself not to look at him as I grab his toothpaste and climb out of the tent. Outside, I find my clothes hanging on a line and pick out my checkered shirt. I go to the wash site, squeeze a bit of toothpaste onto a corner of my shirt, and begin brushing, or rather wiping, my teeth. It's an awkward process, but my mouth feels significantly cleaner afterward, so I chalk it up as a win. Shang stands next to me, brushing his teeth while eyeing me.

When we're both done, we walk back toward the tent in silence. Shang takes out a sweater and pants from his bag and hands them to me. "You can wear these."

"What about you?"

"I'll just sleep in my day clothes like a man."

I roll my eyes. I'm too tired to argue, and plus, I don't like the idea of sleeping in jeans. After the day I've had, I deserve a soft sweater and soft sweatpants, damn it. Shang leaves the tent to give me some privacy, and I quickly change into his clothes. As expected, they're way more comfortable than Mushu's clothes, but they're also so big that the sweater hangs almost down to my knees, and I have to roll up the cuffs of the sweatpants to stop myself from tripping over them.

"I'm done," I call out to Shang.

He climbs back in and pauses, his eyes widening when he sees me.

"What?" I say.

Shang clears his throat and looks away abruptly, zipping the tent up behind him. "Nothing. Uh, bedtime?"

"Yeah." Now that the tent is zipped up, the air feels utterly still, every sound we make painfully clear. Shang's scent envelops me. He smells so good, a subtle warmth that makes me want to snuggle up to him and disappear.

I climb into the "bed," which is nothing more than a couple of towels spread out over the tent floor. I make sure to lie down as close to the edge as possible so as to give Shang more space. I'm so acutely aware of his presence, dominating the small space.

"You don't have to, like, hug the edge," Shang says.

"I'm trying to be considerate."

Shang looks like he's trying to bite back a smile. "Thank you, yes, that's very considerate." He lowers himself onto the towel next to me and lies down on his back, curling one arm behind his head and the other across his stomach.

I turn onto my back as well, and we both stare up at the tent top. The silence stretches on between us, but it's not an entirely uncomfortable one.

"Um—" I say, at the same time as Shang says, "So—"

We both pause.

"You go," we say at the same time. I laugh. Shang turns his head to face me, and I do the same. In the lamplight, his eyelashes cast long shadows across his cheeks. He's so achingly close to me.

"So this is weird, huh?" I say.

"Yeah," Shang chuckles. "Just a few days ago, we were strangers and you were just some finance bro trying to take over my family company and probably strip it for parts."

"What?" I rise up on one elbow. "I would never—"

"I'm just kidding," Shang says, grinning.

I narrow my eyes at him and lie back down, still giving him a dirty look.

"But to be honest with you, I was kind of afraid of that," Shang says. "You hear of these things happening all the time, and with our sales record, I know that our real value lies in our components, not our brand."

"That's not true," I say. "I like your brand."

Shang cocks an eyebrow.

"Okay, I think your brand has a lot of potential."

Shang is wearing a smile I would very much like to wipe off. Possibly with my own mouth. *Ew, why the hell did I just think that? Stop it, brain. Bad brain.*

"In the right hands, your brand could become very . . ." Is it just me or is every word coming out of my mouth sounding super suggestive? "Uh, lucrative."

"Interesting," Shang says. Now it's his turn to raise himself up on his elbow.

I try to ignore the way my blood pressure makes my head feel like it's about to explode as Shang gazes down at me.

"And what are the right hands going to do to our brand?"

Damn it, now everything coming out of his mouth sounds really suggestive. I mentally give myself a shake, trying to yank my mind out of the gutter. What am I, a fifteen-year-old kid with raging hormones?

"Um, a lot of things," I say, fighting to keep my voice even. I raise myself up on my elbow once more so I'm at eye level with him. "But I can't tell you, because we're not partners yet, and that would be proprietary information." Of course, now that I'm looking right at him, it hits me how incredibly close we are. Mere inches separate us. I can see each individual eyelash, the smooth texture of his skin, and the way his nostrils flare ever so slightly as he stares at me.

"Hmm." Shang's gaze moves from my eyes down to my mouth, and I resist the urge to bite my lip. I part my mouth ever so slightly, and am delighted to hear a sharp intake of breath from him. Good, I'm not the only one whose mind is in the gutter tonight.

A moment passes, during which I imagine twining my arm around Shang's neck and pulling him close. But then Shang abruptly turns away and lies back down. Feeling foolish, I settle back down on the towel as well, and we both resume staring at the top of the tent. This time, though, the silence is charged and not at all easy or comfortable. What little space there is between us feels electric, and I'm sure that if our elbows were to bump each other, even a tiny bit, I would spontaneously combust.

Shang shifts, and I stop breathing. He reaches over his head, pauses, and says, "Lights off?"

Disappointment washes over me. Maybe I've miscalculated it after all. My voice comes out in a hoarse whisper. "Okay."

He turns the lamp off and darkness floods the space, so absolute and so fast that I'm a little shocked. I've never known such blackness; back home, I'm used to a city that never quite falls completely asleep. There are always splinters of light coming from the streets below, creeping through my shades, and noises from passing cars. But now there is complete silence and complete darkness, and in the absence of light, I feel other senses firing up.

My hearing has become more sensitive since we came into the tent, but now my skin seems to tingle with the passing of air. As I listen to Shang's breathing, I imagine that I can feel his breath caressing my skin. And his smell— God, his smell is everywhere, and it is intoxicating. A clean smell, which I don't understand how that's possible after the day we've had, but he smells of soap and light sweat and maybe a hint of cologne and it's all I can do to stop myself from burying my nose in the nape of his neck.

From the way Shang is breathing, I can tell he isn't asleep, either. We lie there in silence for an excruciating amount of time, and after a while, the exhaustion of the day catches up with me. Even though I'm still sorely aware of Shang's presence next to me, my eyelids become heavier and heavier, more and more impossible to keep open. At some point, I manage to doze off.

I have no idea when I wake up, but I have a sense of some time passing, maybe an hour or two, and then waking up and finding myself still in complete darkness. But something is different. It takes a moment to realize what it is. I'm warm, comfortably warm, feeling utterly safe. And with a start, I realize it's because somehow, as I slept, I'd turned to my side and burrowed into Shang's arms. Shang's arms, which are at this very moment around me.

Time stops moving. My breath pauses mid-inhale. I don't dare move a single muscle. I lie there, frozen, unsure what to do. I should slip out of his arms; otherwise it's going to be so awkward come morning. But also, I really don't want to. It's bitterly cold, even inside the tent, and I don't want to leave Shang, I want to lie soft in his arms and nuzzle my forehead into the crook of his neck and—

"What are you thinking?" Shang whispers.

I utter a soft gasp. "You're awake?"

"Yeah."

"How long have you been awake?"

"Um. From the time we went to bed?"

"You haven't slept at all?" I say, horrified. "Have I been snoring? Have you been listening to me snore?"

"There wasn't much else to listen to."

"Shang!" I hiss.

He laughs. "For what it's worth, it's a really cute snore."

"I can't believe—" I ease myself up and feel Shang's arms tightening a little around me, his hands wide across my back. I pause, whatever words I was about to say forgotten in the moment. The darkness around us is still complete, so it isn't possible for me to see Shang's expression, but I can sense it, the atmosphere around us turning soft, the unspoken words between us dissipating into thin air.

"Sorry," Shang says, releasing me.

And that's when I dip my head and cover his mouth with mine. No more masks. No more wondering what my dad would do, or what Ranch Mulan would do, or what Work Mulan should do. None of that. I don't even care that it's forbidden, that my company is trying to acquire his, and about all the ways in which that makes this so wrong. All I want to do right now is what real Mulan wants to do, and that is to kiss Li Shang.

Our lips mold against each other's perfectly, moving slowly, softly at first. I've kissed and been kissed plenty of times before, but this is different. It's somehow new and exciting and yet familiar at the same time, like kissing your best friend. It doesn't make sense; Shang is about as far from a best friend as anyone can be, and yet. And yet here we are, our mouths moving in sync, deepening the kiss until my entire body feels like it's on fire.

Shang's hands stroke up and down my back, and I shift slightly so that the oversize sweater I'm wearing lifts up a little, and Shang groans and slides his hand underneath. His palm caresses my back tenderly, slowly, and I arch my back, wanting to savor every touch of his. I brush the side of his face, still kissing him, before letting my hand trail down his chin, grazing that superhero jawline of his before going down to his hard chest. I've never been so turned on in my life. When I slip my hand under his shirt, he gives a soft moan and whispers, "Zhou . . ."

The name sears through my senses, piercing through the haze of the moment. It feels as though the thick atmosphere has just shattered. I lift my head and freeze, hovering above him.

"Are you okay?" Shang says. "Did I—"

"No, it's fine. You're fine." I clear my throat. "Um, I just— I was afraid that the others might hear us."

"Oh." Shang swallows. "Sure, yeah. That's a legit concern."

He carefully removes his hands from my back and I roll off him, grateful it's so dark that it's impossible for Shang to see how red my face must be. Or how guilty. I turn away from him and squeeze my eyes shut. Shang turns as well, though I can't tell where he's facing. The silence stretches on and on, until it becomes so taut that something must break.

"I hope I didn't make you uncomfortable," Shang says. "I'm sorry if I did."

I grit my teeth, willing my tears back. "You did nothing wrong." There's a clear tremble in my voice.

"Zhou, are you okay?"

Stop calling me that! I want to scream. It's hitting me like a gut punch, the lie I've told, this deception I've carried out, and now it's too late to take it back. His family has accepted Mushu and me, even Uncle Hong has been won over, and now I've fallen—

I stop breathing.

I've fallen? For Shang? In such a short time?

No, it can't be. It must be lust, or infatuation. I don't believe in insta-love. I believe in math. I believe in currency. I believe in hard work and being sensible and definitely not falling in love with a man I barely know. A man who's been nothing but kind toward me, a man who does all the cooking so his mother doesn't have to, a man who cuts up food because his mother has arthritic hands, a man who stayed back and rode alongside me and got into a bar fight because of me and—

A man who thinks I am Hua Zhou.

When I speak again, my voice is steel. "I'm okay. That was a mistake. I apologize. It was unprofessional and I won't let it happen again."

"Oh." The surprise and disappointment in Shang's voice is undeniable. He clears his throat, then says, "Okay. Yeah, you're right. I'm glad you—uh, put a stop to it. Let's get some rest. Good night."

This time, when I doze off, I don't wake up in Shang's arms, feeling warm and soft and safe. In fact, when I wake up, it is morning, and the makeshift bed is cold and undeniably empty.

CHAPTER FIFTEEN

The entire way back from the campsite, I can't bear to meet Shang's eyes, and as soon as we get back to the farmhouse, I hurry inside my bedroom. Mushu follows and closes the door behind her.

"Okay, spill," she says.

"What?"

"What happened between you and Shang?"

I look away. "I don't know what you're talking about."

"Uhh, I have eyes, therefore I can see. And you two were all chummy and there was this cute chemistry going on between you yesterday, and then all of a sudden, *bam*, this morning it's nothing but toxic silence between you guys. And I have to say, it's poisoning the atmosphere, so I think you owe it to the rest of us to tell me what happened."

I frown. "I can't tell if you're actually making sense or if you're gaslighting me."

"Obviously I am making sense," Mushu cries. "What is it?" She gasps, bringing her hand over her mouth. "Did he try something in the middle of the night? Oh, that bastard, I should've—"

"No!" I say quickly. "No, nothing like that. It was actually kind of the other way around."

"The other way around?" Mushu lifts an eyebrow. "Uh. You mean, you tried something and he didn't want it? Oh, girl. Okay, I know you must be humiliated right now, and it is pretty humiliating, I won't lie to you, but you've done much worse things."

184

"No, it's not— Wait, I have? Like what?"

"Like the time Cousin Joey celebrated his birthday and you got so excited you blew out the candles?"

I snort. "I was six years old."

"I'm just saying, I don't think Cousin Joey's forgiven you for that one. You know, he's in therapy."

"Because I blew out his birthday candles when we were kids?" I say flatly.

"I'm not saying that's the reason, but I'm not *not* saying it isn't, either."

There is a pause as both of us regard what she just said.

"I think you used triple negatives there, so you went full circle," I say.

Mushu looks ponderous. As she opens her mouth to argue, I continue: "Anyway! I didn't—we didn't—well, we did, but then I stopped and it got all weird."

Mushu's eyes grow so wide they look like they're about to pop right out of her head. "Oh my god. Go back. What do you mean you did? What? You can't just casually drop that in there."

I release a long sigh. "We were making out, okay? Nothing else."

"Nothing else?" Mushu screeches.

"Shh!"

"Sorry," she whispers. "Oh my god." Her mouth turns into a thin line and she looks like she's this close to actually exploding. "Making out!" she squeals.

"You wanna shout that a little louder? I don't think his entire family heard it."

"Sorry, I'm just so excited for you! Wait, so why did you stop? Oh no, is Shang a bad kisser?"

"No." My cheeks warm up as I recall those incredible, earth-shattering kisses. God, no. "Far from it. But at one point he said my name—"

185

"Oh, I love it when they do that. That's so hot."

"He called me 'Zhou,' " I say flatly.

"Ah." Mushu deflates and flops onto the bed. "Damn, talk about a mood killer."

"Yeah. It made me feel so guilty I just had to stop." I look out of the window, unable to face even my cousin. "God, what am I doing here? Deceiving him, not to mention his family. All these people who have been nothing but kind to us."

Mushu sits back up. "Um, nothing but kind to us? Okay, hold up. I mean, are you deceiving them?"

"Yes, I am."

"Okay, technically yes. But do you not remember why we had to do this? His family is so patriarchal you couldn't have done this as Mulan. And even as Zhou, you couldn't just convince them with your flaw- less track record, because they're so sexist. No, you've had to bend over backward to prove that you're man enough to do whatever it is needs doing around here. They're hardly innocent in all this."

I sigh. "Yeah, but Shang isn't like that."

"Really? Stoic hunk of a dude isn't like the rest of his family?" Mushu looks very skeptical, and I find myself wanting to defend Shang.

"He really isn't. At least, I don't think he is. I don't know, I had this image of him as—well—someone like James or Uncle Hong, but he keeps doing things to contradict that image."

"Yeah, well, most people don't fit neatly into one category. Anyway, I get it, it's not the ideal situation, but you've gotta remember what's truly important here."

"The acquisition," I say, at the same time as Mushu says, "Getting laid."

My mouth snaps shut and I glare at Mushu, who shrugs and says, "What? I'm just saying. Look, Mulan, you've always been so respon- sible. Even when we were kids, you were always so caught up with making everyone around you happy, especially your parents. It's so rare to get to see what the real you wants. And in this case, what you really want is obviously that scrumptious hunk of a man."

"The acquisition is what matters here, Mushu," I say, trying hard not to laugh.

"If you say so. But you do a million of these things a year, whereas you definitely do not get laid a million times a year, so . . ."

I can't help laughing at that. "God, I don't know how you make me laugh even when everything is so crappy."

"It's a blessing to be related to me," Mushu says.

"It is," I say, and I really do mean it.

This time around, on the way back to the city, Mushu calls dibs on getting a ride in Shang's car, which makes me both relieved and terrified. I ride in the uncles and aunties' trailer, and I actually find the nonstop chattering and invasive questions kind of fun to maneuver. ("What GPA you got in college? 3.9? Aiya, why not 4.0?" *Well, Auntie, it's kind of tough to get 4.0 at Princeton. I was surrounded by actual geniuses and all.* "Yes, but you are Chinese, you should be better than these American geniuses." "How many children you want, Zhou? I think you better have three. Three is good number of children to have. Two boys to take over business and one girl to take care of you when you old." *Can't the girl take over the business?* "Oh, what nonsense, of course not. Daughter job is taking care of parents.")

My parents moved to America without the rest of their families, so I'm not used to the chaos of a big family like the Lis, but I revel in it. I love their merry atmosphere, the way the trailer is never quiet, because everyone is talking over everyone. I love the good-natured arguments between the uncles and aunties, the way they can never just agree with each other and have to debate everything until someone—more often than not Uncle Hong—shouts, "Okay! We settle down now!" And then they settle for about two minutes before they start up a whole different argument. But the entire time they're laughing and patting one another on the arm or the back with obvious affection, and there is a constant stream of snacks being passed around, all of them homemade.

There are the Chinese Rice Krispies that they had at the campsite, and then there are savory prawn crackers, which I hadn't even known were possible to make at home, though when I think about it, of course they are, because why wouldn't they be? These ones are far superior to any I've had before, tasting of real shrimp and garlic and onion, and are utterly addictive. There are egg wafer rolls—paper-thin, fragrant wafers rolled up like cigars, with toasted sesame seeds sprinkled throughout the batter. I lose count of how many I've had on the ride. There is bak kwa—Chinese jerky, which isn't dry like the American version but tender and sticky sweet and savory, the greasy sauce coating my fingers. They are quite literally finger-licking good.

By the time we arrive back in the city, I think I'm way too full to eat, but the Lis stop off at a Chinese restaurant and I find that, actually, I'm now craving some hot dishes. I'm about to enter the restaurant when Shang arrives. We pause at the door, both of us looking frantically at each other.

"Go ahead," Shang says, opening the door for me.

"Thank you," Mushu says, blithely stepping from behind him. She goes through the door while wiggling her eyebrows at me.

"Um, thanks," I say, ducking my head and hurrying through the door.

Inside, the rest of the family is seated, leaving me to sit next to Shang and Mushu. I silently curse the universe as we settle into our seats. The round table is so cramped that it's impossible not to graze elbows with your neighbor, and each time my elbow touches Shang's, we both jerk apart as though we've been shocked.

The uncles, aunties, and cousins are talking over one another as usual, with Mushu diving right in as though she's been born and raised in this family. Shang and I sit in silence, letting the noise wash over us, painfully aware of each other's presence.

"So—" I say.

"Um—" Shang says.

We stop. "You first," I say.

"Okay. How was your ride back? Did you get grilled about your college GPA?" Shang says.

I laugh. "I did, actually. How did you guess?"

"I grew up with these people," he says dryly.

"They were unimpressed by my GPA," I say.

"Gasp, you didn't have a perfect GPA?" Shang says.

"Okay, but might I remind you that I did go to Princeton? It's kind of a little competitive?"

"Oh yeah, how did I forget when you mention it every other conversation?"

I stare at him in mock outrage. "I do not!"

"It's like that thing people say about Harvard men—how do you find out if a guy's been to Harvard? You don't, he'll tell you within five minutes of meeting him."

"Li Shang, you did not just compare me to a Harvard man."

His dimples appear again and he looks so adorable that my mind is just going *Eeeeeeee*. I can't believe we're having an actual conversation, that we've gone right back to our old banter even after last night. Of course, now that I'm thinking about last night, I go back to feeling awkward.

Luckily, the food arrives then, and I, whose stomach is filled with junk food, dig in gratefully. The meal is plentiful but fast as everyone inhales the food. Unlike the other meals, we don't linger afterward, all of us eager to get home. The group disperses back at Uncle Hong's house and Mushu and I drive to the hospital to visit Baba.

Mama is rubbing Vaseline on Baba's lips as we walk in.

"Hi, Ma."

"Hey, Auntie Li, how's it going?" Mushu says.

"Ah, you girls are back. How was the trip?" Ma places the tub of Vaseline down and comes over to give us a hug.

"It was good. I think they'll sell the company to us quite happily," I say.

Ma's face breaks into a huge smile. "Really? How did you convince them?"

"Oh, you know." I have a hard time meeting my mother's eyes. "This and that. Had a lot of good conversations with them, told them our company's philosophy and stuff."

"She sheared sheep, rode a demon of a horse, herded cows," Mushu says.

"What?" Ma gapes at me.

"Well, I tried herding cows. I failed miserably. Fell into a pile of cow patty."

"That's the polite term for cow dung," Mushu says helpfully.

Ma looks torn between horror and laughter. "Oh, my dear girl. You know, Baba and I have always wanted to take you back to his family farm back in China."

I wrap an arm around Ma and rest my head on her shoulder. "I would love to, Ma. I have a newfound appreciation for farming."

"My goodness, who are you and what have you done with my Mulan?"

"How's Dad doing?" I say.

"Not too bad, I think. The doctor says his vitals have improved, and he'll be up in no time." Ma sighs. "It hasn't been nice going home without him though, so I've been sleeping on the sofa here."

"Aw, Ma!" I cry. "I'll accompany you. I'm sorry I left."

"Well, you had to. But yes, stay at the house. It'll be less empty with you there."

I smile as I watch Ma fussing around Ba's bed, tucking him in more snugly and placing a loving kiss on his forehead before leaving. My parents have set such a high standard for coupledom. Watching them, I know I'll never settle for less than this kind of love, a love that is strong and yet tender-hearted, a love that is worn soft round the edges, like a comfortable pair of socks. I link my arm through Ma's and Mushu does the same on the other side, and together, the three of us walk out of the hospital and drive back home.

The next day, I go to the office early and dive into work. I haven't taken time off in years, and skipping two workdays for the Li family trip has made me feel like I've fallen behind on a million tasks. The morning whizzes by as I play catch-up with everything, having meeting after meeting with the analysts and checking in with clients and investors.

There's a knock at my door and the receptionist pops his head in. "Mulan, there's someone here to see Zhou."

"Who is it?"

"His name is Shang. He's from Wutai Gold."

"Oh! Right. Yes." I straighten up, my hand flying to my hair, flattening any flyaways that might be there. I feel so frazzled. "What time is it?"

"It's two p.m."

"What?" I've missed lunch without even realizing it. "Uh. Right. Shang. You know what, I'll meet him out there." The last thing I want is to have to tell others to call me Zhou again. And anyway, it's too late for that, Shang is here—why is he here? Grabbing my phone and bag, I hurry out of my office.

Shang is waiting at the reception area, his hands stuffed in his pockets. He's wearing a light blue work shirt with the sleeves rolled up to his elbows. I read online once that a shirt with the sleeves rolled up to the elbows is the sluttiest thing a man could wear, and I agree whole-heartedly. God, he looks good.

"Hello, Shang," I say, very much aware that several of my colleagues nearby aren't even trying to hide the fact that they're eavesdropping.

"Zhou," he says, his eyes crinkling at the corners.

The receptionist looks confused. "Zhou is—"

"Right here!" I say. "Anyway, let's go out, I missed my lunch hour and I am starving!" I'm babbling, I know, but I barrel ahead, practically shoving Shang toward the elevator. "So nice to see you again, hope you had a good rest?" I only stop talking when we get in and the doors slide shut, then I let my breath out.

Shang looks amused. "Busy day?"

"Yeah, my workload really piled up while I was away."

"You're a very important person," he says, smiling.

"The most important," I say, tossing my hair over my shoulder. We grin at each other, and I try not to notice the way his cheeks dimple. It's only been a day since I last saw him, but already I'd forgotten how good he looks in person. Those deep brown eyes of his and the intense way he looks at me, my god. His scent fills the elevator, that damn addictive smell that makes me want to nuzzle his neck. "Um, so what can I do for you?"

He takes a beat to answer, and the way his gaze rakes over me makes me blush. Again, I wonder why everything I say sounds so suggestive

192

when it comes to Shang. "You mentioned that you need to go over some numbers?"

It takes me a second to remember that I have indeed mentioned that before. "Oh, yes."

"And the others thought it would be good for me to go through them with you."

"Oh," I manage to say. It's not entirely unheard of for a client to run through the numbers at this stage, though it is uncommon, and I would be lying if I said I wasn't happy about it.

"James offered to do it," Shang says.

My joy shrivels for a second.

"But I kind of, uh, told him I'd do it." Shang shoves his hands back into his pockets and gives me a sweet, bashful smile. "I hope that's okay with you."

I give up trying to fight the smile from taking over my face. "Yes. It is absolutely fine with me."

We go to a nearby bistro for a late lunch. It's the middle of the workday, so the restaurant is practically empty. We grab a seat next to the window and I order a chicken sandwich for myself. Shang opts for a matcha crepe cake. It's hard not to stare at Shang. I've gotten used to seeing him in sweaters and casual clothes, so seeing him in office wear is a new sight. One that I could definitely get used to. And, I realize with a start, this is the first time that it's just the two of us in the real world, without his family or Mushu around. The thought makes me nervous, like I'm a teenager again, out on my first ever date.

"Did you sleep well last night?" Shang says.

"I did, actually. I stayed over at my parents' because my—" I stop myself in time. God, I was about to tell him that my dad's sick and my mom's lonely because of it. *Argh.* The reminder of my lie is sobering.

"Because?" Shang says.

"Oh, um, they just missed me while I was away."

Shang's eyes dance as he smiles. "That's really nice, Zhou. I'm glad you have such a good relationship with your parents."

"Yeah," I say weakly. That damn name again. I hate hearing the name come out of his mouth. Each time he says it, I want to jump up and scream *It's all a lie! I'm lying to you!* "What about you?" I say.

"Oh yeah, after that ride back and then the drive home, I was pooped. I got back to my house, unpacked, did the laundry, and then collapsed into bed."

I gasp. "You did the laundry? What are you, some kind of psychopath?"

"You mean am I a responsible adult? Yes, yes, I am."

"Who does the laundry as soon as they come home from a trip?"

Shang shrugs. "The clothes were damp and dirty and covered in sweat and—let's not forget—cow dung and probably fish scales as well. It would've been a health hazard not to do the laundry."

"Yep, psychopath," I say.

"I think the correct term is antisocial personality disorder," Shang says primly.

"Oh yes. Thank you for mansplaining."

Shang bites back his smile, but his cheeks still dimple anyway. "So your unwashed clothes are still sitting in your laundry basket?"

"If by laundry basket you mean my luggage, then yes."

"You didn't even unpack?" Shang gapes at me. "Wow. You, my love, are an agent of chaos."

The words *my love* hang in the air between us like a neon sign. I'm pretty sure my entire face is beet red, my heart swelling like it's about to spill out through the gaps in my rib cage. *Don't make it a thing. It's just a saying.*

The food arrives then, breaking the delicious tension. I'm starving, so I pick up my sandwich and take a giant bite. Shang watches with amusement as I chew. I don't want to talk with my mouth so full, so I raise my eyebrows at him to say: *What?*

"Nothing, I've just never seen anyone take such a big bite before. It's kind of impressive."

I narrow my eyes, as though to say: *Are you judging me?*

"I'm not judging."

I roll my eyes. Totally judging.

"I swear I'm not."

I finally swallow, then have to drink some water to stop myself from getting hiccups. "I like taking big bites."

"Evidently."

"Okay, Judgey McJudgerson, scientific studies show that there is an actual biological reason why we like taking big bites. It hits all of the pleasure sensors in our mouths, and the feeling of swallowing a huge bite also triggers a feeling of pleasure." I falter a little as I realize that, once again, the words I'm saying are coming out really suggestive. I quickly add: "Also, when our ancestors were hunter-gatherers, they had to eat fast whenever they made a kill."

"I don't know, this all sounds like pseudoscience to me."

I push my plate to him. "Try it. Take a giant bite out of my sandwich." Damn it, did that sound suggestive, too, or do I just have a perverted mind when it comes to Shang?

He picks up my sandwich and does so. He chews slowly as I watch with one eyebrow raised.

"God, can you eat any slower?" I say.

Shang widens his eyes and holds up a finger and keeps chewing. When he finally swallows, he breathes a sigh of relief. "Okay, that was a choking hazard."

"But was it good?"

"Well, yeah, you're right that there's something enjoyable about that, but look at this, your sandwich is half gone in two bites."

"Yup. Enjoyable and efficient."

Shang laughs and shakes his head. "So you finish all your food in under five bites?"

"Well, some foods are more enjoyable when I take smaller bites. Like vegetables, meats, desserts. It's really only the carbs that I just want to stuff into my face. Rice, noodles, sandwiches." I take another humongous bite and Shang grins as he takes a sensible bite of his crepe cake.

"So should we work back at your office?" Shang says.

I quickly shake my head. I chew a lot longer than necessary so I have time to think. When I finally swallow, I say, "How about your place?"

"My office? My office is a really small space in a warehouse where we store and distribute the whiskeys. I don't think it's a very nice environment. What's wrong with your office?"

"It's getting fumigated." As soon as I say it, I wonder if offices actually get fumigated. Why the hell did I say that?

"Oh." A frown creases Shang's forehead. "You guys have an infestation?"

"Yep. Of infests. I mean, insects. Crickets? No. I mean, the other one, the one that eats wood."

"Termites? Jeez. Okay." Shang takes a sip of his drink. "Weird, though, it looked like the space was fully functional just now."

"Oh, yeah. The fumigation will start tonight, so we'll be out of action for a while."

"Right. So where should we go to do the work, then?" Shang says.

Oh no. He's about to suggest my place, and I can't have that because of all the mail I get that says MULAN HUA and the custom fridge magnet that says MULAN and the framed college degree that says MULAN HUA and the—

"Your place," I blurt out.

196

"Oh?" Shang looks surprised. "Really? I mean, sure, I don't mind, but . . ." He searches my eyes and I smile like a maniac. "Okay, I guess. If you're comfortable with that."

"Yeah, of course." *Am I? Comfortable with the thought of the two of us working closely at his apartment?* Now that the thought sinks in, I realize I am far from comfortable, but not because I feel unsafe around him. If anything, it's the other way around. I don't trust myself not to pounce on him. *Stop it.* I can be an adult and do mature, responsible adult things, even if said things are being done with the most gorgeous man alive. "Your place sounds perfect."

Shang lives in a one-bedroom apartment in Bayview, and if anyone had asked me a few days ago what I expected his place to look like, I would have said, *Immaculate. Cold and austere to the point of giving psychopath vibes.* But as I step inside and pause to take my shoes off, I realize how wrong I would have been.

The apartment is neat, yes, but it's also overflowing with life—potted plants line the shelves, along with what seems like dozens of cookbooks, tastefully arranged throughout the space. Instead of the cold, metallic furniture I would have expected before, Shang's tastes run more natural, toward wooden furniture in neutral shades. An eclectic mix of artwork decorates the walls. The overall effect is beautiful and cozy and—if I were to think of all the things I've slowly come to learn about Shang over the past few days—so completely and utterly him.

I follow him through the beautiful living room into the adjoining dining space. His dining table is equally welcoming—a solid wood table that fits six people, with pots of succulents in the center, next to a tray of sauces. There's soy sauce, sesame oil, roasted sesame seeds, and a bottle of Lao Gan Ma chili crisp, all lined up neatly. I wince as I think of my own dining table, a space that is always filled with various clutter. Books that I've been reading, random pens and notepaper, old coffee cups that I haven't bothered to clear away, a scarf that I wore in winter and never got around to tidying up, more books, a cute card a friend sent me, stacks of junk mail I meant to recycle but somehow haven't had time to . . .

The open kitchen is, at a glance, incredibly spotless, especially given how much cooking probably goes on in there. "Oh my god, look how impeccable your kitchen is. I was right, you are a true psychopath," I say. "Am I going to find a severed hand in your fridge?"

"No, I like to keep severed hands in the freezer," Shang says.

I narrow my eyes, stride to the fridge, and open the freezer. There are plastic containers labeled CHICKEN TERIYAKI, SALMON (UNSEASONED), GARLIC HERB STEAK, and so on, all of them neatly stacked. "Who does this?" I cry.

"Um. I do? Would you also like to check the fridge section?"

"I would, actually." I close the freezer door and open the fridge. It looks like a fridge that's been stocked by a social media influencer, all neat rows of containers filled with various fruits and vegetables. I can't remember the last time I cleaned out my fridge. There are possibly new specimens of penicillin growing inside it. I close the fridge door and straighten up. "I don't know whether to be impressed or horrified."

"Why not both?" Shang says, opening a cupboard and taking out two mugs. "Coffee?"

"Yes, please." There are two stools next to the kitchen counter. I pull one out and perch on it, then rest my chin on my palm and study Shang as he moves about the kitchen. This man. This incredible, surprising mama's boy—oh my god, that's it. "Your mom!" I shout.

Shang slides an espresso pod into his coffee maker. "Yes, what about her?"

"I bet she comes here and cleans your place," I say smugly.

Shang laughs. "Close, but no. I go to her place and help her tidy up once in a while. I told her to hire a cleaner, actually, but she keeps refusing."

"Ooh, so you have a cleaner."

"I don't. I just . . . like cleaning."

"Nobody likes cleaning," I say.

"Have you been on TikTok? The number of cleaning videos on there proves you wrong."

"Cleaning videos?"

Shang takes out a carton of milk. "You know, just videos of people cleaning their space."

"The fact that you know about these videos delights me."

Shang shakes his head. "I feel like a lot of things about me delight you. In the worst possible way."

"A little, yeah. Okay but really, this place is incredibly neat. Like, hospital-grade neat."

"Did I not mention that cleaning is one of my many hobbies?"

"No. You said cooking is your hobby."

"And cleaning."

"Cooking and cleaning are your hobbies," I say.

"Yes, is that a problem?" Shang raises his brows as he slides a steaming mug of milky coffee to me.

"No, just surprising is all. Given, you know, your whole family, not to mention your company's brand." I wrap my hands around my mug and take a deep inhale of the rich, nutty scent.

"Are you stereotyping me?"

"A little bit, yeah." I sip my coffee and sigh. "Damn it, I know I've said this already, but you make the most amazing coffee. Is there anything you can't do?"

"Lots, actually. Baseball. Basketball. Calculus."

"Calculus? Am I going to have to take your Asian card away?" I tease.

"Here we go again with the stereotypes."

I shake my head, laughing. How is talking to Shang so easy? With a start, I realize that I haven't once asked myself: *What should I say as Work Mulan?* There's something about Shang that disarms me. Something about him reaches out to me and whispers: *You don't have to play a part with me. You can let your guard down.* And I don't want to fight it. I'm so tired of fighting the real me. But this is so dangerous. I can't afford to go down this road. It could put the entire acquisition at risk.

I watch as he assembles a snack platter of cured meats, cheese, and fruits, then we go to the living room, where we take out our laptops and start going over my analysis of Wutai Gold.

Shang listens attentively as I explain the financial model and valuation that my analyst has come up with. "This is all based on the CIM—the confidential information memo—that was sent our way, plus our projections. This valuation is based on DCF modeling."

"DCF modeling?"

"Discounted cash flow."

"That means nothing to me."

"It's fine, it's just a way of valuing something based on projected cash flows. I tend to be pretty conservative, but I think there are some really great things we can do with your company to get the profit margin up."

"Like what?" Shang says.

"Well, I think we could be a lot more diverse with our target audience."

Shang smiles. "You mean we shouldn't just aim the product at white males ages forty-five to sixty-five?"

"Exactly." I assemble the perfect bite of cracker, jam, cheese, and prosciutto before popping the whole thing in my mouth. "Mmm."

We go on to brainstorm ideas on how to diversify the target market, and for the first time in a long while, I find that I don't feel at all frustrated while working, because unlike my usual meetings with patronizing finance bros, I'm not forced to argue or defend my ideas or tell the other person to stop interrupting or talking over me. I'm not forced to explain why I think this would be a good idea or why that would be a more sensible approach, and it hits me then how exhausting simply existing as a woman, and a woman of color at that, has been in the finance industry. But here, with Shang, I don't have to do any of that. When I share an idea, he simply listens and asks a question here and there for clarification, but he doesn't challenge me. He doesn't play devil's advocate—a thing I abhor with the passion of a thousand suns because the only time people play devil's advocates is when they have no stake in the matter, whereas I have to deal with endless devil's advocates every single time I step into a meeting.

When Shang says, "Shall I cook us some dinner?" I'm genuinely surprised to see that it's grown dark outside.

"What time is it?" I check my phone. It's almost eight o'clock. "Oh my god, I didn't know it was so late. Sorry, I didn't mean to keep you working on this. I can leave now, you probably have plans."

"Yeah, cooking." He says it so simply, in a way that's so different from how he is around his cousins. There is no shame in it, no hiding how much he looks forward to doing it every evening. He doesn't wear his mask around me, either, I realize with a warm glow that spreads throughout my entire body. Shang grins at me. "Are you hungry?"

"Always. But are you sure? I don't want to impose."

"I'm sure." Shang heads into the kitchen, where he peers into the fridge. "How does chow mein sound?"

"Sounds delicious."

"Yeah, and I'll get to see you shovel an ungodly amount of food into your mouth."

I roll my eyes, smiling. "Can I help?"

"Sure. Wash the vegetables, and I'll cut them. Hey, how come I didn't notice you taking giant bites when we were at the ranch?"

"Well, we were with your family then, so . . ."

"So you decided to act like a civilized human?"

"Correct." I hand the freshly washed cabbage to Shang.

"But you don't care about doing it in front of me."

"Nope," I say cheerfully.

Shang laughs. "You know what? I'm honored. It means you're comfortable around me."

"Yeah." My voice trails off in wonderment. This is it. No more roles. No more hiding. "I am comfortable around you, Shang," I say quietly.

Shang looks up from the chopping board. Our eyes meet, and the air between us grows thick. "I am too." He puts down the knife and reaches out, touching my cheek gently, his thumb grazing my skin, and it feels like I'm being touched for the first time. "I really like you, Zhou."

That name again. But this time, I don't let it break me. I accept the stabbing guilt and then push it aside. It's wrong, I know it, but I want this so much. I like him so much, and we're finally here, in a space where we're alone, where we don't have to speak in whispers, where we don't have to be Work Shang and Work Mulan, where we can simply be. I reach up and twine my arms around Shang's neck.

"Maybe," I say, "dinner can wait until after?"

CHAPTER SIXTEEN

Afterward, I dress in one of Shang's buttoned shirts and sit at the kitchen counter, watching as he cooks. I know I'm gazing at him with open adoration, but I don't care, because as he moves around the kitchen, Shang throws glance after glance at me, as though he can't bear to take his eyes off me, even for a minute. The two of us have spent so long trying to ignore or push aside our attraction toward each other that it's a relief to not have to pretend anymore.

"You're gonna burn my chow mein if you keep looking over at me," I tease.

Shang snorts, shaking his head. He sneaks a quick look at me before wrenching his gaze back to the wok. "It's just—you look so cute in my shirt."

"I know," I say with all the confidence in the world.

"You know, huh?"

"Yeah. Listen, I know I've got shortcomings, but not looking cute in a man's shirt is not one of them." My god. Who is this witty, confident person who's comfortable in her own skin and can make jokes without second-guessing herself all the time?

Shang does that laugh of his again, the one that makes the corners of his eyes crinkle, and I can't help but bite my lip as I smile stupidly wide. "Okay, well you're right about this one," he says finally. He finishes frying the chow mein and serves it up into bowls.

"It smells amazing." I stab my chopsticks into the bowl and pick up a huge tangle of saucy, greasy noodles. I take a big mouthful and then have to put my hand over my mouth as I breathe in and out to try and cool the noodles down. I've burned my tongue for sure, but oh my god, it was worth it. The chow mein is savory, with a nice charred flavor from the wok, and the noodles are still chewy, and the sauce Shang has cooked it in hits all the right spots. "Best chow mein I've ever had."

"Wow, high praise." Shang does the same as I did, picking up an extra-huge serving of noodles before shoving them in his mouth. This time though, he hiccups after swallowing and has to gulp some water to help the food down.

I laugh. "Noob."

"You know what, though? You're right. It does taste better when you take a huge bite like that. Whoa. Who would've thought?"

"Me. I would've thought."

Shang's gaze turns tender. "You're amazing, Zhou. There's something about you that just—" He shakes his head. "I can be fully myself around you. Only with you."

It feels as though my heart is both bursting with joy and shriveling up with guilt, all at once. "I agree," I say quietly. God, I want so badly to tell him the truth. All of it. Or at the very least the most important part, that my name isn't even Zhou. But he's also right in that, ironically, despite my deceit, I feel like I can be fully myself around him, and only him.

Shang leans against the counter, looking down at me, then he bends over and kisses me. I set my bowl down and kiss him back. He cups my face with one hand and I love it, I love him touching my face, I love wrapping my arms around his neck, I love kissing him even though our mouths smell of chow mein. Shang's hand trails down my neck, fingering the collar of the button-down shirt, making my skin tingle. With some effort, I push him away gently and say, "Do not get between me and my carbs."

Shang groans. "Really?"

"Yes, really." I pick up my bowl once more. "But I do eat quickly."

"Yes," Shang whispers, pumping his fist.

"See? Now you're glad I take huge bites of my food."

Shang's laughter fills the kitchen. "Yes," he says, dipping his head and capturing my mouth with his once more. "You're right. I am glad about that."

I can't quite remember the last time I was this happy. Maybe when I was away at college and I found myself surrounded by people who were as passionate about numbers as I was? Or maybe the first time my parents took me to Disneyland? I had been very happy then, for sure, bursting with excitement. But I can't remember the last time I felt this prolonged, sustained happiness. And more than just happiness, but contentment.

It's been over a week since we came back from the ranch, blissful, whirlwind days where Shang and I have been practically inseparable. Each morning, I go to work with a huge, dopey smile on my face and a tumbler full of latte that Shang has made on his espresso machine. At lunch, we meet up at a nearby restaurant and hold hands under the table like teenagers. After work, I bounce out of the office and meet up with Shang for dinner. He's cooked for me twice more, and taken me out to a beautiful French restaurant on a different evening.

Then we go home, alternating between his place and mine, and spend the rest of the night in each other's arms. We talk endlessly in bed. Once, we chatted so long that the sky melted from black to light purple before we finally dozed off, minutes before the alarm went off. I had to have three coffees that day, but it was worth it.

On our fifth day together, Shang came to my apartment. I had done my best to tidy up beforehand. As an additional precaution, I gathered everything I could find that said MULAN and drove the box of incriminating items to store at my parents' garage. Of course, my apartment was nowhere near the level of pristine his was, but at least it didn't look like the train wreck it usually is. But when Shang had opened the closet door to put away his clothes, he was attacked by my pile of junk tumbling down on him. I just about died of shame, but Shang had laughed for a full minute before grabbing me and squishing me and then, while kissing the top of my head, he said, "Let's go to the Container Store."

The Container Store. A store that I had only heard of but never set foot in. I was so intimidated at all the different-size containers, ranging from ones big enough to store an entire human body in to ones that are so teeny I have no idea what they're meant for. Maybe paper clips? Shang took my hand and led me around the store, picking out several containers, and within half an hour, we were on our way back to my place. If it had just been me in there all by myself, I would've wandered up and down the aisles, getting increasingly intimidated and frustrated, and two hours later I would've gone home empty-handed.

Somehow, Shang made even tidying up fun. And that is not even an exaggeration. I laughed a million times with him as we went through my stuff and he held up questionable things, like the whisk attachment of an electric mixer (except I'd long lost the mixer) and tiny thongs I'd gotten as a gag gift for my twenty-first birthday.

"Actually, maybe we shouldn't throw these away," Shang said, clearing his throat and putting aside the thongs.

"Stop!" I laughed, snatching them and stuffing them into a trash bag. Or tried to. Shang tackled me and we ended up rolling on the floor, laughing, before it inevitably turned into kissing and more.

The next day was a Saturday, so we worked on my place. Several times Shang would ask me, "What do you think, would you like this? Or maybe something like that?" And each time, I had to pause and really ask myself: *What do I like? What does the real me want for this space?*

And somehow, by the time the sun set, with Shang's coaxing, I had managed to let go of that part of me that's constantly asking: *But what would Baba think? What would my colleagues think?* And we made my place into a space I know I'm going to look forward to coming home to, which is a huge step for me. I've never given a second thought about my apartment. It has always been just a place for me to crash after endless meetings at work, and in the mornings I barely even look at my surroundings before rushing out the door. But now I find myself pausing at random moments—when I'm getting a glass of water, for example, or when I'm shrugging off my jacket—and looking around me with a sense of comfort and pride. This is my apartment, and it's not big or flashy, but it's . . . pretty. My couch, now that it isn't covered with jackets and random articles of clothing, is actually cozy. My kitchen is tiny but functional, and with Shang's help, I've added floating shelves and placed potted herbs in it, sprucing the space up. My bedroom is a place in which I now want to do more than just sleep: That Saturday night Shang stayed over, and in the morning we lounged for a long while in bed, reading, talking, sipping coffee.

I'm so happy that if I were someone else, I would absolutely hate me. But the happiness isn't perfect. For one thing, my dad is still ill, still in a hospital bed. His recovery is going slow, and I make sure to visit him as much as I can while juggling work and my newfound relationship with Shang. Not to mention the fact that I'm still lying to Shang about who I am. Each day, I promise myself that I will tell him the truth, and each morning, he wakes me up with a soft kiss and I feel my determination falter. *Just one more day*, I tell myself. *Give me just one more day of this bliss.* What we have is so precious, so priceless, that I can't bear to break it, because maybe that would break me.

What a thing to think of, when we've only been together for a few days, but already I can't envision going back to a life without Shang.

And I know he feels the same way, because already he's given me a key to his place, already he's cleared out an entire chest of drawers for me, already he's speaking in future terms. "For Thanksgiving, do you want to . . ." "For Easter, shall we . . ." "For Christmas, do you think . . ."

And I don't want to stop this ride. I want to think of spending Christmas with him, wearing matching ugly sweaters and sipping eggnog. I want to do weekend getaways and plan for longer trips and I want so badly to introduce him to my parents. I want it all, everything, every moment of it, and the knowledge that all of it might disappear because of this stupid, horrible lie I've told is excruciating.

On Tuesday, Mushu says, "I haven't seen you in three days, and that's three days too many. Shall we have dinner tonight and catch up?"

I feel a twinge of guilt. I've turned into one of those people who disappear into a black hole just because they're in a relationship. "Sure," I tell Mushu. I send Shang a text telling him I won't make it back for dinner and he replies with:

Ok. Are you still coming over? X

I smile and text him:

Yes x

Dinner with Mushu is exactly what I needed to clear my head. Mushu is the only one who knows the whole truth, so I can be honest and get her advice. As we settle into our seats at the restaurant, a sense of comfortable joy washes over me. I've missed quality time with my cousin.

"So," Mushu says, "Shang is really that amazing in bed, huh?"

I cough. "Mushu! Oh my god."

"What?"

"We haven't even ordered our drinks yet."

Mushu catches a waiter's eye, and when he comes over, she says, "Can we have a bottle of chardonnay, please? Thank you." The waiter nods and leaves and she turns back to me. "Right. Now can you tell me everything? Spare no details."

I laugh. "Oh, Mushu. I needed this."

"Yeah, me too. You've been shacked up in coupledom and forgotten me." Mushu pouts.

"I'm sorry. You're right. I kind of got swept up in Shang. He's so . . ." I sigh.

The waiter comes back with our wine and after it's poured out, we raise our glasses.

"To love," Mushu says.

"I don't know if it's love," I say.

Mushu rolls her eyes. "I've known you all my life and I have never seen you like this, ever. Not even with Nick, and you were with him for two years. Thing is, cuz, I just— I know we joke around a lot and it's hard for anyone to take me seriously—"

"I take you seriously," I say.

"It's not your fault," she says. "I don't take myself seriously. I guess I never felt like I deserve to be taken seriously. Anyway, what I'm trying to say is, I am being completely sincere when I say I think this is the first time that I'm getting a glimpse of the real Mulan, and I like her."

A knot forms in my throat. Mushu and I have always been close, but I never expected Mushu to read me this well.

"I give you a hard time for being the perfect kid and all that, and it's because I feel like you're always playing a role. But now, this thing with Shang, I know that it's not a role. It's just . . . you. And I love that for you. So don't get all stupid and mess it up because you think it's something you're not supposed to do or whatever, okay?"

I nod hurriedly, hiding how emotional Mushu's words have made me. "To love," I say, clinking my glass to Mushu's. Warmth rises from my neck to my face. *Is Mushu right? Is this love?* Of course, as soon as I ask myself that, it becomes painfully, startlingly obvious. I recognize this feeling at last, like finding a long-lost friend, and the realization makes me choke up a little.

"Wow," Mushu says. "Am I jealous? Yes, yes I am. Am I also happy for you? Yes!" She gets up from her chair and gives me a hug. "My cousin in love."

I laugh and wipe at my eyes as Mushu settles back in her seat. "I'm so scared, though. What's he going to do when he finds out I'm not actually Zhou?"

"Oh yeah, ooh. I forgot about that," Mushu says.

"How in the world did you manage to forget about that?"

"I don't know, I've got lots of things going on, you know. I have a roaring social life, as you know—"

"Of course," I say with a smile.

"So I can't keep track of all the details. Anyway, right. The Zhou thing. Oof." Mushu takes a sip of wine and stares off into the distance for a while, deep in thought. Then she snaps her fingers. "I've got it. The perfect solution."

I lean forward eagerly. "Yes?"

"You should legally change your name to Zhou."

I deflate. For a moment there, I'd really thought that Mushu had found an actual solution.

"Why not?" she says. "I mean, he's your dad, so it's not inconceivable that you might want to be named after him."

"So I'd be Zhou Junior?" I say dryly.

"Exactly."

"Okay, aside from all the legal ramifications, I don't know, I don't like the idea of continuing the lie. I want to be honest with Shang. I don't want a relationship based on a lie."

Mushu's expression turns sad. "Yeah, I know. So why don't you tell him?"

"Two reasons: I don't want to mess everything up with the acquisitions, and I don't want to lose him." Even just saying the words *lose him* makes my throat dry.

"Oh, cuz. That's tough."

"And this whole thing with the acquisition, I don't know why I didn't think of it sooner—the fact that we'd be working closely with his family once we buy their company. I guess I thought maybe that my dad would've gotten better by now and I could hand over the account to him, as planned, and I wouldn't have that much interaction with them and none of this would matter in the long run. I didn't foresee any of this happening." I take a deep breath. "I didn't foresee falling in love with Shang and my dad still being in the hospital."

Mushu reaches across the table and takes my hand. "I know. But soon this will all be over. You'll come to the end of the negotiations process and seal the deal and your dad will get better and things will be less up in the air and you'll be able to tell Shang everything then."

I give Mushu a weak smile and squeeze her hand. "God, I hope you're right."

In the morning, I wake up in Shang's arms. I stay there for a few moments, savoring his nearness, then reach over for my phone. I am mid-yawn when I unlock it and find seventeen missed calls from Mama. And Baba. My heart leaps and I sit up abruptly, opening the numerous texts from them. Next to me, Shang stirs and strokes my back, but my attention is fully on my phone.

Mulan, Baba got the green light to go home! Come
to the hospital once you see this!

"Oh my god," I say.

Shang sits up and kisses my cheek. "You okay?"

"Yeah, just— My dad's going to be discharged."

Over the past few days, I've told Shang vague details about Baba
being in the hospital. Shang's face breaks into a smile. "That's great!
Are you going to see him now?"

"Yeah, just as soon as I change."

"Would you like me to come with you?" Shang says.

My stomach twists with guilt. More than anything, I want to
take Shang to my parents. I want to bask in their joy at seeing him,
because of course they would be delighted to know that I've found
someone who loves me the way Shang does. But if I did that, my cover
would be blown and everything would turn to ash. "Um, I would love
to, but—"

Understanding dawns on Shang's face, and he looks so sweet that
I die a little inside. "You know what? It's fine, you should see your
dad on your own right now. I mean, he's just gotten out of the hospital and everything, he probably wouldn't want some random dude
rocking up."

Knowing my dad, I am positive that he would love to meet Shang
immediately, but I force myself to nod. "Yeah, I think I'd better see him
on my own this time. But I would love for you to meet him and my
mom at some point."

"Yeah?" Shang says, smiling and looping his arms around my waist.
"That would be nice. Because you've met all of my family, so it only
seems fair for me to meet yours."

"I know. I want that too." I reach over, kiss him, and try not to
think of the way my lies have snowballed into this awful, tangled mess.

Still, I tell myself, now that Baba is coming home, it'll all be okay. It will be.

I feel like a little kid again when I lay eyes on Baba. He looks tired, but he's standing up and out of his hospital clothes, and tears rush to my eyes as I hurry toward him and throw my arms around him. "Baba!"

"Mulan."

I lean back to take him in. "Oh my gosh. How are you feeling, Baba?"

"Surprisingly good. If I'd known how refreshing a two-week rest would be, I would've done it a long time ago."

"Oh, you," snorts Mama. "Stop spouting rubbish."

Baba laughs. "I really do feel good. A bit sore on my back, though."

"Yeah? I mean, if all you feel is some stiffness, I'd say that's pretty good," I say, wiping my eyes.

Ma hands Baba a peeled tangerine. "Here, you should eat nutritious foods."

"Thank you," Ba says. He turns back to face me. "Tell me everything that's happened at the office."

"Not work already," Ma snaps.

"Oh, you must let me have this one," Baba says. "I've never been away from work this long before."

"Well, don't get too stressed out," Ma warns.

Don't stress him out, I think. Great. I scrap the possibility of telling him what I've done with Shang's family. I focus on our other accounts, giving him a detailed summary of the important updates, and Baba listens for a while, but then he raises his hand. I stop talking.

"Sorry to interrupt, my dear, but I have a feeling we'll be kicked out of here soon, so let's get to the important stuff: Any updates with Wutai Gold?"

My jaw clenches tight as I mentally scramble to knit together a passable story. "Yes, things are progressing really well with them right now, actually. We're through the negotiations process and tomorrow we're going to sign the papers."

"Ah!" Baba's face brightens. "Wonderful. How did that happen? Did you spearhead the whole thing?"

"Yes." I find it next to impossible to meet his eye.

"Oh, Mulan." Baba reaches out and grasps my hand, and when I do look at him, I'm shocked to find him teary-eyed. "I'm so proud of you."

"Ba, I didn't know Wutai Gold meant so much to you."

"It's not that." He squeezes my hand affectionately. "Yes, I thought they would be a good acquisition, but from my conversations with them, I didn't think they'd want to have you as the point person running this deal. My plan had been to have you attend the meetings and have you win them over with me by your side. So the fact that you've managed to handle it and bring it home is . . ." His expression softens as he gazes at me with pride. "So impressive. You are the flower that blooms in adversity."

"Oh, Ba . . ." My eyes fill up once more.

"And this tells me that you are ready to become a partner at the firm, and soon enough, you'll take my place as managing partner."

I've wanted to make partner for so long that for a second, the magnitude of his words doesn't sink in. And when it does, I want to scream with both joy and frustration, because this is not how I wanted to make partner. For years I've thrown everything I have into the job, first one in and last one out of the office, coming in on weekends when needed, only going home when the rest of the world seems to already be asleep, and I was happy doing it because I was doing a damn good job. And now that I'm finally getting what I wanted, it doesn't feel at all good. It feels terrible, it feels like a curse. It's tainted, and it's all my own fault.

But Baba is gazing at me with a familiar expression, the same one he's worn whenever I do something right—when I fell off the beam in gymnastics but then climbed on again and finished my routine, when I graduated from Princeton, when I closed my first deal at the firm. It's a look I treasure, and I don't have it in me to ruin it, not just this moment. And definitely not when my father is still recovering.

So I hug him and say, "Thank you, Ba. I'm honored."

"I'm so proud of you," he says again, patting my cheek. "You're the best kid a father could hope for."

"Only because I got the best dad." I pat his arm and straighten up. "I have to run now, but I'll drop by the house later this evening, after the office."

Baba smiles. "See you later."

I keep my head down all the way to the parking lot, my face burning with shame and anger at my brashness, my foolishness. Once I reach the privacy of my car, I grip the steering wheel tightly and wail. Looking up, I see that I've shocked a passerby. I grimace and mouth a *Sorry*, but they hurry away.

I utter a heavy sigh and let my head drop onto the steering wheel. There's a sharp rap on the car window. Startled, I jerk back up. It's Ma. I roll down the window, my heart thudding so hard I feel it in my throat. "Hi, Ma. What are you doing down here?"

"You left your phone," Mama says, holding it out to me.

"Oh, thanks. I would've been in trouble without it." I take the phone, keeping my eyes on it instead of Mama.

"What's going on, Mulan?" Ma says.

"Nothing," I say quickly. Too quickly.

Ma merely looks at me without saying anything, until I crack. "It just— Everything's a mess, okay, Ma?"

"Oh, Mulan. What is it? Tell me."

"No, I can't— Oh." I watch helplessly as Ma marches around the front of the car and slides into the passenger seat.

215

She closes the door and folds her hands on her lap. "Okay. Now tell me."

I squeeze the phone to keep my hands from shaking. "I don't even know where to begin," I whisper. Though Ma knew of the lie that I had cooked up to save the acquisition, I'm pretty sure she doesn't realize the extent of the whole charade and how out of hand it's gotten by now.

"How about you start by telling me about this nice boy you've been seeing?"

I jump, my head swiveling to face my mother. "You knew?"

"How can I not know when my own daughter is in love?" Ma gently tucks my hair behind my ear.

"Ma," I sob, feeling like I'm all of five years old. "I think I'm going to screw it up."

"Start from the beginning."

And so I do. I tell her everything. Ma listens with rapt attention, uttering a small gasp here and there, making a sad *mm* noise when appropriate, but whatever she does, she keeps her hand on my arm, and the love on her face never fades, not even a little, not even when I tell her about how Shang is falling for me as "Zhou."

When I'm finally done, I still feel terrible, but I feel a little lighter, like the weight crushing my chest has lifted a tiny bit, just enough to allow me some breathing room. I let out a long, defeated breath. "So there you have it. And now I just don't know what to do."

"Oh, Mulan," Ma says again. She places a hand on my cheek. "You do know what to do. You've known all along."

I lift my gaze to meet hers, and I know that Ma is right. I do know what to do. "I need to come clean to him. To his family."

"Yes," Ma says. "And you need to do it before you finalize this deal. A business partnership cannot happen based on a lie. As for the boy . . ." She looks out of the windshield with a little smile. "I think if he loves you, he'll get over it."

"It's a pretty major lie to get over. Technically, he doesn't even know my name."

Ma laughs.

"Ma!"

"I'm sorry, it is a little bit funny."

"You can't say that," I cry. "You wouldn't like it if someone did that to me."

"Oh, I would take a cleaver to their house."

I groan. "See? It is bad!"

"I'm just joking. Or am I? But honestly? Yes, it's bad. But from what you've told me, it seems that it led to true love. Who knows, if you hadn't pretended to be Zhou and done all these ridiculous things, you and Shang might not have found each other. And you are treating each other well, with love and respect, so I think you'll overcome this. He'll see that you were foolish, yes, but beneath the foolishness, he should know that your heart is good."

I nod, feeling tears slip down my cheeks. "I hope so."

"Now off you go and do the right thing."

CHAPTER SEVENTEEN

don't sleep a wink that night. I lie in bed, turning one way, then the other, then back again, and so on and so forth until I give up and turn on my bedside lamp. Shang and I had a call earlier to say good night, but I didn't want to tell him over the phone, so I held it back the entire time. Now, as I check my phone, I find a text from Shang.

> I'm missing someone. She's the funniest
> woman I know.

Smiling, I text back:

> Funniest? That was the best you could come
> up with?

I'm about to put the phone down when three dots appear.

> Shang:
> And the most beautiful. And the smartest. And the
> coolest.

> Me:
> Thank you, that's more like it.

I put the phone down, then pick it up again.

> Me:
> Hey, tomorrow morning can you meet me before
> the meeting?

> Shang:
> I promised my mom I'd pick her up to come to the
> meeting. I can pick her up early and see you at the
> office before the meeting is due to start?

I gnaw on my bottom lip. It's not ideal having Shang's mom in the office as well while I tell him the truth, but I can take him aside for some privacy. All I know is, I need to tell him before I tell his entire family. Ugh, what terrible timing it all is.

> Me:
> Yeah, that works. Maybe come in twenty minutes
> early? I'll make sure to have some breakfast ready
> for your mom so she can eat while she waits.

> Shang:
> Thank you, that's so considerate. X

I place the phone back on the nightstand, flop back into bed, and try to will myself to sleep. It goes about as well as expected.

The following morning, I jerk awake when my alarm goes off. Groaning, I turn the alarm off and push myself up. I must've had less than an hour of sleep. I feel rough, as though I have a hangover even though I didn't have anything to drink the night before. Then reality hits me and I sit up straight. Today is the day when I tell Shang the truth. And his family. And hope it doesn't blow our deal wide open.

Who am I kidding, it will most definitely blow our deal wide open, or at the very least delay it. But my mother is right, I can't go forward with either a personal or professional relationship based on a lie. Best-case scenario, the Lis laugh it off and say they knew all along. Worst-case scenario, they lawyer up and sue the firm for all it's worth, and Baba loses the company he spent the last two decades building from the ground up. Not to mention I'll lose the best relationship I've had in years. Or ever. Great. No biggie.

I take my time getting dressed, applying my makeup with extra care and choosing a navy blue pantsuit. I nod at my reflection and say, "You look like someone who's about to blow her life up." Nope, too negative. "You look like someone on a mission. A really impossible one." Wow, I suck at pep talks. I release my breath in a huff, grab my keys, and leave the apartment.

As promised, I stop by a bagel shop on the way to the office and buy two dozen bagels and four different tubs of cream cheese. I know I am overcompensating and probably trying to assuage my guilt by overfeeding everyone, but at the very least Shang's mom won't go hungry while I have the world's most awkward conversation with her son. When I get to the office, I instruct everyone to please just not call me Mulan when the Wutai Gold people show up.

"Do you want us to call you Zhou?" Josh the analyst says. I guess word has gotten out about me asking Mushu and Gerald to call me Zhou last time.

"No," I say. I am so tired of being Zhou. The last thing I want to hear is anyone calling me Zhou.

They all look at me with apparent confusion. Mushu raises her hand.

"Yes?" I say wearily.

"Is there a name you'd prefer us to use, or are you in, like, a nameless era right now, like a rapper or a yogi?"

"Oh, right." I sigh. God, I'm too tired to even put on my Work Mulan mask and say something professional. Of course I haven't thought of a name for myself. "Just. I need to do something, and can you all just not . . . mention my name at all until after I do the thing? If you need me, I don't know, just tap my shoulder or say 'Hey' really loudly or something."

Mushu nods with a satisfied smile. "Yep, she's in her yogi era. This is Transcendent Mulan. Oops, sorry, not Mulan. She whose name shall never be uttered."

"Okay, glad that's sorted." I hand the bagels over to an intern and instruct him to lay them out nicely in the conference room. Then I signal to Mushu to follow me into my office. As soon as we have privacy, I turn to her and say, "I'm going to tell Shang the truth."

"Damn, okay," she says.

"Today. Right now." I check my watch. "Well, in a few minutes. He's coming here before the meeting with Wutai Gold."

Mushu's eyes widen. "Really? Before the meeting?"

"Yeah, and it has to be before the meeting because"—I take a deep breath—"I'm telling his family the truth, too."

Mushu whistles. "Wow. Have you thought this through?"

I nod. "I can't go through with the buyout knowing that I've lied to them this whole time."

"Okay. I've got your back no matter what."

"Thanks, Mushu."

"Even though I think you're making a terrible mistake. I'm telling you, changing your name legally is the way to go."

"Yeah, okay, thank you." I shake myself, smiling a little as Mushu leaves the office. How does Mushu manage to make me laugh even at a time like this?

I check my phone again. Shang should be here by now. I look up, peering through the glass walls of my office, half expecting to see him arriving with his mom, but the reception area is Shang-less. I open up our text thread and begin composing a message, but then delete it. He's probably on his way, and I don't want him to text while driving.

The minutes crawl along, painfully slow. I sit at my desk, one foot wagging nervously, picking up my phone every now and again in case I've somehow missed a text from Shang. Just then, a message arrives. But it's not from Shang. It's from his mom.

> Auntie Jiayi:
> Hi Zhou, this is Auntie Jiayi. Shang told me to
> message you because he is driving. There was a car
> accident on the road, looks like we will be late to
> the meeting. Shang is very sorry.

"No!" I groan out loud. "Damn it." I quickly type out a reply thanking Auntie Jiayi for the update, then bury my face in my hands. Now what? I don't want to ambush Shang with the news in front of his family; after everything the two of us have shared, he deserves to be told this in private. My palms are so sweaty by now that my phone slips out of my hands and drops onto the floor. I barely register it. *Breathe.* But I can't. There's a fist around my chest and it's squeezing. *Stop that. Stop. Get a freaking grip.* I force myself to take a deep inhale and count to five before releasing it in one long, continuous exhale.

The answer comes to me slowly. It's too late for me to cancel the meeting now; the Lis are probably all on their way. So the next-best thing would be to stall. Yes. I'll tell them that there is a slight delay, that the legal department is still ironing out small kinks—yes, that's good, every contract has kinks—and that we will be ready later today. Or the day after, whatever works for the Lis. And as soon as I can get Shang alone, I will immediately tell him.

I grip the armrest of my chair, tightening and loosening my hands as I go over the new plan. As far as plans go, it's not a brilliant one, but it's decent, and that's the best I can hope for under the circumstances. The Lis aren't going to be pleased about having their time wasted, but they're businesspeople—they are not unfamiliar with delays and minor disruptions like this.

By the time the Li family arrives, I'm as ready as I can be. I greet them at the reception area, giving each one a firm handshake, telling them how nice it is to see them again. I'm leading them into the conference room when Shang and his mother arrive. He hurries out of the elevator as soon as the doors slide open and greets his family but doesn't stop walking until he's in front of me.

"Hey, I'm so sorry I couldn't get here earlier," he says.

"That's okay, don't worry about it," I say.

There's an awkward pause as we both notice everyone in the office—the Lis and my colleagues—is watching us. I clear my throat. "Anyway, I'm glad you're here. Let's get inside." The last thing I need is for the rest of Shang's family and my colleagues to find out about my relationship with Shang. We're not exactly hiding it, but we haven't announced it officially yet, and this is definitely not the most auspicious of times to be doing that.

Everyone files inside the conference room. Mushu is the last one in, and she closes the door behind her.

This is it. I stand at the head of the conference table and force a smile as I gaze down at the expectant faces. "Good morning, everyone, I'm so glad you could make it here today."

"It's very good seeing you again, Zhou," Uncle Hong says. "You are an impressive young lady and we are excited to sell our company to you."

James scowls, but everyone else nods genially.

"Thank you, Uncle Hong," I say. "I'm so honored that you've decided to sell Wutai Gold to us. I know how much the company means to you and I promise you that we will do right by it and preserve your legacy. And that is why we are taking extra care with the contracts to make sure that everything is perfect." The words feel leaden, thunking out of my mouth, awkward and obviously untrue. I keep going. "There are a few kinks that we still need to iron out, but—"

There is a knock at the door. I frown at Mushu, who jumps up.

"I'll let them know not to interrupt," Mushu says, hurrying to the door. She opens it and slides out.

I face the Lis once more. They're looking somewhat less pleased now, except for James, who's looking smug. "Are you saying the contract isn't ready?" he says.

"James," Shang says in a warning tone.

"Well—" I begin, my voice faltering. This is not good. In fact, it is bad. Very bad. Can't possibly get worse.

There is a knock at the door again. "We're having a meeting here," I call out. My nerves are pretty much shot by now, and I can hear the shrill tone in my voice. Could things get any worse?

Then the door opens and Baba totters inside, holding a walking stick and wearing a huge smile. "Ah, I am so sorry to interrupt, but I insisted that I must meet all of you in person while we sign this momentous contract."

Nobody speaks. Everyone stares at him. My brain implodes. I stand there, frozen, my insides warring over what to do. Currently, the part of me that's screaming at me to just up and run and never stop is winning.

Then James blurts out, "Who are you?"

"I'm sorry, I have forgotten to introduce myself. I am Zhou. Hua Zhou. The managing partner of this firm."

I was wrong. It can get worse after all.

After that, there is no saving the meeting. The conference room explodes with noise—mostly angry questions fired like a machine gun, overlapping one another.

"I'm sure there's an explanation—" Auntie Jiayi begins, but is quickly shushed by the others.

"What do you mean you're the managing partner?" James demands.

"Maybe there are many partners in this firm?" Auntie Lulu says.

"Are there also multiple Hua Zhous here?" Uncle Jing snaps.

Within the sheer panic building inside me, my major concern is Baba's health. All of this nasty shock and horror can't be good for his heart. "Ba," I say, "can you maybe wait in your office and I'll explain everything to you in a bit?"

Baba looks around, confused, at the angry crowd, then back at me. For a moment, he looks as though he might argue with me and insist on staying, but then he nods. Raising his hand, he turns to the Lis and says, "I apologize. It seems my arrival has caused some confusion. I will leave. I trust my daughter will resolve this." He walks toward the door and as he leaves, he says, "It was very nice meeting all of you. A real honor."

He leaves behind him a horrible, gaping silence, a black hole that sucks everything into its center. I want to shrivel up into a tiny ball and disappear, but somehow, I force myself to look at them. To see the one face I need to see.

And when I do see it, it is devastating. Shang is looking at me like he's seeing me for the first time, and he doesn't like what he sees. I finally understand the concept of heartbreak. All the relationships I've had in the past, the way it felt when they ended, they were nothing compared to seeing this look on Shang's face. The disappointment and sadness. I feel not my heart but my entire soul ripping itself apart.

"I—" I say. I falter, but somehow, from deep inside me, I find a tiny kernel of strength. I cannot break apart right now, even though I want to. I don't deserve the luxury of falling apart. Not yet. This is my bed, and now I get to lie in it. "I am sorry. I have something to tell you. The real reason behind the delay. And that is that Hua Zhou is, as you just saw, my father, and not me. I am Hua Mulan. The day before you were supposed to meet with my father, he had a heart attack and was hospitalized. The last conversation he and I had was about Wutai Gold and how much this acquisition meant to him, and I didn't want to lose it. I felt from your reputation and the correspondence you've had with my father that you wouldn't take me seriously as a daughter, a woman, so I felt that I had no choice but to pretend to have been Zhou all along. I wanted to do right by my father, and in doing so, I did a very bad thing to all of you, and for that I am so sorry." My voice trembles as I speak, but I manage to get all the way to the end without breaking down. I look at Shang, willing him to understand, to empathize, but he still looks so disappointed that I know without a doubt that we are over.

"Well," Uncle Hong says, getting out of his seat. "We are leaving now."

"I told you," James mutters loudly as he stands.

There are unhappy murmurs all around as everybody stands and files out of the conference room. I wait until Shang nears me. I reach out to touch his arm, but stop short of making actual contact. "Shang—"

He drops his eyes, turning his face ever so slightly from me.

My throat closes up. I let him go. I can't talk to him without bursting into tears right now, and I can't have that on top of everything. I simply stand there and watch all of them leave. Mushu hurries toward me, wraps an arm around my shoulders, and squeezes.

"Thanks, Mushu," I whisper. I sniffle, then gather whatever pieces of myself I can muster up, and leave the conference room. I pretend not to notice everyone peering over their cubicles as I make my way to Baba's office.

I knock before coming in. "Ba."

He is gazing out of the floor-to-ceiling windows. "They left, then?"

"Yes."

"You pretended to be me?"

I now feel like a little kid who's broken my dad's priceless vase. "Yes." My voice comes out in a whisper.

"Why?"

"I— From your emails with Shang, it was clear they wouldn't agree to deal with anyone other than Zhou."

Baba finally turns around to look at me. "That's the surface reason. What's the real reason?"

"I don't know, Ba. You'd just had a heart attack. I thought we were going to lose you." My voice breaks then. "I didn't want to lose you, and I didn't want to lose the deal, because it felt like losing you."

"Mulan," Baba says, and though his voice is sad, there is a world of love in his eyes.

"I'm sorry, Ba. I ruined everything."

Like many Chinese parents, Baba isn't the type to hug, but he does so now, albeit a little awkwardly. Then he releases me and says, "Let me tell you about the time I left the gate open and lost all Grandma and Grandpa's sheep."

I laugh-sob. "You did not do that."

"Oh, I did. Thirteen sheep, they had, and all of them gone, just like that. It was their livelihood. We nearly starved but for the help of our neighbors and family."

"Ba," I say again through my tears.

"We all make mistakes, Mulan."

A mistake. It seems ridiculous to think of this awful mess as a mistake. More like a failure on a massive scale. I'm grateful that Baba doesn't hate me the way everyone does right now, but I'm still left with a giant wreckage that I've created, and no idea how to fix it.

CHAPTER EIGHTEEN

I've never once hated living alone. I love the solitude my apartment gives me, the way it's the one quiet place I can return to after a long, hectic workday. But this evening, when I walk through the door, the silence hits me hard. My apartment feels so empty, devoid of a soul. I stand in the hallway and see the ghost of Shang on the couch, reading a book. When I look straight at the couch, he disappears. I can still smell him, though.

"Stupid," I say out loud, just to have some kind of noise in the dead silence. I shake off my shoes and walk off, then come back to put them away neatly. Even now, I can't deny that the peace that comes with having a tidy, uncluttered place is gratifying.

I put away my coat, then go to the bathroom to wash my hands. Even the bathroom is spotless. Shang and I did a visit to Target, where I found a pretty glass tray for the bathroom, along with a matching soap dispenser and toothbrush holders, and just that one minor change spruced up the entire sink area. Everywhere I look, my apartment is painted with memories of Shang. How? We've only gone out for a few days.

The sadness inside grows into a boulder, crushing me. I look into the mirror as I wash my hands. I look so tired and haggard, not at all like a twenty-something-year-old. Sorrow and worry line my face. I splash my face with some cold water, then walk out of the bathroom and into the kitchen.

It's worse in here. The kitchen is where Shang and I spent most of our time together. Aside from the bedroom, that is. And in here, we worked as a team, me washing the ingredients while Shang chopped them up. Shang cooking the meat and vegetables while I got the rice cooker going. A quick kiss on the back of his neck as I reached past him, a squeeze of my arm as he slid past, an affectionate hand brushing through my hair. A hundred different ways of touching each other. We couldn't keep our hands to ourselves, not even while cooking, and it wasn't even sexual most of the time; it was just us wanting to reach out and touch each other, as though we were extensions of the same spirit.

Tears burn my eyes. I take my phone out of my pocket. I texted Shang earlier in the day, but all he said was:

I need some time.

It's not unreasonable, nor cruel. He hasn't even said a single angry or hurtful thing to me, and I know I deserve them. I deserve to be called a liar, a dishonorable thing, a coward, and he hasn't said anything of the sort. Even now, after the way I have betrayed him, Shang remains kind. He needs time. I can give him that, at least.

Brushing away my tears, I stuff the phone back into my pocket and shake my head, as though trying to shake off the memories of Shang. I blow out my breath.

"Come on, Mulan," I say out loud. "Get it together." Just because I've made a giant mess of everything else doesn't mean I should let my new good habits fall on the wayside, too. I'm going to cook myself dinner. I open the fridge and there's the last straw.

The refrigerator is filled with neatly lined up containers, all of them stocked full of fresh ingredients. It is this final reminder of Shang that breaks me. Uttering a short cry of pain and rage, I slam the fridge shut.

God, he was so good for me. So, so good. And I've done nothing but ruin it all.

"Stop," I say out loud to the whirling rage of self-hatred inside my head. "Stop it."

Instead of stopping, it grows in intensity, overwhelming me. I crouch down on the floor, hugging my knees to my chest. Even just standing feels too much right now. Everything is too much, all of it. All my life, I've felt pressured to hide my true self, because everything centers the men in my life. Trying to impress them, or prove them wrong, or make sure they're not disappointed. My father, my schoolmates, and later, my colleagues, my clients, and now the Lis. With all of them, I've scrambled to put on the right mask, and I'm so good at it, have done it for so long, that I didn't even know the real me anymore.

Until Shang.

All my life, I've been masking—and it feels like having to suck my stomach in all the time, and it's only with Shang that I've been able to let everything go and completely relax. A sob wrenches out of me as I think of how I was when I was around Shang. I was still the hard-working finance bro, responsible and intellectual and confident, and I was still the loving, filial child. But I was also something more. I was a goofball around him. I was fun, and silly, and brash. When was the last time I was brash before Shang came into my life? I'd been so uptight that my idea of risk was jaywalking across an empty road. But Shang brought out that part of me. He also brought out the selfish part of me, the one who, for once, isn't thinking: *What would Baba do?* The part of me that knows exactly what it wants and isn't afraid to go for it, no matter how irresponsible. Shang brought me back into myself, a self that I'd thought was missing. And I don't want to lose that self again.

That realization brings me a tiny bit of peace. Sniffling, I uncurl and push myself off the floor. I go into the bathroom and splash cold water over my face again before looking in the mirror. My reflection stares back at me, and I see myself then: A very flawed person, someone who's made so many mistakes, so many bad decisions. But also maybe someone who's made bad decisions because of the right reasons. Someone driven by love and duty. Someone driven, period.

I force myself to go back out into the kitchen, open the fridge again, and this time, I grab a cloth bag from the cupboard and start taking things out from the fridge.

Ten minutes later, I'm back in my car. I make a phone call. "Ma, don't bother cooking."

When I arrive, my parents greet me with happy but confused smiles. "What are you doing here?" Ma says.

I hold up the bag of ingredients. "I'm going to make dinner for you guys."

"Oh my," Ba says. "I think we have some antidiarrheal tablets left from our last trip."

"Ba!" I snap, and he laughs. "Hey, Baba, can we talk for a second?"

"Always."

"I'll let you two chat," Ma says, taking the bag of groceries from me and bustling into the kitchen.

In the living room, I plop down on the sofa with a big sigh. Now that I'm actually here, seeing my dad in person, I find it hard to know where to begin. "Um, so . . ." I flail mentally. Baba is looking at me with so much expectation in his eyes that it's paralyzing. Expectation. That's it. That's where I can start. "When I was a kid, I overheard Auntie and Ma talking, and how Ma couldn't have any more children because of me."

Baba's face falls, and it looks as though he's about to say something, but he stops himself and gestures at me to keep going.

"And Auntie said, 'What a shame because of Mulan you had to

have that awful operation. And she isn't even a boy!' And ever since then, I knew that I had to make it up to both of you, and I've been doing it my whole life. I have this intense fear of letting you and Ma down because—"

"Oh, Mulan," Baba says. "You work so hard. You are—" His voice cracks then, and he takes a shuddering breath. "Oh, Nu er, I am sorry you heard your auntie say that. I never, not for a moment, regretted having you as my child. You are worth ten sons. Twenty!"

A weight that I hadn't even noticed was there before is suddenly lifted off my chest. "Really? You never secretly wished for a boy?"

"Hah!" Ma shouts from the doorway.

Baba and I both jump.

"Mulan, what is this rubbish?" Ma cries. "Do you really think that your baba and I would rather have had a son?"

"Ma, but Auntie—"

Ma snorts, and flaps a hand dismissively. "Oh, my sister. She's stuck in the old ways. And do you not remember your cousins? Kenny and Keith? Such terrors they were. Within the first hour of visiting they'd broken our TV. I bet Auntie only said that because she's jealous that she doesn't have a daughter."

I laugh through my tears. "Oh, Ma."

Ma hurries over and envelops me in a fierce hug. "You are everything we wished for."

"And more," Ba says, reaching over and grasping my hand.

"I'm sorry I messed everything up with Wutai Gold," I say when Ma lets go of me. "I know you really wanted to acquire them."

"Oh, Mulan. I did want to acquire them, yes, but not for the reasons you think. I wanted you to acquire them. I wanted you to assess them, not just purely with your mind, but with your heart and your instincts. You are so good with numbers. But what we do is so much more than numbers. Anyone can look at the numbers and make a decision to buy or not, but you want to know my secret? Why I have such a good success rate?"

I nod.

"Because I look for something off the page. I look for resilience. It is the one thing that drives someone to succeed, because they will get up again and again, no matter how many times it takes. And that's what I saw in Wutai Gold. It's what I see in you. And I wanted you to see that for yourself. It takes a special gift to see how a struggling company can become successful because of the people behind it."

A light dawns inside me. So that's why he wanted me to take Wutai Gold home. "I understand."

"I know you do. And I'm proud of you. For everything you've become." He touches my cheek and smiles, nodding. "Shall we start cooking?"

"Yes," I say, wiping the last of my tears away. We stand, me giving my dad's arm one last squeeze, and make our way into the kitchen, where Ma has taken out the pork, scallions, cabbage, and other ingredients that I've brought.

We chat as I chop up the scallions the way I've seen Shang do, then mix them into the minced pork. I add ginger, Shaoxing wine, salt, pepper, soy sauce, sesame oil, and oyster sauce before stirring it all up with a pair of chopsticks. Then I take the bowl over to my parents, as well as a pack of premade dumpling skins, and say, "Let's make jiaozi."

"My goodness, Mulan, where did you learn to do this?" Ma says, picking up a dumpling skin and placing a dollop of pork filling on it.

My mouth turns into a thin line before I finally say, "Shang."

"Ah," Ma says, her expression turning soft. "And how are you two doing? Have you talked?"

I shake my head, keeping my focus on the dumpling I am folding. "He says he needs time."

"Time heals all wounds," Ba says. "It's a Chinese saying."

"Pretty sure it isn't, Ba."

"I'm sure there's a Chinese version."

"There is, actually," Ma says. "In Chinese, we say 'Time's a great healer.'"

"Huh," I say, crimping my dumpling closed and placing it on a plate. "I like that."

Somehow, despite everything falling apart, I feel a semblance of peace, right here in my parents' kitchen, making dumplings with them. The physical act of folding dumplings is a great way of channeling the frustration and sadness inside me, and the easy conversation keeps my mind off the bleak mess of my life. And the conversation I had with them has eased such a weight from me. A weight I've carried for decades, a weight I probably would've carried for the rest of my life if I hadn't met Shang. I have no idea what will happen between Shang and me, but I hope that I might one day be given the chance to thank him for everything he's done for me.

With three pairs of hands working, it isn't long before all the pork is used up and we end up with two big plates of dumplings. I heat up the wok, then place the dumplings in carefully. I splash in some water and close the lid. Halfway through, I pour in a cornstarch slurry, then close the lid once more before getting to work on the dipping sauce. When I turn around, I find my parents gazing at me with wonderment.

"You really learned all that from Shang?" Ma says.

I shrug, my cheeks growing warm.

Ma and Ba exchange a look. "I've been trying to get her to learn how to cook basic dishes all these years and all it took was a boy and *poof*, she's a chef," Ma says.

I groan. "Whatever, Ma."

They both cheer when I finally announce the jiaozi is done and slide them out onto a plate. I put another plate on top of it and flip it over, revealing a crispy layer on the bottom. My parents *ooh* and *aah* at the sight. I step back and admire my handiwork.

"Wow, can't believe that actually worked."

"Was that the first time you made this dish by yourself?" Ba says.

"Yeah. I wasn't sure if I would burn it or not. Anyway, dig in."

We dip the jiaozi in the homemade sauce and take a bite.

"Mulan!" Ma says, her mouth still full of jiaozi. "This is so good, oh my goodness. I am shocked."

"Okay, Ma, you don't have to be, like, so surprised." I take a bite and my eyes go wide. "Oh wow, these are good. Good job, me."

"These are delicious. Even better than the ones your mother makes."

Ma smacks Ba's arm. "He's right, though. These are better."

I sigh. "Well, I guess if our firm gets sued to the ground I'll open up a dumpling shop."

"No use worrying about that right now," Ba says.

And, somehow, sitting here in my parents' house eating dumplings, I manage to not worry about things, just for a bit.

After we finish eating, I allow myself a peek at my phone. No texts from Shang, but there is one from Mushu, asking me out for drinks. I could really use a drink right about now, so I reply and tell Mushu I'll meet her at our usual bar. I kiss my parents goodbye and leave, and half an hour later, I'm in the heart of the city, in an upscale bar called Ginger Flower.

Mushu arrives looking as fabulous as always, wearing a silk dress with a cutout that shows off her abs.

"You look nice," I say.

"Thank you. You look tired."

"Rude."

"Well, you're beautiful, so you can get away with looking tired," she says.

"After the day I've had, I am tired." I pour wine into Mushu's glass and we clink glasses.

"I'm sorry about how things went down," Mushu says. "You okay?"

I take a long sip of wine. "I'm about as okay as I can be in this situation, I guess."

"You'll be okay," Mushu says firmly. "I know you. You're strong. Stronger than anyone I know, including myself."

"Thanks, Mushu. You know, you sell yourself short."

"Not really. I just tell it like it is. Look at me, I took this job at Eighty-Eight because I had no idea what else to do after college and I really thought I'd have it figured out by now, but nope."

"You will. I know it. You're way too vibrant and capable not to."

Mushu coughs and waves a hand in front of her face. "Okay, enough of that. Change of subject before I feel too awkward and duck out."

Smiling, I tell Mushu about making jiaozi with my parents.

"Aw, that is so sweet. But wait, you make jiaozi now? Who are you and what have you done with my cousin?"

"That's what my parents said, too. Am I really that bad of a cook?"

"You weren't bad, you just . . . never did it."

I laugh. "True."

"So what are you going to do about Wutai Gold?" she says.

"I'll apologize to them, obviously, but I'm not sure when and how to do it. I doubt any of them would give me the time of day now. And they have every right not to."

Mushu looks at me with concern. "And Shang?"

I sigh. "He says he needs time, so." I take another gulp of wine and look out the window for a while, letting my mind wander. It's a weeknight, so the area isn't too busy. I'm watching a couple strolling down the street hand in hand when the mention of Wutai Gold catches my attention. I turn back to Mushu. "What?"

"I didn't say anything."

I swivel in my seat, scanning the place. I could've sworn I heard someone say Wutai Gold. Then I see him. James, sitting two tables away. *Argh.* I grab the drinks menu and hold it up like a shield. I lean forward and hiss, "James Li is here."

"Where?" Mushu looks around.

"Don't look. He's there, to our left." I cock my head.

Mushu peers over the menu, then ducks behind it again. "You're right."

"Just when I thought the day couldn't get any worse."

"Well, at least he hasn't seen us."

I nod, thanking my lucky stars that Ginger Flower keeps its lighting very, very dim. The place is only half full, and most patrons are speaking in low voices, unlike James, who seems to be the only person speaking at full volume. I roll my eyes at his obnoxious loudness. But then I catch more of his conversation and for the first time, I think that maybe there is some good to James's loud voice after all.

"I think he's . . ." My voice trails off as I peer over the menu, this time to look at the man sitting across from James. My mouth drops open. "No way."

"What?" Mushu says.

"He's having drinks with Richard Foreman."

"Who?"

I sigh. "Mushu, I love you, but you are in the wrong industry."

"Tell that to someone who cares. Who is it?"

"It's our biggest rival? Remember? The guy who was so obsessed with my mom that he tried to destroy Eighty-Eight Capital?"

Mushu's mouth turns into a perfect circle. "Ooh, that guy. Yeah, I remember now. Why is James meeting with him?" She gasps. "Do you think they're plotting revenge?"

A pit opens up in my stomach and despair floods me. "Very

possible." I can definitely see James talking with Richard about what I've done, and Richard using it to his own advantage, maybe giving James advice on how to use this as an opportunity to sue the hell out of us.

I listen harder, closing my eyes so I can better focus on the two men. There are gaps in the conversation, but I manage to catch the gist of it, and somehow, it's even worse than I'd expected.

James: "Thank god that deal fell apart."

Richard: (Laughing) "Eighty-Eight Capital is small fry, not worth spending time talking about."

James: "I don't know why Shang didn't take you up on the offer to meet up. I swear, I love my cousin, but he's just not a visionary."

Richard: "No, he isn't. He shouldn't be the CEO of your company."

James: "Fucking right he shouldn't. I don't know why they voted him in. My whole family acts like sunshine comes out of Shang's ass."

Richard: "It's a good thing you and I see eye to eye. Your company is too traditional, it's a relic, a dinosaur. It won't make it past your generation. You know that, don't you?"

James: "I do, that's why I've been urging them to sell for the longest time. I just didn't foresee Shang wanting to sell to Eighty-Eight Capital."

Richard: "Well, now that that's no longer on the table, we should make our move. My team is drawing up a proposal as we speak, and I will have it sent to you by Monday."

James: "And you're still good on our deal?"

Richard: "You will get a very nice cut of the package."

James: "Good. I fucking deserve it, after all the shit I've had to put up with."

They clink glasses.

James: "Out of curiosity, what are you going to do with Wutai

Gold? That Eighty-Eight Capital bitch, whatever her real name is, kept yammering on about diversifying our customer base."

Richard: "Like I said, Wutai Gold is a relic. Your brand is worth very little, given your aging customer base. The real value is in the proprietary information. Your recipe, your technique. Everything else will be broken down into parts and sold off."

There is a beat of silence.

James: "Damn. The end of an era. Can't say it won't make me sad."

Richard: "I'm sure your cut of the deal will make the sadness easier to bear."

James: (Laughing) "Fucking right it will."

I've heard enough. "Let's get out of here," I whisper to Mushu, who nods. I put some cash down on the table, and then we stand and leave as discreetly as we can manage. Outside, I notice that Mushu's grabbed our bottle of wine as she left.

"I've got good priorities," she says when she sees me looking at the bottle.

"Never mind the wine. Oh my god. Richard Foreman and James."

"Yeah, that's messed up. So he's trying to get this deal done behind everyone's backs?"

"I don't know if that's possible. He'll still need the board of directors to agree, but I think he's going to let them think that it's a similar deal to ours when it isn't. He's going to destroy their company," I say.

"Damn, and for what?"

"Did you not hear them? For money. James is getting a cut on the side."

"That little worm. We should march in there and tell him what a piece of shit he is."

As much as I would love to do that, I force myself to take a beat to ponder. "No, we have the advantage. They don't know that we overheard them."

Mushu frowns. "Are you going to tell Shang?"

"I have to." I take out my phone and call him. I'm so swept up in what I've just found out that I don't even hesitate until I hear the dial tone. I fight the urge to hang up, and stay on the phone, counting the number of rings. After the fifth one, he picks up.

"Hey," Shang says.

"Shang, don't hang up," I say quickly. "It's me, Mulan. Uh. Zhou. But I'm really Mulan. Uh, anyway, I need to tell you something about James and Wutai Gold. I heard—"

"Uh, Mulan, I'm going to stop you right there," Shang says. "I cannot discuss matters of the company with you any longer. I'm sure you understand. And I still need some space to think. Have a good night." With that, he hangs up.

I stare at my phone, emotions storming inside me. "He hung up."

"Damn it. I'm sorry. Are you okay?"

I blow out my cheeks. "I—I can't think about him right now. His family company is in trouble. I need to warn them."

"Yeah, I don't think any one of them is going to talk to you. Or me. Or anyone at Eighty-Eight Capital."

"Oh god, you're right," I groan. I pause. "Maybe Auntie Jiayi might talk to me."

"Shang's mom? Really?" Mushu looks skeptical. "I mean, no shade, but if I were his mom I wouldn't talk to the person who hurt my kid."

I wince. "I know. But she's so kind and she seems to be the most levelheaded person in the family. Anyway, it's worth a try, right?"

"Sure, I guess so. Are you going to call her now?"

"It's so late. I'll text her."

It takes us over fifteen minutes to compose what we think is a decent enough text to send. I start off by apologizing for everything once more, then say I have urgent information about the company that involves Richard Foreman and James and that though I understand that Auntie Jiayi has no reason to trust me, I really need to relay the information to someone at Wutai Gold.

I hit send, and exhale. "There. That's that. All right, I'm going home. With any luck, in the morning I'll wake up and find that this whole day has been nothing more than a bad dream."

Unfortunately, I don't wake up to find that the previous day was just a dream. I do, however, wake up to a reply from Auntie Jiayi.

> Auntie Jiayi:
> Hello Mulan. We should talk. I will meet you at
> Lamian Paradise at eleven a.m.

I sit bolt upright. Holy crap. I can't believe that Auntie Jiayi is willing to meet up with me after everything that's happened. I quickly type out a response.

> Thank you so much, Auntie. I'll be there.

I spend the morning bustling around my apartment, trying to pass the time by doing various chores. Several times, I think of Shang and how cleaning is his hobby. And now I can't keep my mind off him as I clean. I rehearse what I'm going to say to Auntie Jiayi.

I arrive at Lamian Paradise well before eleven and perch nervously on my seat. This is even worse than waiting for my finals to begin. When Auntie Jiayi arrives, I jump out of the chair and greet her awkwardly, unsure if she would want a hug from me. Luckily, she does, enveloping me into her arms. I close my eyes and will the tears back. It's a close battle, but I win.

We sit down and I pour some chrysanthemum tea into Auntie Jiayi's cup. "Thank you so much for meeting me, Auntie."

Auntie Jiayi nods. "I am curious about what you have to say. But before that, I just have to ask: Why?"

I lick my lips before replying. I've rehearsed this a dozen times, but now that Auntie Jiayi is sitting in front of me, looking concerned and sad and so terribly present, all of my carefully crafted words have dissipated from my mind. "I didn't want to disappoint my father," I say finally.

"Ah." Auntie Jiayi takes a sip of her tea. "I understand this. I've been wondering, you know, ever since we found out about it. Because you seemed like such a nice girl, not someone who would lie to us. But there is one other reason why you felt you had to do what you did."

I look at her quizzically.

"The fact that you're a woman, and you're right: There would've been nothing you could say to win my brothers over if you hadn't lied to them. I know this is a fact. I grew up with my brothers, and I have had to lie and go about things in sneaky, roundabout ways to be heard by them."

Guilt coils like a snake in my belly. "Thank you for saying that. It still doesn't excuse what I did, but I appreciate you acknowledging that part of it. I'm so very sorry."

"I know," Auntie Jiayi says simply. "I can see it on your face. You're not someone who is used to lying."

"No."

"Another question: What about my son?"

I didn't think I could feel any worse, but I do now. Oh, how I do. "I think he's probably done with me. I don't blame him, by the way."

"Not that," Auntie Jiayi says, waving a flippant hand. "I mean, what you two have—or had—what is it?"

I'm so taken aback by this that the answer blurts out of me before I realize it. "Love." There it is, raw and true in its simplicity.

Auntie Jiayi smiles, and her eyes crinkle at the corners, just like Shang's. In that moment, she looks so much like Shang that a knot forms in my throat. I take a sip of my tea to try and clear it.

"Ah, I knew it," Auntie Jiayi says. "Because I could see in Shang's face also, you know. I have never seen him so happy before."

"I haven't been that happy before, either," I say quietly. "But it doesn't matter now anyway, because I told you, he's done with me."

"Oh, that." She flaps her hand again. "What rubbish. Of course he is not done with you. He just needs some time to sulk a little. He can be quite sulky, you know, that Shang."

I laugh. "Good to know. To be fair, though, if I were him, I would be very sulky, too."

"Oh yes, of course. If I were Shang I would thunder everywhere. But never mind, he'll get over it."

"I hope you're right."

"Okay, so now tell me, what is this urgent thing about James and Wutai Gold?"

I lean forward and tell Auntie Jiayi everything I overheard last night. I'm surprised to find that Auntie Jiayi doesn't seem in the least bit shocked by the news. In fact, she hardly reacts at all until I finish speaking. Then she says, "Hmm."

That's it? I've just told her about a whole conspiracy that her nephew has cooked up to stab them all in their backs and all she says is "Hmm"?

"You look surprised," Auntie Jiayi says.

"Yeah, I kind of am, because I was expecting you to, I don't know—"

"Be angry? Be shocked?"

"Yeah, actually."

Auntie Jiayi smiles. "You young people, always having such big reactions."

I bite my lip, thinking of how raucous the Li uncles and aunties are around one another.

"Is it really so shocking, this thing?" Auntie Jiayi continues. "James has always wanted to sell the company. His heart's never been in it."

"Yeah, but this firm he wants to sell to—they're not going to keep Wutai Gold's legacy going."

Auntie Jiayi sighs. "The Wutai Gold legacy. You ever heard of this saying: Zhong nan qing nu? Heavy male, light female. It means: *Men are worth more than women.* That is the real Wutai Gold legacy."

I grow sad listening to Auntie Jiayi. None of this is news to me, of course, but hearing it coming from Auntie Jiayi somehow makes it that much worse.

"For years, my brothers have told me to shut up, be quiet, listen when men are talking. I still care about the company, so when I have good ideas, I suggest it to them. But I can't just say the idea, oh no. If I did, they will ignore it because it came from a woman. No, I have to say it in little pieces here and there, make them think it's their own idea. And it's tiring, but I do it. I sacrifice for the family, because I love them." Auntie Jiayi sets her teacup down. "But I do not love Wutai Gold."

I look at Auntie Jiayi, really seeing her for the first time. Not as an auntie, or a mother, or a sister, but as a person in her own right, an individual with her own dreams and goals. For the first time, I see beyond the laugh lines of Auntie Jiayi's face and I can imagine Auntie Jiayi as a young woman, moving from China to America, full of youthful vibrancy and hope for the future.

"What was it like for you, when you first came here?" I say.

Auntie Jiayi gets a faraway look in her eyes. "Exciting. Oh, so exciting! You know what America is called in Chinese? Mei Guo. *Beautiful country.* And it is. San Francisco is very beautiful, isn't it? When I first arrived, I thought: This is a different place. And I will be a different person. I watched the Americans, you know, especially American women. Even the way they walk is different. They walk with a purpose, big strides, like they are all so important, going to important meetings and making important decisions. I thought to myself: Yes, this is who I will be. I will be an important person, too."

"You are important," I say, my voice almost breaking with earnestness.

Auntie Jiayi scoffs. "No. I'm not. When I try to walk like them, my brothers and sisters-in-law say: 'Why are you walking like a man, Jiayi? Walk like a woman. Don't embarrass us.' Every time I tried to make a change, they stopped me, they told me don't be stupid, what would people say? This is a Chinese phrase that people always say: Ren jia kan. *Everyone will look*. Don't do this or that, because ren jia kan. Everything I did that was outside of the norm, they'd say: 'Stop that! Ren jia kan!' And it would embarrass me enough into stopping, because what could possibly be worse than being judged for being different?" The last few words are said loud enough to turn heads at our direction, and Auntie Jiayi smiles and says, "See? Ren jia kan."

I nod. I'm familiar with that phrase, too. Not so much from my parents, but from other parents who disapproved of the way that my parents raised me.

"The thing is, I was scared. My husband had passed away, I had a child, and I only had a high school diploma from China. I didn't speak English like you kids do, so I couldn't get a real job. So I listened to my brothers. I was—still am—grateful to them for looking after me and Shang. They built Wutai Gold out of nothing, and I thank the Merciful Goddess every day that she has blessed us with this. But what they seem to have forgotten is that it was me who gave them the idea to start a whiskey distillery."

"What?" I cry. My head spins with this newfound knowledge.

The corners of Auntie Jiayi's mouth curl up into a small smile. "Oh yes. Back in China, who do you think made all of our baijiu? It was me and the other aunties, of course. We were the ones who harvested the grains and fermented them and built our own homemade distillery using buckets and dough to keep it airtight and all that. All the men ever did was drink the liquor once it was done. What do they know about distillation? We couldn't find baijiu easily when we first moved here, so I made it in our garage. And one day, I said to my brothers, 'Why don't we make bigger batches and sell to our neighbors?' And so we did."

"That's amazing, Auntie," I say. I still can't quite digest the enormity of this news. To think that without this woman sitting in front of me there wouldn't even be a Wutai Gold to speak of is staggering. And knowing the way the men in the family have continuously disparaged and belittled her despite her contributions is enraging. "I'm so sorry that you were never given the recognition you deserve."

Auntie Jiayi shrugs. "This is their legacy."

"I hate that they did that to you."

"Yes, well. It is who they are. It's okay, I see the younger generation, like you and Shang, and I have hope. You kids are so strong, look at you, Zhou—I mean, Mulan—you stand up straight, you dress like a man, you talk like you know everyone will listen, and they should, because you are a very smart person."

I look down at my pantsuit. "Do I really dress like a man?"

Auntie Jiayi laughs. "I have been listening to your ideas, you know. During our meetings? They are very good. My brothers are very foolish to not want to work with you. If they really care about saving their precious legacy, it's very clear they should work with you."

"You really like my ideas?" The little kid inside my heart is grinning with excitement at this.

247

"Yes. Why wouldn't I like your ideas? They are very good."

Whether it's the talk or the tea or hearing Auntie Jiayi's story, the beginning of an idea starts to sprout in my head. "I might have one right now that might prove to your family that I have what it takes to save their brand, but I'm going to need your help."

Auntie Jiayi leans forward, her eyes shining. Once again, I'm struck by the vibrancy of her. Once more, I see the younger version of Auntie Jiayi, her face bright with a million possibilities, her heart wanting to do something bold, something that would make ren jia kan. And I realize that maybe this isn't just my second chance, after all. That maybe it's also Auntie Jiayi's second chance to make a statement. To finally be heard, and acknowledged for all the wisdom she's carried with her and shared with her family. To claim her credit for helping build the company into what it is today.

"I am in cahoots with my future daughter-in-law," Auntie Jiayi says.

I laugh. "Okay, Auntie, calm down, you're going kind of fast for me."

"We talk business now."

And so we do.

CHAPTER NINETEEN

The thing about being a VP at a private equity firm is, I have a million contacts in various industries. And I know exactly which ones to call now. I stride back into the office with my head held high, and I'm struck by what Auntie Jiayi had said, how women here walk with purpose. It's true, and I savor the walk. It's only possible because of all the sacrifices that people like Auntie Jiayi have made. I ignore the looks from the other employees and nod at Mushu, who jumps up and follows me into my office.

"How did it go?" Mushu says.

I fill her in as quickly as I can, then say, "We're going to show them that Wutai Gold is worth saving, and I know exactly how to do it. Make a list."

Mushu takes out her phone and looks expectantly at me.

"All right, that banquet that's happening tomorrow night—"

"The Women Entrepreneurs one?"

"Yes. Who's organizing it again?"

Mushu doesn't skip a beat. "Alicia Lopez."

"Oh, nice! I met her at a conference last year." I scroll through my contact list and find Alicia's name. I tap dial and put the call on speakerphone.

Alicia picks up on the second ring. "Mulan, girl, it's been a while. How's it going?"

"Hey, Alicia! It's been way too long. I'm here with Mushu."

Mushu calls out, "Hey, Alicia, how are the kids?"

"Adorable monsters as always. Kevin has teeth now, if you can believe it. Makes breastfeeding super fun. Not."

"Ouch," I say, wincing. "Anyway, I know you're really busy, so I'll get to the point. I'm calling about the Women Entrepreneurs Awards."

"Yes, what about it?"

"Is it too late to be a sponsor?"

"A sponsor? Are you kidding? Of course not. It's never too late. All right, I'll put Eighty-Eight Capital on the list."

"Actually," I say, "could you put Wutai Gold down instead?"

"The whiskey company? Really?" Alicia pauses. "I've seen their ads. Why do they want to sponsor our event? They know it's not a thing celebrating cis white males, right?"

"Yeah, they're thinking of changing their brand, branching out a little."

"Okay." Alicia sounds hesitant.

"We will donate two large crates of the finest Wutai Gold whiskey."

"Done," Alicia says immediately.

I laugh. "Well, that was easy."

"Free whiskey? You are speaking my language."

"In exchange for Wutai Gold banners and posters at the event."

"Fair enough."

"And you're having the event at the Regency Court?"

"That's right."

"Great, thanks, Alicia."

"See you there!"

I end the call and turn to Mushu. "Who do we know at Regency Court?"

"The events manager, Brooke Tanaka, used to work at Phillips and Jones."

"How do you remember all this?" I say in wonderment. Once again, I scroll through my contacts list, locate Brooke's name, and make the call.

"No, not the taupe one, I said beige." Brooke's voice snaps out of the phone. "Hey, Mulan, it's total chaos here. What's up?"

"I won't take long. Are you managing the Women Entrepreneurs Awards ceremony?"

"Yes, hence the chaos. Um, can someone please get Ricky down from up there? He's breaking like a million health and safety codes right now. Sorry, what were you saying?"

"The drinks—they'll be made in-house?"

"Yep."

"We're providing whiskey for the event and I would like to have one or two new cocktails using the whiskey, if possible?"

"Sure, let me connect you to the bartender."

"Thank you, Brooke."

"For fuck's sake, Ricky—" The call is abruptly cut off.

Mushu and I stare at each other. "Funny how I used to think finance was the most stressful industry to work in," I say. "Sounds like event planning is even worse."

"Really? Sounds great to me. You get to boss people around, throw a shit fit over taupe versus beige. . . ."

A text message from Brooke comes in.

Brooke:
Sorry, hung up by mistake. Here's the bartender's contact.

I call Susie the bartender and explain the situation and what I would like.

"Don't worry," Susie says. "I gotchu." She hangs up.

"Oh." I give Mushu a look. "That was quick."

"I like Susie. I have a crush on her."

251

"You don't even know what she looks like."

"I'm not shallow," she says. "By the way, I like this plan, except the part about providing them with two large crates of Wutai Gold's finest? Can I ask how you're going to swing that? Are you going to drain your savings? Embezzle money from the firm? I am always down for some embezzlement."

"Mushu, you should so not be in finance." I sigh. "No, Auntie Jiayi is going to source us the whiskey."

"Damn, Auntie Jiayi showing up. You know, I bet she'd make an excellent mobster. She's sweet, she's gentle, she's slightly terrifying."

"I don't disagree. Our work isn't done. Who do we know in the media? We want them to know about Wutai Gold's new look."

Mushu rattles off names of publicists and influencers, and we get to work calling them one by one. Then I call in a favor from a design company we acquired some years back and ask them to come up with a simple, elegant design for Wutai Gold. By the time we're done, I am exhausted. I sit back in my chair and let my head fall back. "Oh no," I say, jerking upright. "Now we need to find the right outfits."

Mushu jumps up. "Heck yeah we do! Come on, we're going shopping. I know just the place."

"This is never a good sign," I say, recalling with painful clarity the outfits Mushu made me buy for the ranch.

"When have I ever led you wrong?"

"Not even going to answer that one." Laughing, we leave the office in search of the perfect banquet outfit.

Surprisingly, the boutique that Mushu takes me to is pretty freaking amazing. It's a small, understated shop a block away from Union Square called, simply, Posy's.

"Posy Lee is a second-generation Chinese American whose designs blend Chinese-inspired clothes with modern American fashion, which results in beautifully unique outfits," Mushu says by way of introduction.

Posy and I both stare at Mushu, before we burst out laughing.

"What?" Mushu says.

"Did you memorize that from the bio page on my website?" Posy says.

"I have a photographic memory," Mushu says.

"You literally can't remember a single thing about finance," I say.

"Let me clarify," Mushu says. "I have a photographic memory when it comes to things I care about."

I'm about to tease Mushu again when I realize that, in fact, Mushu is right. When it comes to things like these, Mushu's knowledge is practically encyclopedic. She's proven that again and again this entire day. All I had to do was say, *Who was the person in charge of . . .* and Mushu would immediately tell me. She knows everybody in the city.

"Mushu," I say in wonderment, "you are wasted at Eighty-Eight."

"I know," Mushu says with her usual flippant confidence.

"No, really."

Mushu pauses, looking slightly taken aback. "Okay. I mean, sure, but it's not like I'm drowning in job offers."

"No. But we're about to attend a banquet for female entrepreneurs," I say. "And I think that's what you should be. You don't need a job offer. You're going to create your own business."

"Doing what?" Mushu says.

"Event planning," I say.

"Oh, she would totally be perfect for event planning," Posy chimes in. "You would, Mushu."

Mushu wrinkles her nose like she's about to tell us both that we're being ridiculous, but then her expression turns vulnerable. "You really think so?"

"Yes!" Posy and I say in unison.

"Well." Mushu looks down at her feet. "Well, shit. Okay. I will think about it."

Posy and I grin at each other.

"All right," Posy cheers, "now that we've done that, let's look for the perfect outfits for you two."

We spend the next hour trying on various outfits, each more beautiful than the last. Posy likes using meticulously embroidered Chinese silks, and many of the dresses have elaborate Chinese beasts like dragons and phoenixes on them. Others have delicate plum blossoms in an elegant spray.

Mushu picks a red backless dress with a tiger embroidered onto the hip. "Business in the front and party in the back," she says, turning around and showing off the back.

Peeping out of my changing room, I give her a thumbs-up.

"Show me yours," Mushu says.

I step out of the changing room and Mushu and Posy gasp.

"What do you think?" I say.

"You look like a goddess," Mushu says.

"The wrathful kind," Posy adds.

"Is that a good thing?"

"Yeah, who wants to be the merciful kind?" Mushu asks. "All the hot ones are villains."

I turn to look in the mirror. The dress I have on is gold, with a dragon swirling around it in a darker shade of gold. Every time I move, the dress shimmers under the lights, making it look as though the dragon is moving. It's long-sleeved and doesn't show much skin, but it hugs my body in all the right ways and somehow makes me look, as Mushu and Posy said, dangerous in the most alluring way. It's impossible to take my eyes off the dress. And I know beyond any doubt that this is the right dress for me. It's both feminine and powerful at the same time. Exactly how I want to be from now on. No more alpha male façade. I want to be myself—both feminine and strong.

"Posy, you are a magician," I say.

Posy bows.

Later, as we walk out, I marvel at our success: "I can't believe we actually managed to find outfits for tomorrow."

"See? All you had to do was trust me," Mushu says.

The next afternoon, Mushu comes over and we get ready for the event together. When we're done with our hair and makeup, I put on my dress and then survey my reflection in the mirror. I look stunning, quite literally; I am stunned whenever I catch a glimpse of myself. Who is this badass, beautiful woman who looks ready to take on the world? It's me. And I have a company to save.

The Regency Court hotel is a luxury hotel in the heart of San Francisco. The awards ceremony is in the Grand Ballroom, and its name suits it perfectly. Seating five hundred guests comfortably, the already opulent space has been decked out to the nines for the event. There are spectacular flower arrangements everywhere, along with beautifully set tables and state-of-the-art lighting that makes the large space seem somehow warm and intimate.

Mushu and I are greeted by Alicia Lopez as soon as we arrive. "Oh my god," Alicia screams, "look at you two! You are a vision."

"Thank you, you look amazing as well," I say.

"Yeah, didn't you just come back from mat leave?" Mushu says.

"Yes, that's why my boobs look amazing." Alicia leads us deeper into the ballroom. She'd instructed us to come early, so there are no guests yet. "The posters you sent arrived safely and we've got them set up at the bar."

Sure enough, there are two big posters flanking the bar. The design is simple yet refreshing, showing a bottle of Wutai Gold whiskey with a feminine-looking hand next to it holding a whiskey glass filled with amber liquid.

"Hi," the bartender says. "Are you Mushu and Mulan?"

"Susie the bartender," Mushu breathes, her face lighting up. She turns to me and says, "See, I told you she's hot."

Susie laughs. "Thank you. And so are you. Come try the drinks. I've created two. This is the Wutai Gold punch. It's a fun twist on an oldie. Milk, vanilla extract, and I added blended banoffee to it."

"Banoffee?" I say.

"Banana toffee."

I take a sip and close my eyes in ecstasy. "Oh my gosh, that is yummy. It tastes like a dessert."

"I love it. It's so rich and creamy but you can still taste the spice of the whiskey," Mushu says.

I take another mouthful and let it linger on my tongue, savoring the comforting sweetness.

Susie smiles. "I'm glad you like it. The second cocktail is the Wellness Drink. It's got freshly squeezed lemon, honey, ginger, and turmeric. All stuff that's good for you. Aside from the whiskey, of course." She winks as she slides the glasses over to us.

"Oh, this definitely tastes like something I would chug while doing yoga," Mushu says.

We all laugh.

"This is so good," I say. "I can't decide which one I like more. They're both brilliant, thank you, Susie. Everyone's going to love them."

Brooke Tanaka arrives, looking as frazzled as she'd sounded on the phone. She hugs and kisses everyone. "You all look incredible," she says. "How are the drinks?"

"Perfect," I say.

Brooke beams. "Susie's a genius. No, table twelve can't have peonies, because Gilly Anders is allergic."

I'm confused for a moment, then I realize that Brooke is speaking to her earpiece. Brooke sighs and turns back to us. "I don't know why I thought being an event manager was a good idea."

I nudge Mushu, and she stumbles forward a little. "Uh, Brooke, I was wondering if I could pick your brain about event planning one of these days?"

Brooke's mouth drops open. "Mushu! Are you thinking of doing it?"

"Maybe?"

"Oh my gosh! You are going to be brilliant at it. This is totally your calling."

Mushu smiles bashfully. "Really?"

"Yes. You'd be perfect at this. No better job in the world—wait, why are they removing the lilies? Gotta run." With that, Brooke rushes off.

Mushu turns to us, her eyes shining. "Phew, the adrenaline."

I grin at my cousin. I can't recall the last time I've seen her this excited about something.

"Mulan," someone calls out.

We all turn to find Auntie Jiayi.

"Dang," Mushu says.

I agree with her. Auntie Jiayi has opted for a shiny black gown worthy of the Met Gala. It has a stiff collar that plunges into a deep neckline, revealing very ample cleavage. Gone is the timid, quiet, unassuming auntie I knew. In her place is an empress.

"Auntie Jiayi," I say, "you look— Wow."

"Thank you, dear, you look very nice, too. And you, Mushu, very sexy."

I introduce Auntie Jiayi to Alicia, who thanks her profusely for the whiskey donation. Susie presents Auntie Jiayi with the cocktails, and Auntie Jiayi downs the Wellness Drink in one long gulp. When she sees us staring, she shrugs and says, "Oh, I don't want to be sober when my brothers come here, they will give me headache."

"They agreed to come?" I say nervously.

"Yes, of course. I tell them it's big event with many businesspeople for them to make new contacts with."

"Did you tell them the businesspeople are all going to be women?" I say.

Auntie Jiayi gives me a look and starts in on the punch. Her heavily lashed eyes widen. "Oh my, this one is very nice, like drinking a dessert."

"Thank you, ma'am," Susie says.

"Hang on," Alicia says, "so your brothers, who make up the rest of the board of directors, don't know that this is the Women Entrepreneurs Awards ceremony?"

"No," Auntie Jiayi says blithely, drinking more of the punch.

Worried that this might annoy Alicia, I say, "Um, I think—"

But a devilish grin has appeared on Alicia's face and she says, "Excellent. I love shenanigans. I love them even more when they involve showing men that women should be taken seriously."

I breathe a sigh of relief. "Right, Mushu and I are going to, uh, make ourselves scarce for a while. There's a real danger that the Li family might leave once they see me, and I want to make sure they have some time to take all this in and see the reactions of the guests to these cocktails."

Auntie Jiayi reaches out and squeezes my hand before giving me a nod that says: *You've got this.* Mushu and I walk out of the ballroom and locate the powder room. Fortunately, the Regency Court is so fancy that the bathroom has chaise longues in it. We settle down and exhale slowly.

"You did well," Mushu says.

I glance at her. "Yeah? You think they'll like it?"

"Objectively, those cocktails are delicious, and I don't even like whiskey. Everyone is going to love them, and if the Lis can't get their heads out of their butts long enough to see it, then that's not on you."

I shake my head, snorting. "Mushu, what would I do without you?"

"Nothing good."

"Agreed."

We spend the next half hour chatting on the chaise longue and listening to the growing noise of the crowd outside. Then the sounds of hundreds of people chatting and laughing turns low and is replaced by someone speaking into a mic.

"I think it's safe to go inside now," I say.

We leave the bathroom and slip back into the ballroom, where we find our assigned seats. Brooke and Alicia have kindly put us two tables away from the Wutai Gold table. Far enough away not to be spotted, but close enough for me to be able to watch them.

I recognize Shang before my mind catches up, like my entire being is poised to spot him. I know it's him before I even see his face, from the now-familiar figure of him, the way he sits, the shape of his head, and the broadness of his shoulders. He's wearing a tux, and damn it if he doesn't look good.

I swallow and pick up my water glass, willing my heart rate to slow down. I hope he doesn't see me. Not yet. But I also will him to see me. I want to see the look on Shang's face when he takes me in wearing this dress. I want to know if I'll still have an effect on him the way he does on me.

Alicia is up on the stage, thanking everyone for coming.

"Tonight, we are excited to celebrate the most dynamic, the most exciting, the most influential women entrepreneurs," she says, her voice loud and clear over the speakers. Everyone cheers and claps.

Well, almost everyone. I can see that the Li uncles are openly confused, looking around while frowning. Uncle Hong leans over and says something to Auntie Chuang, who for her part looks like she's enjoying herself. James looks bored as he swipes at his phone with one hand, his other arm slung over the back of his chair. Even the way he sits is somehow douchey. How does he do that? Sit in a douchey way? Does he try hard to be douchey, or does it come naturally?

"Judging by the sneer on your face, you're looking at James," Mushu says.

I startle and uncurl my upper lip, turning my attention back to Alicia.

"The women we are honoring tonight have not only excelled in male-dominated industries but also made the world a little better for other women," Alicia says. "The success of their businesses will pave the way for future generations so that hopefully by the time our children enter the workforce, they won't have to deal with as much patriarchal bullshit as we did, huh?" She winks at the audience, who clap and hoot.

The Li family is now looking markedly uncomfortable. Uncle Hong is looking around warily, like he's expecting something to come out at any time to ambush him. I suppose that, technically, this is a sort of ambush.

"Before we start giving out the awards, I'd like to take a moment to thank our sponsors. Tonight was made possible thanks to the following companies: Pigeon and Heart, Small Galaxy Travel . . ." As Alicia reads out the list of sponsors, everyone cheers for them. "And last but not least, Wutai Gold, who have kindly donated the fine whiskey, which I trust we are all enjoying?" More hooting, though there is also a confused murmur scattered around the ballroom, presumably from people who are familiar with Wutai Gold's alpha male ad campaigns.

"And now, for our first award: Most Promising Brand of the Year goes to Rabbit Habit!" Alicia announces to an enthusiastic round of applause. "Who doesn't love their ethical, cruelty-free products. . . ."

As Alicia continues talking, some of the tension leaves my shoulders. I watch the CEO of Rabbit Habit climb onstage to accept her trophy. For a while, I lose myself in the moment, savoring this night, this event that celebrates women who have worked their asses off to break through the glass ceiling. I clap hard when the CEO of Rabbit Habit finishes her acceptance speech, cheering along with everyone else in the audience. More awards are given out, and each time, I applaud vigorously, grateful to be present here.

When all the awards have been given out, the waiters glide out with appetizers. I get up from the table and move away from the side of the ballroom where the Lis are seated. Instead, I visit other tables, talking to many guests and asking if I could record a short video of them. Everyone here is kind and supportive and hyped up, and before long, I have enough footage. I go back to my table and open my video editing software. With Mushu's help, we come up with a one-minute-long video and upload it to every social media platform we can think of. Armed with her phone, Mushu begins the work of sharing it, tagging every influencer she knows, which is a lot of influencers.

I watch the view count go up, slowly at first, steadily, then blowing up rapidly, growing exponentially, and I lick my dry lips, unable to believe that it's working so well. By the time the meal is over and people stand up to move onto the dance floor, the view count is at over two hundred thousand, and I am ready to face the Lis.

CHAPTER TWENTY

It is Shang who spots me first. He's standing at the bar, holding a glass of Wutai Gold punch and frowning at it thoughtfully as he sips, when he glances up and sees me. He does a double take, his mouth slowly opening as his eyes widen, taking me in. His gaze is surprised and admiring and intense all at the same time, and he places his glass down at the bar without even looking at it before walking toward me.

"Was this your doing?" Shang says.

I nod, searching his face for clues as to how he feels about all of this. Is he angry? Disappointed? Betrayed? "We'd mentioned it when we were brainstorming for ideas on how to reach a new audience." There is a slight tremor in my voice.

"We did," he says softly.

"I ran it by your mom, and she loved the idea."

Shang tilts his head back for a second and makes an *ooh* sound. He looks down at me again. "So that's how you got enough whiskey for the banquet." He looks over his shoulder to where his family is sitting. Auntie Jiayi lifts her cocktail glass and winks at him. Shang snorts. "She's not even trying to hide the fact that she's watching us."

"Um, yeah. Did you know that your mom is a badass?"

"Yeah," he says simply. His gaze rakes over me once more, slower this time. "Zh—Mulan. Damn it."

"I'm sorry," I say quickly. "I never meant to deceive you like that.

Well, I guess technically I did, but I never meant to take things as far as we did. I didn't know I was going to fall in love with you, it was only supposed to be about business."

Shang gives me a strange look, so I continue talking. "I suppose maybe that makes it even worse, actually. Look, I wasn't thinking straight, okay? Bad decisions were made. By me, yes. I guess I just thought—"

"Mulan," Shang says, "wait."

My mouth snaps shut.

"Back up a little. You fell in love? With me?"

I shrug, feeling my face reddening. "Sure, yeah, it's not a big deal. I fall in love with a lot of things. Sunsets. Puppies. A really good pumpkin spice latte."

Shang merely watches me with a slightly amused expression on his face.

I sigh. "Yes, Shang. I fell in love with you, okay? And I know what I did was highly irresponsible and ethically catastrophic and you never want to see me again, so maybe we can move on from the whole falling-in-love part? I need to tell you something about—"

"Why do you think I never want to see you again?" Shang says with genuine confusion.

I gesture. "Uh, because of the whole 'I pretended to be Zhou' thing?"

"Were you pretending when we cooked together? Or when we snuggled up on the couch and binge-watched *Love Is Blind*? Or when we kissed?"

"No! Of course not. None of that was a lie. It was only the whole thing about my name, but everything else was real."

Shang takes one step toward me. "Exactly. I know that. I was there with you the whole time, remember? I know that that was the real you." Another step, and he's suddenly so achingly close to me.

I want so badly to reach out and take his hand, but if he pulls away I don't know how I would bear it. *Please take my hand.* He doesn't. Instead, he reaches out and caresses my cheek.

"All I said was that I needed time," Shang says gently. "When that whole thing happened, my mind was a mess. I couldn't think straight. Hell, I went home and I went into the kitchen to cook and I just— I forgot what I was doing and I stood there for ages with my knife in one hand and an unpeeled parsnip in the other. I was not exactly functional. So yeah, I asked for some time, but Mulan, I never once thought that you and I were over. I'm sorry that I didn't make that clear. I'm sorry I let you think that we were done."

This can't be real. After everything I've done, all the lies I've said to him, he can't be this kind, this loving. I lift my hand and pinch my cheek (the one he isn't currently cupping). It hurts. "This is real," I say in wonderment.

"Yes."

"You're not breaking up with me?"

"No."

"Why not?"

"Because I'm in love with you, Hua Mulan."

This moment is perfect, and I never want to forget it. The way my entire body sings, the words Shang has just said, the exact intonation of his voice. I want to sear every aspect of this moment into my brain, sew it into the fabric of my memory so I can take it out in the quiet of the night and replay it over and over again.

I stand on tiptoes as Shang dips his head and our mouths meet in a painfully sweet crush. I lose myself in the kiss, leaning completely into Shang, feeling his hands holding the small of my back, pushing me even deeper into his embrace. My hands are lost in his hair, and I can't get enough of him, of his mouth on mine and his body against mine.

"Whew, girl, you are going to get lucky tonight," a guest says.

We break apart, grinning guiltily, and I clear my throat and straighten my dress.

"You look ravishing in that," Shang whispers in my ear.

His breath makes my skin tingle, and just like that, I'm biting down hard on my lower lip. I shake myself. Even though I want nothing more than to rush home with Shang and tumble into bed with him, my work here isn't over.

"You're getting that look on your face," Shang muses.

"What look?"

"The one you get when you're about to do something you don't think you'll be very good at, but damn it you're going to give it your best shot."

"That's a look I get? That is very specific."

"Yeah, you get it a lot. You had it before you rode Slugger, and before you descaled the fish, and before you sheared that sheep, and—"

"Okay, thanks for the reminder. I am now traumatized." I take a deep breath, turning to scan the crowd for Uncle Hong and the rest of the Lis. "I need to speak with your family."

"All right. Lead the way." He takes my hand and squeezes it and, together, we plunge into the crowd.

James's look of boredom turns into a sneer when he sees me, an expression that I have to fight hard not to mirror, because *ditto, James.*

"What's she doing here?" He sees that we're holding hands and groans. "Seriously, bro? You guys are still together after what she did?"

"What we are is none of your business," Shang says. He shifts his attention to the uncles and aunties. "Uncles, aunties, Mulan has something to say to all of you."

I release Shang's hand and step forward. Now that the Lis' eyes are riveted on me, I feel like a little kid about to enter the principal's office. "Hi, everyone, thank you for coming tonight."

"Is this her idea?" Uncle Hong says, looking around in confusion.

"Yes, it was my idea."

"And mine," Auntie Jiayi says.

All heads turn to face her, and she lifts her cocktail glass in a toast. "I am, as youths call it, going inside my villain era."

The others continue staring in confusion, and Auntie Jiayi frowns at me. "Mulan, did I say it wrong?"

"No, you got it. Uh, anyway, yes, as Auntie Jiayi said, this was our idea."

"What is the meaning of this?" Uncle Hong snaps. "First you trick us, lie to us, come to our family ranch, then you trick us again to get us to come here?"

I raise my hands. "I really am very sorry about it. But the thing is, I needed you to come tonight because I wanted you to see what Wutai Gold can become. Look around you. Most of the guests here are women of all ethnicities between the ages of thirty and fifty. They are a much younger crowd, much more diverse, and every single one of them loves your whiskey." I take out my phone and send them a link. The Lis look down as their phones beep. "I just sent you a video. Please watch it, it's only a minute long."

There is silence as they swipe at their phones. The video plays.

It opens with Malika Bridges, a Black woman who owns a tech startup that develops games for women, holding up her glass and saying, "This has Wutai Gold whiskey in it? Seriously?" She takes a sip and her eyes flutter shut for a second. "Damn, it is so good. I never knew they were this good. This is liquid gold!"

It switches to Ann Kwok, a Singaporean woman with an

266

environmentally friendly company that uses bamboo fiber to make paper. She, too, is holding up her glass. Laughing, she says, "No way, Wutai Gold whiskey is so old-school boring." Then she takes a sip and her eyebrows disappear into her hairline. "*Whaaat?* Girl, this is so f— ing good, what the f—?"

It switches to another woman, and another, and another, all of them having their drinks and loving them. It ends with a close-up of Wutai Gold whiskey, beautifully shot by the ad company I have acquired, and the words *Everyone deserves good whiskey.*

I wait for everyone to finish watching, then clear my throat. "I shot that video tonight. All those reactions? They're real. None of these women had to be paid to say they loved the whiskey. They just did. Because it's true—your whiskey is good, and when a product is this high quality, sales should not be down. The only reason why they are down is because your practices are outdated. Your target audience is aging out, it's shrinking. Meanwhile, in one evening, I have created a viral video for your product. This video you're watching right now has over a hundred thousand views on Instagram, and double that on TikTok. You need new blood. That's me. I am your new blood. I will take your whiskey and I will make sure it gets into the hands of every whiskey enthusiast out there of every race and every gender. I will continue your legacy. The name Wutai Gold will be upheld, it will strengthen and grow and remain for generations."

There is a pregnant silence. The uncles and aunties look stunned. I have no idea how they will take my words. Based on their expressions, it really could go either way. But whatever their reaction, I no longer care. I've said my piece and shown them what I bring to the table. The rest is up to them.

As though hearing my thoughts, James slams his palm on the table. "You can't listen to her. She lied to us!"

"She only lied about her name, and nothing else," Shang says.

"I also lied about growing up on a farm in China," I pipe up. "I was born and raised here. Uh, that is all." At the look on Shang's face, I say, "I just want to be really honest going forward."

"See?" James cries. "You heard her. She's done nothing but lie ever since she came into our lives, and—"

"You're not being entirely truthful yourself," I say.

Eyes widen. Eyebrows are raised.

"What are you talking about?" James scoffs.

"Your meeting with Richard Foreman from Foreman and Byrde."

James's face pales. "Wait—"

"I happened to be at Ginger Flower. I heard what you said."

"James, what is she talking about?" Uncle Hong says.

"Nothing, she's making shit up like she always does."

"James met up with Richard Foreman at a bar called Ginger Flower two days ago," I say. "During which time they talked about Richard's firm acquiring Wutai Gold."

"It's a good deal," James hisses.

"Yes, for you," I say. I turn to Uncle Hong. "But not for the company. You won't be retaining any rights, no creative say, nothing. Because Richard Foreman wants to break your company down and sell it for parts. And James wants to go for it because he gets a cut on the side."

Auntie Chuang gasps and turns to her son. "James, what is she saying? Is this true?"

"No," James says, but there's a telling quaver in his voice, and though he is no doubt scrambling to come up with a lie to save his ass, he's so obviously panicked and taken aback that it quickly becomes clear to everyone that he's been exposed.

Uncle Hong's face falls, and he looks a lot older than his seventy years. "Er zi," he says. *Son.* The heartbreak in his voice is palpable and even though I despise James, it hurts to see Uncle Hong looking so small and vulnerable. He's looking at James like it's the first time he's seeing him. "A firm that wants to break up our company?"

James looks desperately around the table, searching for some help. When it becomes obvious that there is none coming, his expression of panic hardens. I actually see the change happen, as though he is a trapped animal who realizes there is no escaping and what remains is a fight to the death. His upper lip curls up into a look of such contempt that Uncle Hong flinches at the sight of it.

"Yes," he hisses. "Because I want out. I can't wait to be rid of this joke of a company."

"Joke?" Uncle Hong croaks. "How can you say that, James? This is legacy, this—"

"Fuck legacy!" James screeches. People at other neighboring tables stop talking and turn to stare, but he keeps going. "Do you know what it's like growing up as a Li? From as far back as I can remember, you and Ma said shit like: 'When you join the family company, when you start working at the family company . . .' Did you ever stop to think that maybe I didn't want to join the company?"

Uncle Hong and Auntie Chuang look aghast. "Why didn't you want to join the family company?" Auntie Chuang says. "It is what has given us our livelihood, otherwise we will be—"

"Homeless, out on the streets begging for food," James finishes. "Yeah, you always drill that right into my head." He taps on his temple. "Did I have a say in what to major in at college? Nope. Did you ever bother asking me what I really want to do?"

Uncle Hong utters a small, shocked laugh. "Well, of course you want to keep working in the family company, like Shang."

"No I don't!" James snaps. "I never did, okay? I wanted to be a writer." His voice breaks then. "I'm not like Shang, the fucking perfect

269

son," he spits, throwing a venomous glare in Shang's direction.

"A writer?" Auntie Chuang says, as though the concept of being a writer is entirely foreign to her.

What is going on right now? Why am I— My god, am I actually feeling empathy for James, of all people?

And I am. James's anguish is palpable. He's still repulsive, but I understand the complicated blessing and curse that a family company brings with it. The pressure of continuing it for our parents' sake, combined with all their expectations. The awareness of all the sacrifices that our parents had to make to build the company from scratch, and the expectation on us to ensure its longevity. I am lucky, I realize now, to have a natural affinity for finance. I can't even imagine if I were like James and wanted to do something completely unrelated.

"Yeah, Ma," James says. "A writer. Of books." He actually mimes reading a book, as though he doesn't think his mother knows what they are. "Did you guys never notice how much I loved reading as a kid?"

"Of course we noticed," Auntie Chuang says. "We told everyone how you are a gifted child."

"Right, because that's all that matters, right?" James says. "What other people think. You never even stopped to think: *Huh, my son likes reading, maybe he's into writing as well.* Of course you didn't. It was all about Wutai Gold. We—" He gestures at the cousins, who look torn between embarrassment and sympathy. "We're nothing but your little projects that you had so you could mold us into exactly what you desired. Nothing more than an extension of yourselves." James leans back, looking satisfied. "So yeah, I want to see the company end. I want to see it broken into many little pieces and sold for parts. Because this fucking company has ruined my life." He goes for a smug smile, but his lip trembles like he's barely holding back his tears.

My breath comes out in a hiss. That was surprisingly heavy, coming from James. And judging from the looks on Uncle Hong's and Auntie Chuang's faces, they've been hit hard by his admission, too. They look like they're this close to wailing.

Then Auntie Jiayi says, "Oh, grow up, James." She glares at him. "What stopped you from being a writer? You have a nice home. You have a computer. You have health care. What is it you want to write? Books?"

James, looking shell-shocked, gives a tiny nod.

"So why don't you write books? Are your mama and baba physically pinning you down on the floor so you can't write?"

"No, but—"

"Most writers have a day job," Auntie Jiayi says. "You have a day job, too, but you don't have a spouse or little kids to look after, so why don't you write after work? Or wake up early to write? What are you doing in your free time?"

"Wh—" James's eyes dart to and fro frantically. "I mean, I have a lot of things going on. I go to the gym, I have to clean my place, I hang out with my buddies—"

"Exactly," Auntie Jiayi says. "You have a lot of things going on. And not one of them is writing. Because you don't put writing as your priority. Aiya, James. Yes, I agree with you, family company is complicated, it's both a good thing and a bad thing. But look at what it has given you. An education. Perfect English, not like ours, broken and ugly. You can use that perfect English to write a book, but you don't. You choose to go out with friends, drink and be merry, and then you come back and you blame your parents for having a family company."

"I—" James starts to say, then he seems to deflate, sagging back into his seat. He lowers his head and doesn't say anything.

Once more, I find myself feeling bad for James. No matter how unpleasant he is, it's never an enjoyable thing to watch someone getting told off like that. But god, I am impressed with Auntie Jiayi. She's hit the nail right on the head. I look over at her and when our eyes meet, she winks at me.

Then Auntie Jiayi stands, moving in such a regal way that everyone's eyes are dragged to her.

"I have seen enough," she says. "I see a very bright and talented young person here." She gestures at me. "I see change, and a very scary thing is change. I see something different. But I also see growth. I vote to sell Wutai Gold to Eighty-Eight Capital."

"You?" Uncle Jing says. "You're calling for a vote?" There is so much disdain in his voice that it makes me wince, but Auntie Jiayi doesn't seem fazed in the least bit.

"Yes, I am. I am a shareholder."

"You are a woman," Uncle Xiaotian hisses.

"Yes, I am aware. And it is women who will save this company," Auntie Jiayi says smartly. "But if you'd rather stay the course and drive the company into the ground, it is okay. I am happy to watch."

"I vote alongside my mother," Shang says.

"I vote also," Auntie Lulu says.

Her husband, Uncle Xiaotian, looks at her in shock, and she shrugs. "I like this girl Mulan."

"Yes, I vote too," Auntie Jamie says.

She nudges Auntie Chuang, who takes a sharp breath, then says, "Yes."

"You all are in-laws!" Uncle Xiaotian snaps. "You don't have a vote."

Christopher slowly raises his hands. "Um, us G-two kids have a vote, and I vote to sell to Eighty-Eight Capital."

Ryan nods. "Yeah, I do too."

"Same," Thomas says.

I gape at them in disbelief, but they look at me and smile, and my heart quickens. It's happening. It's actually happening. Then the last person I thought would speak up does so.

"I vote yes also," Uncle Hong says quietly.

His brothers look as though he's just murdered their puppy, but he ignores them. Keeping his gaze on me, he says, "When I came to this country, I only had one wish: the American dream. This dream is what drives this country. It is built by immigrants, all of us who have left our countries behind. Our children cannot speak our mother tongue. All for the American dream. I thought that in order to succeed, you have to sell to Americans, and Americans to me meant big, manly Caucasian men. I forgot about my fellow immigrants." He looks around at the ballroom, filled to the gills with women of color, now dancing on the dance floor. A wistful smile touches his face. "My fellow immigrant families," he says again, softly this time. "You are all so strong," he murmurs to the crowd in general. "I forgot what real strength is. This"—he gestures to the ballroom of women—"is real strength. This is what Wutai Gold stands for. So, yes, I vote to sell to Eighty-Eight Capital."

It takes a while for his words to sink in, and when they finally do, my mouth goes dry. "That makes majority," I say softly.

"It does," Shang says.

My voice shakes as I meet Uncle Hong's eye. "So we have a deal?"

He nods. "We have a deal."

I whoop. I rush over to him and engulf him in a tight hug while everyone around us claps. Amid the clapping and cheering, I hear Uncle Hong say softly into my ear, "Please take care of it."

"I will," I say. "I promise." And I mean every word of it.

EPILOGUE

There is a hot breakfast waiting for me when I come out of the bedroom, my hair still mussed. Actually, calling it *a* breakfast seems inaccurate, given there are so many dishes on the dining table that it looks more like five different breakfasts. There are pumpkin pancakes, a few dim sum favorites like shao mai and har gao, jian bing—Chinese crepes filled with eggs and scallions and shredded chicken—and cold, spicy sesame noodles.

"Oh my god," I say, gaping at all the food.

"Morning," Shang says, walking into the dining room carrying two mugs of coffee. He hands one to me and leans down to kiss me.

"How? Why?" I say.

Shang grins and pulls out a chair for me. "You're a pretty heavy sleeper."

"Or you are the world's quietest cook?"

"Gonna go with heavy sleeper."

I can't keep my eyes off him as I lower myself into the chair. "But why? There is so much food here."

"It's your first day as a partner at your firm. I didn't want you to go to the office hungry. Anyway, we can save some for your parents. Your mom was the one who told me all your favorite breakfast dishes."

I blink. "My mom?"

"Yes. There's a group chat."

"A group chat? Who's in this group?"

"Both our moms. And me," Shang says, smirking. "It's called the Foodies."

My mouth drops open in mock outrage. "You didn't think to invite me to this group?"

"Are you a foodie?"

"I eat food!"

"This group is for serious cooks and food enthusiasts only," Shang says.

"You smug bastard." I take a big bite of cold sesame noodles and my eyes flutter closed. As with everything else Shang cooks, it's delicious. "Thank you for doing this. And for creating the group chat. I bet my mom loves it."

"She does, actually. Every morning I wake up and find like a dozen messages in there already. Our moms wake up really early."

I laugh, shaking my head. "Unbelievable." This man. I lean forward, smiling, eyes bright. This is the best moment. My smile widens. Over the past month, ever since the awards banquet, I find myself thinking: *This moment is the best moment, I want to memorize it.* Except there are so many of these moments. My days are now moments like these, bright and sparkling, stitched together. "Hey," I say, "I love you."

"Good, because I'm in love with you, too." Shang meets me halfway, kissing me just the way I like, soft and slow.

At the office, I knock on Ba's door. When I enter, I hold up a container. "Ba, I have some jian bing here for you."

Ba's face breaks into a smile. "Ah, jian bing! My favorite."

"Shang made it."

"Excellent," he says. "Come sit down, Mulan."

I sit across the table from my father. He gazes at me fondly. "Look at you," he says. "Eighty-Eight Capital's newest partner. I couldn't be prouder."

It's all I can do to whisper, "Ba."

"Can I give you some advice?"

I nod.

"Don't be the first one in and last one to leave the office," Ba says.

I laugh. "What, why? Isn't that what partners do?"

"Sometimes, yes. But I also want you to have a life outside of all this. I didn't come to this country so my daughter can sacrifice her youth for work."

"Okay, Ba. I won't."

"Good, now let's talk business."

At noon, I leave for my lunch hour. I walk quickly, eager to get to the corner bistro. Mushu is already there, and she's got our usual table by the window. I break into a smile when I spot her. It's been weird not having Mushu around in the office anymore, and I relish our regular lunches.

"I ordered your usual," Mushu says when I slide into my seat.

"Thanks. How was your weekend?"

Mushu blows air through her lips, making a *thp-btb* sound. "Exhausting. Brooke Tanaka is a demon. We had three events, back-to-back."

"Oh yes, I saw the photos. You looked incredible at all of them."

"That goes without saying."

"All original Posy Lees?"

Mushu nods, then gives me a wicked grin. "You know, she mentioned she's starting up a wedding dress line."

"Shang and I have been in a relationship for less than two months," I say flatly.

"I'm just saying, when you two inevitably get engaged, you know who's a badass event planner?"

"I would not dream of going to anyone but the best event planner the Bay Area has to offer," I say.

"Just to clarify, that would be me, yes?"

"Yes, Mushu!" I laugh. "Of course it would be you."

"Good, because I've talked about this with your mom and she agreed to disown you if you went with anyone else."

"Has everyone in the world been talking to my mom behind my back?"

"Yes," Mushu says simply.

I shake my head, still beaming. My eyes soften as I look closely at Mushu. There are so many subtle differences with her now. Even the way she sits is different. Relaxed and happy and confident. "I love this job for you."

Mushu meets my eye, and we gaze at each other with the kind of understanding only two women who have grown up with each other can have. "Thanks for pushing me to do it."

"Thanks for helping me save my career."

"Always."

At the end of the workday, Baba and I make our way to Lamian Paradise. Everyone is inside, and it is chaos when we arrive. Hugs and handshakes are given all around, and Uncle Hong says, "Sit next to me, Zhou. The big Zhou," he adds with a wink at me.

I roll my eyes, taking a seat next to Shang, who kisses the side of my head.

Uncle Hong pours some tea for Baba, briefly switching to Mandarin. "We're so happy about the company's performance."

"Mulan has done very well with it," Ba replies.

Uncle Hong nods. "She is a bright young woman, you must be very proud of her. We are all very pleased with the numbers, aren't we?" He looks around the table, and Uncle Jing and Uncle Xiaotian nod, albeit a tad grudgingly.

"She is my future daughter-in-law, of course she is a bright young woman," Auntie Jiayi pipes up.

Shang turns beet red. "Ma!"

"Hush, future son-in-law," Ma says.

Now it's my turn to blush. "Ma!"

The younger generation is more enthusiastic than the uncles—save for James, who just mutters something into his tea. I don't care. The numbers don't lie, and Wutai Gold is doing better than ever before. Shang, as CEO, still gets creative control, but he and his team have been surprisingly easy to work with, and I always look forward to our check-ins.

"Okay, no more shoptalk," Auntie Chuang says. She turns to Shang. "Shang, when are you proposing to Mulan?"

"Go back to the shoptalk," I say.

Everyone laughs. The conversation moves on to the topic of the holidays, which aren't too far off in the distance now. As we argue good-naturedly about which one of us should get to host them, Shang reaches out and places a warm, callused hand on mine.

I look up and find him gazing at me with tenderness, and I think, for the millionth time: *This moment. This one is the best moment.*

Of course, given the fact that I will later find a million more moments where I think, *Nope, this one is even better*, I am wrong about this one being the best, but I'm not mad about it.

THE END

ACKNOWLEDGMENTS

What a dream and an honor it is to be able to write a *Mulan* retelling for the Meant to Be series. I first watched Disney's *Mulan* when I was a kid in Singapore, and I can still remember how pivotal the film was for me and my friends. We have of course learned about Mulan from our Chinese history lessons, but to see her as a Disney princess on the big screen was—and I am not exaggerating here—life-changing. She was beautiful, she was funny as hell, she was smart, she was brave, and most importantly, she looked like us. My friends and I cheered and cried at the scene where Mulan managed to climb up that pole and retrieve the arrow, and to this day, whenever I see that scene, I still get teary-eyed.

When the wonderful Jocelyn Davies reached out to my agent to ask if I would be interested in writing Mulan's story for the Meant to Be series, I said to my agent, "TELL HER YES! I WILL DO ANYTHING! I will do it for half a banana!" Fortunately, my agent did not tell Jocelyn about the half a banana, though she did convey my enthusiasm to Jocelyn, and thus was this story born. Thank you to Jocelyn, who has been such an incredible editor to work with and whose vision helped make this story a million times better than I first imagined.

I want to share a bit about my background and why this book means the world to me. My grandparents all came from China to Indonesia at different ages. My maternal grandfather was actually sold when he was five years old and brought to Indonesia and sold as an indentured servant at the wet market. They literally sold him by the pound, and he fetched a low price as he was so skinny. The family that bought him brought him up as a servant/companion for their own son, and he was often beaten for any minor infractions. Despite his rough upbringing, he was able to save up enough money to start a small trade, and later on, develop it into a big company.

My other grandparents were more fortunate. They moved to Indonesia with their families, but their lives were not without hardship. To avoid xenophobia, they all had to change their Chinese names and adopt Indonesian ones. Chen became Sutanto, and Ho became Wijaya. Though they all wanted to integrate into their new country, they have always held firm the belief that their descendants should never forget where they came from. My family still celebrates most Chinese holidays such as the Lunar New Year, the Mid-Autumn Festival, and the Dragon Boat Festival. We also have Chinese names in addition to our legal Indonesian names. When my daughters were born, I chose their Chinese names with care and pride: Ruyi, which means "as intended," and Shiyang, which means "stone of the sun."

It breaks my heart that none of my grandparents are alive to see me write this book, as I know it would've meant the world to them. When I told my parents that I got this contract, my mom cried and told me that they would've been so proud to know that their granddaughter is writing a retelling of China's most famous woman warrior. There are no words to express my gratitude as the chance to write this story, and I hope that I have handled it with the care and love that it deserves.